# Guess Who's
# Coming to Die?

A THOROUGHLY SOUTHERN MYSTERY

# GUESS WHO'S COMING TO DIE?

## PATRICIA SPRINKLE

**WHEELER**
**CHIVERS**

This Large Print edition is published by Wheeler Publishing, Waterville, Maine, USA and by BBC Audiobooks Ltd, Bath, England.
Wheeler Publishing is an imprint of Thomson Gale, a part of The Thomson Corporation.
Wheeler is a trademark and used herein under license.

The text of this Large Print edition is unabridged.
Other aspects of the book may vary from the original edition.
Set in 16 pt. Plantin.

---

**LIBRARY OF CONGRESS CATALOGING-IN-PUBLICATION DATA**

Sprinkle, Patricia Houck.
  Guess who's coming to die? : a thoroughly southern mystery / by Patricia Sprinkle.
    p. cm. — (Wheeler Publishing large print cozy mystery)
  ISBN-13: 978-1-59722-544-1 (lg. print : pbk. : alk. paper)
  ISBN-10: 1-59722-544-4 (lg. print : pbk. : alk. paper)
  1. Judges — Fiction. 2. Georgia — Fiction. 3. Large type books. I. Title.
PS3569.P687G84 2007
813'.54—dc22
                                                          2007011142

---

BRITISH LIBRARY CATALOGUING-IN-PUBLICATION DATA AVAILABLE

Published in 2007 in the U.S. by arrangement with NAL Signet,
a member of Penguin Group (USA) Inc.
Published in 2007 in the U.K. by arrangement with
Lowenstein-Yost Associates Inc.

U.K. Hardcover: 978 1 405 64190 6 (Chivers Large Print)
U.K. Softcover: 978 1 405 64191 3 (Camden Large Print)

Printed in the United States of America on permanent paper
10 9 8 7 6 5 4 3 2 1

# CAST OF CHARACTERS

**MacLaren Yarbrough** — Georgia magistrate and co-owner of Yarbrough Feed, Seed, and Nursery

**Joe Riddley Yarbrough** — her husband, co-owner of Yarbrough Feed, Seed, and Nursery

**Walker Yarbrough** — their younger son, insurance salesman

**Cindy Yarbrough** — wife of Walker Yarbrough and recent heiress to Weinkoff hotel fortune

*Members of Magnolia Ladies' Investment Club*

**MayBelle Brandison** — real estate developer

**Meriwether Wainwright DuBose** — owner of Pots of Luck catalog company, wife of Jed DuBose

**Rachel Ford** — international lawyer from New York, now runs a poverty law clinic in town

5

**Sadie Lowe Harnett** — ex-wife of New York magnate

**Nancy Jensen** — financial partner of the club and wife of the CEO of Middle Georgia Kaolin

**Willena Kenan** — outgoing senior partner, one of two primary stockholders in Kenan Cotton Factors

**Wilma Kenan** — her cousin, incoming senior partner, also primary stockholder in Kenan Cotton Factors

**Augusta Wainwright** — queen of Hopemore society, primary stockholder in Wainwright Textile Mills

*Other Important Characters*

**Charlie Muggins** — police chief, Hopemore, Georgia

**Isaac James** — assistant police chief, Hopemore, Georgia

**Slade Rutherford** — editor of the weekly *Hopemore Statesman*

**Grover Henderson** — stockbroker adviser to the club

**Clarinda Williams** — MacLaren's housekeeper

**Dexter Baxter** — custodian of the Hopemore Community Center

**Linette Shields** — Wilma's housekeeper

**Hetty Burns** — Willena's housekeeper

# 1

If my husband, Joe Riddley, tells you, "Mac-Laren can't get out of my sight without stumbling over a body," remind him that this one time, it was all his fault.

Outside my office at Yarbrough Feed, Seed, and Nursery, our little town of Hopemore, Georgia, was enjoying a gorgeous day in May with the sun not too hot, a frisky breeze, and puffy white clouds floating like great dollops of Cool Whip overhead. Early perennials and bedding plants were in full bloom. All the trees had new leaves. Even the pines looked fresh.

Inside at my desk, I was grumpy as all getout. I had gotten back from a two-week bus tour of Scotland that hadn't turned out to be as restful as I had hoped. I had badly injured one hand, a couple of bodies had shown up, and I had nearly made a third.[1]

[1] *Did You Declare the Corpse?*

Coming back to a pile of bills, invoices, and catalogs didn't do a thing to improve my mood.

With my good hand I picked up a fancy envelope perched on top. Creamy and small, the size for personal notes, it was far and away the best-looking thing on my desk. *Judge MacLaren Yarbrough* was handwritten in a fat, round script I didn't recognize.

As I reached for my letter opener, I glanced across the office. Joe Riddley was watching me from his desk with the expression he reserves for those occasions when he knows I will love a present. When he saw me looking his way, he opened a new seed catalog and began to peruse it with the same fervor financiers bring to the *Wall Street Journal.*

We have known each other for sixty years and been married for more than forty, and we share an office at the back of our store. He does the ordering and manages our big nursery out at the edge of town. I handle the store and the financial end of things. Generally, we work real amicably together. If he gets tired of me, he settles his red YARBROUGH cap on his head and goes down to the nursery and drives the forklift. If I get tired of him, I grab my pocketbook and run over to Myrtle's Restaurant for a slice of chocolate pie with three-inch meringue and sugar beads on top. It works for us.

Joe Riddley has been known to occasionally arrange for wonderful surprises, so I slit open the envelope with a tremor of anticipation. "What's this?" I asked in an innocent voice.

"A welcome-home present from Cindy and Gusta." If I didn't read it soon, he was going to grab it and read it for me.

Even if I was disappointed it wasn't from him, my heart beat faster. Augusta Wainwright was the richest woman in town, and Cindy — wife of our younger son, Walker — had recently inherited her grandmother's entire estate. Since her grandmother was the last of the Weinkoffs of the Weinkoff hotel chain, Cindy and Walker finally had enough money to keep their family in the style to which they had already grown accustomed. Joe Riddley and I no longer lay awake at night wondering how they would ever meet their enormous mortgage, car payments, credit card debt, and private school bills.

Had Gusta and Cindy decided to send us around the world?

My bags weren't even unpacked. I could leave tomorrow.

Full of hope, I tugged out a creamy note card and read two sentences: *You are invited to become a member of the Magnolia Ladies' Investment Club. We meet at seven thirty p.m. on the second Monday of every month in the Wainwright Room of the Hopemore Community Center.*

There was no signature or phone number for an RSVP. The aristocracy presumes that people who receive an invitation to join them won't turn it down.

Before we get on with this story, I need to correct any misapprehension you may have that "small town" equals "small bank accounts." A number of our nation's wealthiest families live in the small towns where their ancestors started businesses that became international corporations. These families have already found what the rest of the populace is looking for: lifelong friends, good neighbors, and space to build lovely, gracious homes away from crowds, traffic, and hassles. Our own little Hope County — located in that wedge of Georgia that lies between I-20 and I-16 — has birthed Wainwright Textile Mills, Kenan Cotton Factors, DuBose Trucking Lines, and Middle Georgia Kaolin.

The Magnolia Ladies' Investment Club was organized in the 1950s to provide a place for the women of the Wainwright, Du-Bose, Kenan, and Jensen families to get together, consume a lot of liquor in private, and talk about whatever very wealthy women discuss when not constrained by the presence of plebeians. They originally dabbled in the stock market only to give their meetings a semblance of purpose. After Gusta was widowed and assumed control of her own money, however, she also took control of the investment club. They added other members and became serious about investment strategies. At some point they drew up a charter and bylaws that limited membership to "Hopemore's ten most influential women."

For which read, "richest and most socially prominent."

They had lost two members in the past six months. Edith Burkett had been murdered the previous fall[2], and Pooh DuBose had died in her sleep while I was away. Cindy had taken Edie's place, but there wasn't a single reason I could think of why I ought to take Pooh's. Like most other women in town who did not belong, I generally referred to the group as "the Moneyed Women's Investment Club."

[2] *Who Killed the Queen of Clubs?*

I looked across the office and saw Joe Rid-dley waiting for me to jump up and down with joy. I gave him a sour look instead. "Okay, it was logical that Cindy got invited once news of her inheritance got around. But how on earth did I get nominated? And why? Except for Gusta, most of the current members are a lot closer to Cindy's age than mine. I scarcely know them."

He scratched one cheek and pretended to think that over. "You know most of them. There's Gusta and Meriwether —"

Augusta Wainwright was the widow of the last Wainwright of Wainwright Textile Mills and had been the self-styled queen of Hopemore society since she'd learned to toddle. And yes, I knew Gusta and her granddaughter, Meriwether DuBose, real well. Meriwether was married to attorney Jed DuBose and mother of little Zachary DuBose. She was also starting her own busi-ness, Pots of Luck, which was a catalog company specializing in pots of all sizes and shapes, and doing real well. Meriwether had her daddy's business sense.

"And the Kenan girls . . ." Joe Riddley wasn't being chauvinistic. Everybody called the cousins "the Kenan girls," although Wil-lena was forty and Wilma fifty. I think that was in deference to their state of being what

my mama used to call "ladies-in-waiting."
Until two perfect husbands appeared, they
occupied themselves running — some said
ruining — Hopemore's social and civic
clubs.

"I don't really know the Kenans." I was
beginning to feel balky about this. I picked
up my letter opener and amused myself by
stabbing little holes in the thick invitation
instead of in Joe Riddley's hide.

"They've gone to our church for five
generations, Little Bit." He was getting
exasperated, too. "And Willena's real savvy
where money is concerned. You might just
learn something. And you and Nancy Jensen
have served on a lot of church committees
together." Nancy Jensen was married to
Horace, owner and CEO of Middle Georgia
Kaolin.

"We don't socialize with the Kenans or
the Jensens," I pointed out. The old coot
seemed to have the membership list memo-
rized. I gave him a quick glace to see if he
had written the names down to prod his
memory, but his eyes were peering at me
with that earnest expression he gets when
he's trying to convince me do so something
he thinks is for my own good.

"It's not a social club. You might learn
something from these women. Take May-

Belle Brandison, for example."

"You take her. I don't want her. She's a snake." MayBelle could outtalk and outdeal anybody in three counties when it came to real estate, but that didn't earn her a place on my favorite-people list. I hadn't liked her even back when she was a poor, pushy girl in my son Ridd's class. As far as I was concerned, money had not improved her a whit.

"It would be a chance for you to get to know that Ford woman better — the lawyer."

For the first time, he had my attention. Rachel Ford was the director of our Poverty Law Center and a mystery to me. Striking rather than pretty, she was a tall, rangy woman with olive skin and naturally curly black hair cut to fall above her shoulders from a center part. Her long, intense face was marked by brows like straight dark slashes above eyes that were an unusual shade of blue-gray. I'd deliberately sat by her at a couple of functions to try to get acquainted, but while she would talk about her work, the only personal information I had gleaned was that she was half Jewish and half Catholic, "which is why both my hands move when I talk." Between her Jewish and Italian ancestors, I wondered who

14

had bequeathed her those eyes. She seemed uninterested in the two important Southern questions: "Who are your people?" and "Where do they come from?" As far as I knew, Meriwether DuBose was the only friend she'd made since she had come down from New York to take the Poverty Law Center job.

"She can't earn much," I pointed out. "How did she get in the club?"

"Maybe she inherited money, like most of them."

"I don't think so. Money has a way of showing up in clothes, cars, houses, or something. Her clothes are nothing special, and Meriwether says she is doing most of the work herself on that old house she bought, a little at a time."

"She drives a BMW."

"A very old one."

"Maybe she banks it all. Or gets alimony, like Sadie Lowe. She's in the club, too."

"Take that grin off your face. Sadie Lowe is one more reason for me not to join."

All you need to know about Sadie Lowe Harnett at this point is that she was thirty-seven years old, a former model and soap opera actress, with several millions from a New York divorce settlement tucked away in her sizable bra — and that men's faces

15

invariably went goofy when she came into a room or conversation.

"You are being asked to fill Pooh's slot." He picked up his catalog and turned a page like seeds were all he had on his mind. He added casually, "It was one of her last requests."

Pooh DuBose had been my old and valued friend as well as the widow of the founder of DuBose Trucking Lines. I would miss her terribly. But I also hoped that once she had arrived in heaven, she had met up with her memory. It had predeceased her by a couple of years.

"If Pooh expressed any *recent* opinions about my taking her place," I pointed out, "she had no idea what she was talking about."

"It's an honor, Little Bit." Exasperation oozed from each syllable. He knows me well enough to read between my lines.

"Sure it's an honor. Cindy made that clear when she was invited. But you and I both know each one of those women — with the probable exception of Rachel Ford — has more money than we'll ever see. I don't play in their league, or even want to. Besides, I have enough to do without taking on a new organization."

I not only work full-time, belong to a slew

of business organizations, and serve on too many church and civic committees, but I am also a county magistrate. Many magistrates in small Georgia counties combine judicial duties with a full-time job. As if to illustrate my point, a deputy stuck his head in our office door. "Judge, do you have time to come down to the sheriff's detention center and hold a bond hearing for me? And I'd like this search warrant signed."

I repressed a sigh and tried not to look at the work piled on my desk. "What you got?"

"A young man who has been robbing Mexicans while they are at work. We caught him red-handed, rifling one of their houses. My hunch is that if we search his garage before he gets back to it, we'll find stuff he hasn't disposed of yet."

Joe Riddley chuckled. "Sounds like somebody had better explain to him that 'Mi casa es su casa' is not to be taken quite so literally."

Every deputy at the detention center wanted to know about my vacation, so it was nearly an hour later before I got back to the office.

"Joe Riddley has run over to the bank," Evelyn Pratt, our store manager, informed me.

Evelyn had been creating a new window

17

display of bedding annuals in a bright blue wheelbarrow. When she was busy or bothered, she ran her hands through her wiry red hair, which changed colors depending on which brand of dye she'd bought at the drugstore. Right now it was carrot orange and stood on end from her exertions.

"You might check your hair," I advised as I headed to my office.

I glared at Joe Riddley's desk and settled at my own to wait. He'd have to come back sometime.

I was busy with payroll when I got a call. "Did you have fun in Scotland?" Augusta Wainwright, being a queen, never bothers to say who she is when she calls.

I told her I had, not liking to bring up murder and mayhem on the telephone. You never know when the White House may be listening in and get the wrong idea.

"Have you seen my great-grandson since you got back?" Gusta never misses a chance to bring up little Zachary Garlon DuBose. "He is growing so quickly, he's almost in nine-months clothes, although he's not quite six months old. And do you know, the other day he actually said 'Gamma' when he saw me?"

Anybody knows that clothing manufacturers deliberately size infant clothes to give doting relatives cause to brag and that five-month-olds don't talk, but ever since Zach was born, Gusta had carried on like he'd be ready for a pro sports team or Harvard within the year. I made appropriate sounds and prepared to get off the phone so I could return to work.

"Did you receive your invitation?" she inquired.

I was a tad annoyed that she didn't bother to say which invitation. "I got several," I replied. "The homeless shelter invited me to send them a check to refurbish their kitchen, the church invited me to the choir's spring concert —"

I have known Gusta all my life and consider it is good for her soul for me to heckle her from time to time. She has so few friends still alive who are brave enough to remind her that she lives on the same planet with the rest of us.

"Your invitation to the Magnolia Ladies' Investment Club." I could picture her looking down her nose at me through the telephone wires.

"Oh, yes, but I'm not in that league, Gusta, and we both know it."

"Nonsense. You don't have to invest but a hundred dollars a month. That won't reduce you to beans and bread. Besides, not all of us are as rich as we used to be."

I figured she meant that the Dow Jones was down three points that day. For Gusta, that could mean a significant loss if she sold all her stocks, but she wasn't selling. Gusta clutched her pennies like a drowning man clutches a life preserver. Besides, most of her income came from Wainwright Textile Mills, plus checks and cash from slum rental properties her husband left her in three counties. No matter what the market did, Gusta would never be reduced to beans and bread. I was fixing to say that I hadn't made up my mind yet about joining, but she swept on.

"I told the others what an asset you will be to the club. We are getting too many young women and too much frivolity, frou-frou, and fluff. We need an older member who is practical and down-to-earth, not all wrapped up in clothes and hairdos. You will add maturity and common sense to the group. Well, I need to go now. I don't have time to talk on the phone all day."

I went to the ladies' room and checked my reflection in the full-length mirror on the back of the door. I saw a woman who had gotten up at dawn to get her hair done before coming to work. Who had recently powdered her nose and refreshed her lipstick. Who was wearing a new peach pant-suit that looked real becoming when she put it on.

It would never look quite so becoming again.

As soon as Joe Riddley got back from the bank, I picked up the discussion where we'd left off. "While I am sensible of the honor you and Cindy have bestowed upon me — and don't tell me you had nothing to do with it, because it wouldn't have occurred to them to invite me if you hadn't sneakily connected my name to Pooh's vacancy — anyway, while I know it's an honor, you and I both know I don't belong in that club. And since you got me into this, you need to write the letter turning them down. It should be a real nice letter, since these women are some of our best customers, but I'm not feeling particularly nice at the moment. I've got too much else to do to be thinking up sweet phrases for 'thanks, but no, thanks.' "

He held up one big hand. "Don't be hasty, now. With that new superstore eating away at our profits, it might be smart for you to make a pile on the stock market so we can retire."

"You wanting to retire?" I knew the answer to that, just as he knew we have enough to retire on whenever we want to, including a stock portfolio I've been building for years. I've done it by buying companies I trust to give me a good product at a good price with good service.

"Not anytime soon, but a little extra money never hurts."

I picked up the creamy envelope and held it between us. "But who knows what that group invests in? You know I never buy stock in companies whose products I do not personally use. How do I know whether the products are any good or the executives honest and intelligent?"

He settled his cap on his head. "Given the ancestors of some of the members of that club, corporate integrity may not be high on their investment agenda. Maybe that's why they want a judge in the group. Besides, you aren't investing our life savings, and the programs ought to be interesting. They've got some hotshot Augusta stockbroker who comes out each month to talk about how to invest wisely. Think of all you'll learn." He chortled. "Willena may be learning a few things, too. The two of them seem to be dating."

That got my attention. "Willena is dating? When did this happen?"

"While you were away. They played golf

together several times and ate at the country club both Friday nights. Had a kid with them last week. His son, I understand. He's a widower, so Cindy tells me. And has been handling Willena's portfolio for years. They started going around together back last winter, but they didn't go public until a couple of weeks ago."

"This sounds serious. How old is he? Where's he from? He's not after her money, is he?"

"Hold your horses, and I'll tell you what I know. He's a stockbroker, like I said, and he looks like he's around forty-five. Nice fellow, from what I could tell from meeting him at the club. He grew up in Augusta and still lives there, but went to college somewhere up north. His firm suggested him to Willena when her old stockbroker died. Now you know everything I do."

I chuckled. "Is he the spitting image of Granddaddy Will?"

He laughed, too. "I can't rightly say." He was already halfway out the door.

"Maybe we can get you into the investment club instead of me," I called after him. "Threaten them with gender discrimination or something."

He turned back. "Face it, Little Bit. As a judge, you need to know the movers and

23

shakers in town. And a monthly lecture on investing and a chance to discuss stocks with smart women who know what they're doing is a heck of a lot more interesting than most meetings you go to each month."

Sometimes it annoys me how well that man knows me.

Before I could think of another good excuse, he urged, "Give it a try. You've been wanting to do something with Cindy. Now you've got a chance. Take them up on their invitation. What can it hurt?"

We would soon find out.

## 2

The next Monday evening I stood, alone and awkward, in the Wainwright Meeting Room of the Hopemore Community Center after handing over my membership dues and first month's investment check to the Magnolia Ladies' Investment Club. The room was full of big hair and big money, and I had neither.

What I did have was a cup of punch in my right hand, a plate of brownies balanced on the bandage on my left, and no place to set either down. Given how often people attend stand-up social functions where food is involved, wouldn't you think evolution or the good Lord would have provided a third hand somewhere along the line? I hovered between the big-hair group and the big-money group, trying to figure out how to eat my refreshments and which group to join.

A voice murmured at my shoulder, "I

25

haven't met you yet, Judge Yarbrough."

Grover Henderson, the Augusta stockbroker who had given a very interesting talk on current trends in international markets, looked down at me with twinkling blue eyes and a smile that was tentative enough to be charming. I found myself responding with twinkles of my own. Grover, like Joe Riddley, was one of those men who get better-looking as they get older, and the kind of man who makes single women drool and married women sit up a little straighter. He had a nice strong chin, broad shoulders, and graying hair that was receding except for a cute little tuft in front that he combed over to one side. His tan looked like he'd gotten it on a golf course or tennis court rather than under a sunlamp, and he wore his navy blazer and loafers with a casual ease that implied he'd be equally at home in a tux or jeans.

"Do you already know all these women," he asked, "or shall I introduce you?"

"I know most of them. I've lived in Hopemore all my life. If it wouldn't give you a fair estimate of my age, I'd tell you I was a flower girl in Augusta Wainwright's wedding."

We laughed and looked over to where Augusta, possessor of a bank account any

Third World country would envy, held court. Her silver head wore an invisible tiara, and her long, aristocratic neck was craned toward Rachel Ford, who stood nearby. Gusta occupied a throne set conveniently near the refreshments table so she wouldn't have to juggle a plate and cup in her gnarled old hands. That would have been her granddaughter's doing. Meriwether Wainwright DuBose was both prettier and kinder than her grandmother. She was also possibly richer, now that Pooh had died, for Meriwether's husband was Pooh's heir. I suspected that Gusta was campaigning to find out how much Pooh left, and I hoped Jed and Meriwether wouldn't tell her.

Currently Meriwether was fetching Gusta a second cup of punch while Gusta told Rachel about Meriwether's new baby. Gusta invariably referred to the child as "my great-grandson," as if that defined him. I sincerely hoped it wouldn't.

Rachel was nodding in all the right places, but wore that glassy-eyed look single businesswomen tend to get when other people talk about babies.

"I don't know much about Rachel," I told Grover. "She's not from around here."

"No, she grew up in New York and was in a firm that specialized in international law before she moved down."

I lifted my punch cup and took a sip while I considered Rachel. Unlike the other women in the club, who had dressed up for the meeting, she wore a white turtleneck and black slacks, but maybe Joe Riddley was right about her having money tucked away. The turtleneck looked like silk, and the slacks were so well cut they had to be expensive. Her earrings were emerald studs, while another emerald sparkled on one long, slender hand, which made me think international law paid well. It seemed to have worn her out early, though. She was as skinny as an underfed pullet and had dark circles under her eyes.

Grover's attention was across the room, where the big-hair contingent was having a lively conversation. Nancy Jensen (blond), wife of the CEO of Middle Georgia Kaolin, was telling MayBelle Brandison (a lot redder than she used to be) about how stingy her husband was, while MayBelle, the sharpest real estate developer in three counties, was lamenting that she couldn't make as much in middle Georgia as she would if she moved up to Atlanta. I considered joining that conversation long enough to point out that some folks — including MayBelle's long-suffering ex-husband — kept reminding her there was nothing to keep her in Hope County since her divorce. But why bother? MayBelle was one of those women who would rather suffer and think up new ways of inflicting suffering than get on with life. Besides, Hope County still had a lot of trees left standing and a good number of acres that hadn't been covered with houses, and MayBelle wouldn't be content until she had bulldozed all the trees and built a Brandison McMansion on every quarter acre in the county.

Speaking of divorce, the third member of that group was Sadie Lowe Harnett, a brunette with the kind of curves that spell trouble. When she had divorced a New York magnate several years before, newspapers had claimed she'd won a seven-figure settlement, but I had still been surprised to hear that she had been invited to join the investment club. She grew up in Hopemore and was in school with our son Walker. In their high school days, Sadie Lowe had been infamous for doing most of her socializing in backseats down near the water tank. I wondered who had suggested her for membership and how she had gotten voted in.

It was a safe bet she had not been proposed by Wilma Kenan, who hovered around the refreshment table like a nervous bee. While I watched, she moved one tray an inch to the left and another an inch to the right, being the fussiest woman God ever made about things that don't matter. She called it being a perfectionist. I called it wanting things done her way. Because her family had been making money from cotton, both in the United States and abroad, for generations, she generally got her way.

Joe Riddley opined that Wilma's attitude toward life had been shaped by the obstetrician who delivered her, who (so Joe Riddley claimed) must have taken her face between his two hands and pressed hard. That might explain why her eyes were too close together, her nose long and sharp, her lips little more than a bow, her chin long and pointed, and her mind so narrow, you could measure it in millimeters. Nobody ever set a table, conducted a meeting, ran a government, preached a sermon, fixed a car, or styled her hair to quite suit Wilma.

Tonight she was in charge of refreshments, and had brought the ingredients for the punch in gallon jugs, claiming it was a secret family recipe. A few minutes ago she had gone back to the kitchen to mix up another batch. Now she poured it into the punch bowl and stirred it a couple of times with the silver ladle she had also brought from home. When she noticed I was talking to Grover, though, she dropped that ladle and shot across the room to intervene.

Ignoring me, she peered up at my companion with an expression in her brown eyes that reminded me of a cairn terrier's when it's on the eager lookout for a rat. "Do you have everything you need, Grover?" She had one of those voices that are nasal and sharp even when the person is intending to be charming. She put a hand on his arm as if it had a right to be there and gave him what looked like a smile she practiced in front of mirrors. Wilma had never found the perfect man, but she had never stopped looking. "Keeping myself ready for Prince Charming," she often said, pursing her bright lips and touching her stiff blond curls with polished nails that were never chipped or broken.

"I'm fine," he assured her, turning his pleasant smile in her direction.

Wilma squeezed his arm. "You're damp! Don't you have a raincoat?"

"I brought an umbrella, but I forgot to take it when I ran out to my car for something." He spoke absently, looking again toward Sadie Lowe. She stood with one hip stuck out like she knew he was looking.

Wilma gave Grover's elbow a gentle tug

to bring his attention back to her. "I'll give you a call about next month's program. I have a few ideas. As Granddaddy Will used to say —"

That's when I stopped listening. When Wilma got to talking about her great-granddaddy, she could go on forever.

I pitied Grover. Earlier that evening, the club had elected Wilma senior partner (which is what they called the president) for the coming year, succeeding her cousin, Willena. Poor Grover would be in for a rocky year. On the other hand, I had gotten the impression he was Wilma's broker, too, so maybe he was adept at handling her.

Speaking of Willena, I didn't see her with either the moneyed crowd or the big-hair contingent. She must still be in the ladies' room washing mascara off her cheeks. After Willena had passed the torch of the presidency to Wilma, Wilma had presented Willena with a sterling-silver bar set, complete with a stainless-steel corkscrew with a sterling-silver handle and a monogrammed silver shot glass. Willena was known to be fond of mimosas or chilled white wine at almost any time of day, and always cried at the drop of a hair bow. She had been so overcome by the gift that her mascara had run down her cheeks like clown lines.

"Go clean up your face," Wilma had commanded. "You look like a raccoon before breakfast."

Nobody seeing them together would have ever guessed the two women were related. Whereas Wilma was thin and short, Willena was large and tall, with soft, floury skin, fluffy brown hair, and eyes the exact same shade of brown. Wilma favored tailored dresses and pantsuits with dainty, prim jewelry. Willena wore dangling earrings, ruffled blouses, long strands of showy pearls, and full skirts in bright colors. The only thing their closets had in common was that each outfit they wore probably cost more than my annual clothing budget.

Two more things the cousins shared were an absolute conviction that old William Robison Kenan — for whom both were named — had been God's perfect gentleman, and a firm determination to each find a husband just like him.

They also shared tight fists. As soon as Willena was out of earshot, Wilma had confided to the rest of us, "That bar set cost seven hundred dollars. I paid for it, but I move that I be reimbursed from the treasury."

If she was hoping for a second to her motion, she was disappointed. "We never gave a present before and didn't authorize one this year," Gusta informed her tartly, and that was that.

With Wilma claiming all of Grover's attention, I decided to make a run to the bathroom before the meeting resumed. After refreshments, we still had to reconvene to decide how to invest our money that month. I had no clue what the investment procedure would be, but given the way some of those women liked to discuss every penny they spent, it could take a while.

I trotted down the hall, admiring the sheen our new custodian was getting on the beige tile floors of the community center and thinking about the shipment of summer bedding plants that we'd received that day at the store. I hoped we hadn't ordered too many and that ours would be bigger and more unusual than those at the superstore. Maybe we ought to concentrate on selling in quantity to landscapers and not try to compete when the superstore could set prices below what we could afford to match.

That was as far as I had gotten when I pushed to open the ladies' room door. It wouldn't budge.

I shoved again and felt it give a little.

Puzzled, I knocked, but got no answer. I put my shoulder against the door and put all my weight behind it. Something slid on the other side and the door opened far enough for me to stick my head in.

Forever after, I would wish I hadn't.

Willena lay crumpled facedown on the floor. One hand clutched her throat. The other was out, as if she had been opening the door when she collapsed. Her ruffled white blouse and the taupe tiles around her were drenched in blood.

# 3

I bent nearer and saw a glint between her fingers, like something was stuck in her throat.

My first impulse was to try to jerk it out, but I had enough wits left to grab her wrist first. I found no pulse and could smell the odors a body releases after death. I know not to bother a murder scene, and that was what this had to be. Now that I was down at her level, I saw what the weapon was. Nobody commits suicide by sticking a corkscrew in her own throat.

Wilma's crab cheese puffs, brownies, and punch roiled inside me, preparing to return. I backed out of the bathroom and into the hall, taking deep breaths and hoping I wouldn't throw up on the custodian's shiny floor.

Part of me wanted to run down the wide hall to the safety of our meeting room, screaming for help. Part of me wanted to run out the doors and keep on running. Let somebody else discover this body. I'd had more than my share of that kind of experience lately. But most of me felt real sad for Willena. Forty is young to die. Especially when you have only begun to live. Like Wilma, Willena had come back to Hopemore after college to wait for Prince Charming. Until he arrived, she had occupied herself with clubs and committees, but again like Wilma, she had seemed perpetually on tiptoe, waiting for a future that never arrived. I scarcely knew her, since she was between my two boys in school and belonged to clubs like the Daughters of the American Revolution instead of the Rotary and other business clubs. Neither she nor Wilma had ever worked. Wilma had used her botany degree to create a beautiful garden, while Willena used her art history degree to furnish her house with art and antiques.

Where Wilma was fussy and precise, Willena was so laid-back, she practically lived lying down. Lines of discontent had begun to radiate from her eyes and bracket her mouth in recent years, though, and she had become increasingly hard on those who disagreed with her. Cindy had asked not long before, "How will anybody know when

Willena goes through menopause? Her whole personality is menopausal."

I wondered what she and Wilma might have been like had they found careers they enjoyed, or married and raised families. However, the Kenan girls were each waiting for a wealthy Southern gentleman who lived up to all the mythic stories about their namesake ancestor and who either had roots in Hopemore or was willing to live there. Those are hard to come by.

Had Grover lived up to Willena's expectations? Had they begun to move toward making a match? She had looked happier that evening, and she and Grover had shared a private laugh before the meeting.

Happy or not, nobody ought to die at the hands of somebody else.

Why was I doing all that thinking about Willena? So I didn't have to move. I ought to get the wheels of investigation turning, but my feet were glued to the floor. The building was dim and vast around me, with unlit rooms stretching off into the distance. Our own meeting room was off the back hall, around a distant corner. The air throbbed with hush and menace. I cringed against the wall and tried not to panic, but a murderer had struck in the past half hour and could still be around. Given how far this hall was from the custodian's office and our meeting room, if he or she had sights on me, would anybody hear me if I yelled?

I like to think I would have overcome my heebie-jeebies in another second, but my daughter-in-law speeded the process. She came through the front door shaking her umbrella, and even in dim light and far away, I recognized her tall, lean grace. Cindy is as elongated and elegant as a Thoroughbred horse, with large brown eyes and cheekbones that will make her beautiful even when she's ninety.

She looked down the hall and saw me. "Mac?" she called uncertainly.

"Yeah. It's me." I was glad to find that my voice didn't tremble. "Is it still raining outside?"

"A real frog-strangler. Are they ready to meet again? I went to call the kids, since Walker's out of town. Didn't want them killing each other while I was gone." She sounded blessedly normal.

I hurried in her direction. I certainly didn't want her heading in mine.

She propped her umbrella against a pillar, where it began to create its own small puddle. "I wish somebody would figure out why we can't get a cell phone signal in this building, and fix the problem."

When she fluffed her thick brown hair, I noticed enviously that it fell right into place. She gave me a bright smile. "Are you taking a lipstick break?" That was her circle's latest euphemism for exercising natural bodily functions. "Maybe I ought to do that, too. Sometimes this group can go on awhile, trying to decide how to invest our millions."

Actually, while most of the members might have millions to invest, the club permitted an investment of only one hundred to three hundred dollars a month per member. This was a learning experience, like schoolchildren pretending to invest and reading the papers for a month to keep track of certain stocks.

Why was I quibbling over semantics when Cindy was heading toward the ladies' room? I concentrated my entire will on getting her back to the meeting before I made my necessary call.

"I think they're about ready to start," I told her, forcing my legs to move down the hall at a halfway normal pace, "and I'm finished. Let's go on in. You can go to the bathroom later." I grabbed her elbow, hoping she didn't realize I was holding her to keep myself from shaking. "How did you get in from outside? Wasn't the door locked?"

She turned and gave it a puzzled look. "No. Somebody else must have unlocked it. Good thing for me — I didn't think of that, and I'd have been stuck out there."

I mulled that over while we headed down the hall. She is six inches taller than me, so I let go of her elbow and permitted her to outstride me; then I stopped and called, "I forgot. I need to phone Joe Riddley. It's time for Lulu to go out."

That was not a lie. It *was* time to let our beagle out, and I *did* need to phone Joe Riddley — in the worst way. I wanted to beg him to come get me out of this and remind him it was all his fault I was there. Still, Cindy gave me the puzzled look I deserved. She knew full well that Joe Riddley has had dogs all his life.

I gave her what I hoped was a rueful smile. "I guess I just want to hear his voice, after being away from him so long." Her face softened like she completely understood, and I could have hugged her for loving my younger son so much. Instead, I flapped one hand toward the hall that led to the meeting room. "Go on, honey. I won't be but a minute."

She hesitated, then went. I hurried back toward the glass front door.

The community center had a ledge over the doors, but gusts of wind blew rain in to dampen my clothes. I took deep gulps of moist, clean air scented with fresh-mowed hay, newly blooming creamy magnolias, and rain. Only when I was sure my knees weren't going to buckle and I could speak without my voice wobbling did I punch the autodial for the police station. While I talked, I turned in a slow circle to keep my back from being exposed too long in any one direction.

I was real disappointed when Chief Charlie Muggins picked up the phone.

Chief Muggins is part bantam rooster, part chimpanzee, and part polecat — the least desirable parts of all three. He is also one of the few people on God's green earth whom I cannot abide. He struts around Hopemore like he personally keeps the peace, when in reality he stirs up more animosity and illwill than most of our criminals combined.

Whatever I feel about Charlie, the feeling is mutual. I didn't want him selected for police chief and he didn't want me appointed magistrate. But Joe Riddley would ask you to take all that with a grain of salt. He claims that making us work together is one of the ways God keeps us both humbler than we might be otherwise.

"Chief, it's Judge Yarbrough." We always use titles when we speak to or about each other in public. "I'm over at the Hopemore Community Center for a meeting, and Willena Kenan is lying dead in the ladies' room. Murdered."

"I can't hear you. Can you speak louder?"

The reception would be better out in the rain, but I didn't relish getting soaked. "It's Judge Yarbrough at the Hopemore Community Center. Willena Kenan has been killed."

He whistled. "Willena Kenan. Are you sure?" Charlie worships the gods of money, influence, and publicity, so he would put his best efforts into finding her killer. However, for the same reasons, chances were slim that he'd suspect any member of the investment club. Except me, of course. Sure enough, his voice crackled over the wire. "What did you do to her?" Charlie is eternally hopeful that he'll catch me one day committing a major crime.

I was too numbed by what I'd seen to rise to his bait. "I didn't do anything to her, but somebody did. It looks like she was stabbed in the throat."

Bile rose in my own throat. I hurried over to the edge of the cement and horrified my mama up in heaven by spitting off the community center porch. Soaked and miserable, I got my voice back and shouted, "We're having a meeting right now, and I haven't told anybody else about finding her yet, so if you'll get right over here —"

"You found her?"

"Are you coming or not? If you are, I'll go back in and pretend nothing's happened until you get here. If not, hang up and let me call the sheriff."

With that perversity peculiar to cell phones, the line miraculously cleared, so I must have nearly deafened him as I bawled that last sentence.

"The center isn't in the sheriff's jurisdiction," he reminded me. The sheriff handled the county, while the police department handled crimes committed within the city limits.

"We both know that, but somebody has to get over here right this minute. If you don't —"

"I'll be there in two shakes."

Before I headed back inside, I waited to hear the siren. Considering that he was less than two miles away, Chief Muggins didn't need to wake all the babies in town getting there, but he had himself a new cruiser with all sorts of bells and lights he seldom got to use. I knew he'd seize this big chance to show them off.

# 4

As soon as I heard him coming, I hurried back to the meeting. The group had taken their seats and were looking around, waiting for Willena and me to return so they could start.

"MacLaren," Gusta called in her imperious old voice, "we are ready to begin our investment procedures." She sounded exactly like she used to when she taught my kindergarten Sunday-school class and called me back from the refreshments table. She even patted the chair beside her in the same old way. "Did you see Willena?" she added as I took my seat at the end of the third row. "We are all waiting for her."

I had to clear my throat before I could answer. "I think Willena would want us to go ahead." I spoke loud enough for Wilma to hear.

She dithered around a minute, then went to the table up front. "Very well. Who has a suggestion about what we should invest in this month? And I've forgotten. How much do we have to spend?" Poor Wilma, I couldn't remember her ever being elected president of a club before. That was usually Willena. Wilma was usually secretary because she was a whiz at keeping detailed minutes. No wonder she was nervous.

MayBelle stood. "Nancy had to leave. She wasn't feeling well. But she's left me her report."

When we'd elected officers, Nancy Jensen had been reelected financial partner, their fancy name for treasurer. I remembered seeing her talking with MayBelle, and then, about the time Wilma had joined Grover and me, she had looked around the room and gone out the door. I had passed her coming back in as I went out. Her face was flushed and damp.

Was she returning from killing Willena? The thought chilled my soul.

MayBelle moved toward the table, consulting a sheet she held. "We took in eighteen hundred tonight and have the four thousand we carried over. Do you want to discuss the matter that came up before the break, or wait until Willena gets here?"

"I'd like —" Cindy began, but Wilma interrupted.

"Since we're running late — I'm sorry our refreshments took more time than usual —" She stopped.

As an actress, Sadie Lowe was used to speaking on cue. "They were simply delicious," she breathed. "Well worth the wait."

"Thank you." Wilma gave her a tight little smile that approved of the sentiment, if not of Sadie Lowe herself. "So, since we are running late, I suggest we divide tonight's money equally between Microsoft and Southern Company, which we already own, and hold our discussion of the carry-over funds until next month's meeting." Nobody who had ever served on a committee with Wilma was surprised that she made her own views known rather than asking for other people's. Wilma always knew best.

Rachel objected. "Last month we discussed buying some medical stocks, to diversify our portfolio, and you asked me to look into several. I'd like to recommend —"

I stopped listening. I didn't care what they did with my hundred dollars. I was hearing Chief Muggins's siren scream closer through the night. I was also trying to remember who had done what during the break.

Seemed to me as if everybody had come and gone at one time or another, but all I could remember clearly was Nancy, because she and I had passed at the door, and Wilma, who had buzzed in and out of the kitchen like a little bee. That image was reinforced by the yellow cotton pantsuit she wore with a black-and-yellow-striped silk scarf and yellow flats. Wilma had shoes to match each outfit.

She also had three full-time maids, so I'd been surprised to see her doing the kitchen work herself. I had asked whether Linette, her housekeeper, was sick, and she had said that Linette and Lincoln — Linette's husband, who was Wilma's driver and general handyman — had gone down to Dublin to visit their son. "Besides," Wilma had added with her tight smile, "my crabmeat cheese puffs and the punch are family recipes that I don't share even with Linette."

She had refused my offer (halfhearted as it was) to help her before the meeting, telling the custodian to carry stuff in from the car and asking Willena to assist her briefly in the little kitchen that adjoined our meeting room. At the beginning of the break Wilma had hurried back to the kitchen to put the cheese puffs in the oven and mix up the first batch of punch. She had called coyly as she left, "Don't be insulted that I'm shutting the door, but I don't want you all taking notes."

MayBelle called through the shut door, "You know we're all dying to put that punch recipe on the Internet." To us, she had whispered, "Wanna bet there isn't a drop of liquor in it?"

We'd stood around and waited for more than ten minutes. Some folks went to the ladies' room at that point, but I couldn't remember who. When Wilma came out, she'd boasted that she had put black-walnut brownies in the oven as soon as the cheese puffs came out, and they'd be ready in a jiffy. After that she had trotted back and forth spreading a feast of fruit, raw vegetables, dips, and the cheese puffs. But she had never been out of our sight more than a few seconds except when she was mixing the second batch of punch.

Anybody but Wilma would have used the community center's trays and their perfectly adequate punch bowl, but she had brought silver trays from home, along with a silver punch bowl and ladle. Like I said, Wilma was the fussiest woman God ever made.

"Bless her heart," I had murmured to Gusta, "if serving refreshments puts Wilma in such a dither, I hate to think what being senior partner will do. How on earth did she get nominated?"

Gusta leaned close so nobody else could hear. "We rotate the position one year at a time. Her election was a mere formality." I did some calculations and figured out that I had Augusta and Cindy between me and the time when I'd have to decide whether to decline or resign.

MayBelle was right about the punch: It was strictly teetotal. Still, it was cold and delicious, although it tasted a lot like one in our church cookbook, which was nothing but bottles of chilled ginger ale and strawberry soda and a big can of pineapple juice poured over pineapple sherbet. We had finished off the first batch pretty fast, being so thirsty from eating nuts while waiting for the crabmeat cheese puffs, but Wilma cooed, "Isn't it lucky I brought enough ingredients for a second batch?" and went to mix some more while the brownies baked.

It was while she poured that second batch into the punch bowl that she had noticed me talking to Grover and had sashayed over to join us. Poor Wilma, she was flushed with happiness tonight, between getting elected senior partner and the success of her refreshments. I hated that her special evening was about to get spoiled.

The picture rose before me: Willena lying on the floor with her skirt hitched up and the backs of her white knees bared, her gold high-heeled sandals gleaming in the fluorescent light. Her evening had gotten spoiled, too.

Earlier I had complimented her dangly earrings, thinking they were green and white glass chips. She had said, "Aren't they nice? They belonged to Grandmother Sarah." Now I decided they must have been emeralds and diamonds, and wondered if they were still in her ears.

She had clutched her cardigan around her. "Is it cold in here, or is it my imagination? I'm freezing." The cardigan was tawny cotton, appliquéd with palm trees and tigers to match the jungle print of her skirt, and with it she'd worn a ruffled white blouse.

"I feel fine," I told her. "Maybe you're coming down with something."

"Maybe so. Listen, have I given you the latest petition about saving the wolves?"

In the last few years, Willena had gotten Concerned About the Environment, with capital letters. She had joined the Sierra Club and liked to corner people at inopportune moments to encourage them to save various endangered species.

"I am all for saving whales, manatees, and rain forests," I told her, "but I'm a bit ambivalent about wolves. Besides, we don't have many of those in Hope County. Can I interest you in saving a few impoverished children? We have a number of those."

She shrugged. "They can always get a job." She opened her purse and rummaged around in it. "I have a copy of the petition here somewhere."

Catching a glint of steel, I inquired, "I hope you have a permit for that gun?" It seemed odd to me that somebody who talked about saving endangered species would carry a weapon designed to maim or kill her own.

"Of course." She found what she was looking for and handed me a sheet of folded paper. "You can duplicate this and hand it out to as many people as you want."

Willena could be pushy, narrow-minded, and hard to get along with, but I couldn't imagine who hated her enough to kill her. Besides, whoever had done that murder would have ended up spattered with blood from head to toe. I looked at Wilma in her pale yellow cotton, MayBelle in her sleek tangerine linen, Sadie Lowe in a stark white crepe pantsuit, Meriwether in a mint green cotton sweater and matching skirt, and Rachel and Cindy, elegant in black and white. It was inconceivable that any of them had committed a vicious, bloody murder. Maybe for once Charlie Muggins had what he usually expected: a murder committed by a wandering tramp.

But how did a tramp unlock the front door? Dexter Baxter, the community center custodian, had manned the door and greeted us each by name. Surely he had locked the door once we were all inside, for he had said he'd be down in what he called "my office," the janitor's room near the kitchen. I suspected he was watching a movie on a cast-off VCR somebody had given him, and I'd heard he was partial to horror movies. Would he have left the center doors unlocked?

The siren wailed to a stop outside. Everybody but me darted quick, uneasy looks toward the door. Five minutes later by my watch, heavy boots clumped our way. Chief Muggins is small, but walks like a man of stone.

All that time, Wilma plowed ahead with the business at hand. She had just repeated, "Remember, we only have eighteen hundred to invest this month. I suggest we buy more Microsoft and Southern Company. We don't want to spread ourselves . . ." when she trailed off. Chief Muggins had strutted into the room, thumbs hooked in his gun belt.

Someday he is going to lose his pants that

way. I sincerely hope I am there to see it.

"Evenin', ladies." He swept off his hat, and his thin yellow hair shone in the light. "What kind of meeting is this you all're havin' tonight?"

Gusta drew herself to her full and most regal height. "We are the Magnolia Ladies' Investment Club."

Chief Muggins is not generally a respecter of women. His ex-wife went to live in Atlanta after he hit her once too often. But in that instant I could see him registering the faces in that room and tallying up the financial worth of the group. He gave a deferential nod all around. "Sorry to disturb you, ladies, but we have a little matter of murder in the bathroom down the hall. I have to request that you not leave until we've secured the building and I've been able to ask you a few questions."

I don't think anybody but me heard a word after *murder.*

Necks craned. Eyes darted around the room. Gradually it began to sink in that we were still one member short.

"Who . . . who is it?" Wilma's voice quavered, and she leaned her hands on the table in front of her for support. A low rustle of whispers moved around the circle.

Chief Muggins crossed the room and laid

a hand on her arm. "I'm afraid it's your cousin, Miss Willena."

Nobody looked real guilty, that I could see. Most gasped. Rachel exclaimed, "Oh, my God!" like New Yorkers are prone to do. Sadie Lowe dropped her purse and bent to pick it up. Cindy and Meriwether both grew pale. Gusta sat ramrod straight and regal.

Wilma staggered with a little cry, and would have fallen if MayBelle hadn't caught her and steered her to an empty padded chair. She lowered Wilma into it, then asked the chief, "Are you absolutely sure she's . . . gone?" The last word was obviously May-Belle's second choice.

"Absolutely." His eyes roamed the refreshment table. "Did you all have wine?" When we all shook our heads, he added with his customary tact, "She seems to have been killed with a silver corkscrew."

Wilma keeled sideways. Her head hit another chair with a thud.

# 5

MayBelle knelt beside Wilma, rubbing her temples. "Somebody get me some water."

When I jumped up, Chief Muggins ordered, "Don't leave this room."

"The kitchen is right there." I pointed to the closed door.

He jerked his head toward the punch bowl, which was still half-full. "Get some of that."

I grabbed a cup, filled it with Wilma's family recipe, and rushed it over to MayBelle. She was now giving Wilma's cheeks sharp little pats, like some trainer on a televised boxing match. Without looking to see what was in the cup, she flung its contents into Wilma's face.

Wilma pushed her away and struggled to sit up, gasping. "Look what you've done! You've ruined my clothes!" She glared at MayBelle, then must have remembered why she'd fainted in the first place. "Is it true?

Willena's dead?"

MayBelle nodded. "I'm afraid so, honey." Her hands trembled and her eyes were frightened.

Wilma covered her face and seemed to shrink in her chair.

"No discussing the crime," the chief commanded, then immediately broke his own rule. "Did any of you see anybody come in or leave this building?"

We exchanged blank stares and shook our heads in unison.

"Did any of you leave the room since the meeting began?"

An uneasy silence fell.

"You went out," Sadie Lowe reminded Cindy. "You were gone the whole time we were having refreshments."

The chief swung around in Cindy's direction like a chimp ready to pounce. Cindy's dark eyes burned with indignation. "I went to call my children, and I had to go all the way outside to get a signal. This building is hopeless for cell phones. But I didn't see anybody out there."

"Did you go to the bathroom?" he barked.

"N-no." I wished she had sounded more definite.

"How long were you gone?"

"Fifteen minutes? Maybe twenty?"

Sadie Lowe looked at her watch. "More like thirty. We had a long break."

"Standing out in the rain?" Chief Muggins demanded, hard to convince.

Cindy bristled at his tone. "I had my umbrella. It's in the front hall now, drying off."

Charlie looked around at the others. "Anybody here able to verify she was outside the whole time?"

Nobody could. I got up and moved over near Cindy, who looked like she expected to mount the steps to the guillotine any minute. When I took her hand, she flinched. "Don't let him get to you," I whispered. "He's big on intimidation."

"Sadie Lowe, you went out, too," May-Belle remembered.

Sadie Lowe shrugged as if we were discussing a trip to the beauty parlor. "I did go down to the bathroom, but Willena was alive when I left her, throwing up in one of the stalls. I left her some cream to take off her mascara. It had run," she added to the chief, as if that explained everything.

Meriwether spoke up. "I went into the ladies' room as Sadie Lowe was coming out."

Sadie Lowe leaned toward Meriwether. "But we all know you didn't kill Willena.

Why should you?"

Meriwether looked pale. "Of course I didn't. But Willena came out of the stall while I was there and said she'd eaten something for dinner that disagreed with her. I helped her wash her face. She was repairing her makeup when I left and said she'd be right back." Her voice shook on the last phrase.

"Anybody else leave this room?" the chief snapped.

Wilma raised one hand weakly while the other still covered her face. "I was in and out of the kitchen all evening, fixing refreshments. It was my turn to furnish them."

"Did you go to the bathroom?"

"When would I have had time?" She made it sound like she had personally prepared and catered a meal for hundreds, but she did have a point. She started rubbing her hands together as if they were cold. They made a dry, whispery sound in the silent room while the chief looked over the group.

"Okay, anybody else?" he finally asked.

Nobody spoke, but Meriwether turned and looked at MayBelle, as if waiting for her to say something.

MayBelle's lips twitched with annoyance. "Okay," she admitted, "I ran to the bathroom for a few seconds. Wilma was heating up cheese puffs in the oven, and I figured it might be a while before she got the table ready. Meriwether was leaving the bathroom as I went in." She added in a defiant tone, "Willena was still alive and bitching when I left. Her hands were shaky, and she was having trouble getting her mascara on straight."

"You were gone a long time," Gusta remarked.

"I went to see if Dexter had fixed the toilet in the men's room. It's been running, and he had said he would fix it today, but he still hasn't." That year MayBelle chaired the committee that ran the center. She looked at Sadie Lowe. "You were gone a long time, too. You weren't here when I got back."

Sadie Lowe shrugged. "I went out on the porch to have a smoke." She turned and raised one eyebrow in Rachel's direction. "Right after I saw you go out the front door."

We all swiveled to look at Rachel. Now that I thought about it, I remembered that drops of moisture on her hair had caught the light like diamonds while she was listening to Gusta talk about little Zach.

"I went to my car," she explained. "I had left a tray here at a luncheon last week, and wanted to take it out so I wouldn't forget it later." That sounded harmless enough, so why did she sound like she was defying us to correct her?

"Did you see Mrs. Walker Yarbrough out there?" The chief jerked his head toward Cindy.

Rachel hesitated. "No, I didn't. She wasn't on the porch or steps out front when I went out or came back in." She threw Cindy an apologetic glance.

Cindy's lips twitched in annoyance. "I went down past the big red-tip bush to get a better signal. I saw you, though. Talking to Grover." The last three words sounded like an accusation.

"Me, too," Sadie Lowe said in a voice like a cat's purr.

Rachel's nostrils flared. "He had something he wanted to give me. A prospectus. We came right back in. And I didn't see either one of you." She glowered at Sadie Lowe.

"I was down at the far end of the porch in the dark," Sadie Lowe told her. "Maybe you smelled my smoke?"

Rachel shook her head. Sadie Lowe shrugged and gave the chief a smile that visibly raised his blood pressure.

"How did you get back in?" I asked Rachel. "Wasn't the front door locked?"

Rachel shook her head. "Cindy must have

unlocked it."

"It wasn't me," Cindy objected. "I didn't even think about it when I went out."

"So somebody from outside could have gotten in!" Wilma peered at the door anxiously.

The chief scratched his chin. "Coulda been a tramp," he agreed. "I'll check with Dexter." He looked around the room again, as if taking inventory. "That's everybody, then, except Miss Augusta and the judge, who found the body. I think we all will agree Miss Augusta is innocent."

*Innocent* wasn't a word I'd apply to Gusta, given some of her past history, but I let it go. Some of the others were looking at me as if finding a body constituted creating one.

Wilma raised a weak hand and let it drop. "Nancy Jensen, our treasurer, was here, too, but she had to go home early. She got sick."

"Did she leave the room?"

Wilma hesitated. "For a minute or two."

"It was much longer than that." Gusta was rubbing one of her vein-knotted hands over the other. I didn't know if she was worried or if her arthritis was bothering her.

"Nancy is chairing the golf club committee annual dinner this year," Meriwether explained quickly. "She said she wanted to look at the ballroom to get some idea of

63

how she might decorate the tables."

"Did anybody notice when Mrs. Jensen left or how long she was gone?" The chief made the question sound like an accusation.

Nobody spoke. Finally I said, "I don't know when she left, but she came back in here as I went out."

"She told me she didn't feel well and was going home," MayBelle added.

I had the feeling most of the women were holding their breath.

"I saw her come out the front door and look around, then she went right back in," Cindy volunteered. "Then right before I came in, she ran down the steps to her car."

The chief raised his eyebrows. "None of you knows if she went to the ladies' room?"

We all shook our heads. He stood there turning all that over in what passes for his mind. Finally he came to the conclusion I'd expected him to reach all along. "What it boils down to" — his sharp polecat gaze flickered as he looked straight at me — "is that Mrs. Jensen needs to account for her time, Mrs. Walker Yarbrough has a stretch of time when she was supposedly out on the sidewalk in the streaming rain making a call but nobody saw her, and Judge Yarbrough found the body."

That got Cindy and me a lot of glances we neither wanted nor needed, but they were nothing compared to the grief Joe Riddley would give me when I got home. There was no way he was going to admit it was his fault I'd found Willena.

The chief rolled smoothly on. "Mrs. Brandison, as the last person known to leave the ladies' room before the judge found the body, are you certain Miss Kenan was alive at that point?"

MayBelle stood to her full height and gave him the look she gives contractors who don't fulfill their contracts. "Very much alive. She told me to make sure Wilma saved her some crabmeat cheese puffs for her to eat tomorrow when . . ." The words *she felt better* hung over us.

"They all got eaten," Wilma wailed — as if that made any difference now. After somebody dies, the strangest things pierce you.

"Mac was here when MayBelle came back in," Gusta informed the chief, looking down her nose at him. "She was refilling her punch cup for the third time."

Trust Gusta to have counted. Still, I appreciated it when she added, "Then she talked a long time with Grover Henderson and ate a couple of brownies. I saw her leave, and she wasn't gone long enough to kill anybody."

"It wouldn't have taken long," the chief assured her. He looked around at the group of women. "Who is this Grover Henderson, and where is he now?"

The entire group looked toward Wilma. She threw MayBelle a silent, piteous plea.

MayBelle had been taking charge of things all her life. She took charge of explaining Grover now. "He's a stockbroker who comes down from Augusta to talk about investing each month. He left when the refreshment break was over. Since he has so far to drive and is a single parent with a teenage son, he has asked to be excused from the last part of the meeting, when we decide what to invest in. Nancy Jensen, our financial partner, usually calls him the next day and tells him what to buy for us."

That was all true, but it didn't tell Chief Muggins anything about the effect Grover had on women. He had come in that evening a little late. MayBelle had immediately sailed over to meet him and put a proprietary hand on his arm. As he went to the podium, Nancy Jensen — who sat on the front row — had let her skirt ride up to expose her big knees. Willena had stepped up to share whatever it was that made him laugh. Wilma sat through his whole presentation with a foolish simper on her face, then asked such a dumb question that anybody could tell she primarily wanted his attention. Willena had leaned over and whispered loudly, "Don't go making such a fool of yourself." Rachel had gone outside with him during the break, and I'd seen Sadie Lowe give him several of her special come-hither smiles. Only Gusta, Cindy, Meriwether, and I seemed unaffected by his charm.

"Can you give me his address and phone number?" Chief Muggins asked.

"Grover wouldn't!" Wilma yelped. She turned and flung herself onto MayBelle, sobbing noisily. I didn't particularly like Wilma, but I sincerely pitied her. Willena had been like a baby sister to her, and they were the last of the Kenans.

Even crusty old Gusta made a small grunt of compassion, while MayBelle patted Wilma's shoulder and said, over and over, "It's okay, honey. It's okay."

Chief Muggins hooked his thumbs in his belt. "At the moment I am leaning toward the conclusion that somebody slipped in while Mrs. Walker Yarbrough was down off the porch" — he put extra emphasis on those last three words — "and that we'll find evidence of that on the scene. I know all of you ladies and where to find you. Please don't leave town without checking with me. I'll want to talk with some of you again tomorrow. Will that be acceptable?"

If looks could wither a person, he'd have withered under mine like a roach under pesticide. He wouldn't have been asking if his tactics were acceptable if he'd had a batch of welfare mothers in that room. He wouldn't have been letting them go home, either.

"I don't have a ride," Wilma whimpered. "I came with Willena."

MayBelle took her arm. "Come on. I'll drive you home. Will Linette and Lincoln be back yet?" When Wilma shook her head, MayBelle told the rest of us, "I'll stay until they get there."

Folks with raincoats had left them spread on chairs out in the tiled hall, to save the meeting room carpet. I helped Gusta put on a practical gray all-weather coat. Meriwether had a floral raincoat with a matching umbrella. Rachel donned a large black cape that made her look like Zorro. Sadie Lowe had a transparent raincoat that showed off her outfit.

"Let me get on my rain boots," Wilma insisted to nobody in particular. "I don't want these shoes to get ruined." Not one soul who knew her was surprised that Wilma was worrying about yellow shoes while her cousin lay dead. She took a pair of clear plastic shoes that fit over other shoes from a large cloth carryall and sat to pull them on. They were still wet and muddy from carrying in refreshments before the meeting. She then put on a soft yellow raincoat, opened an umbrella patterned after an impressionist painting, and picked up the bulky carryall.

That whole time Maybelle was prowling up and down the hall demanding, "What the hell happened to my raincoat? Has anybody seen it? It's rust brown, and I left it right there." She pointed to an empty chair.

A murmur of denial filled the hall.

I sidled over to Charlie and murmured, "Rust brown would conceal bloodstains real well, don't you think? I hope you all will look good for that coat."

He frowned, but called to one of the deputies, "Thad, would you take a description of her coat, in case we come across it?"

I wasn't through. "If she was throwing up like that, maybe somebody gave her poison or something."

He looked down his nose. "The woman

was obviously stabbed, Judge. You saw her yourself. You stick to your bench and leave the detecting to me."

I wanted to say, *I would, if you'd do any detecting,* but he was already moving away, and I had two more things to say. "Shouldn't we all get tested for bloodstains and stick around until you take fingerprints from the ladies' room? And don't you want to check for footprints in the hall before we tramp all over it?"

He waved my first suggestion aside like a polecat batting flies. "No need to inconvenience anybody, Judge," he assured me. I was about to point out that murder is generally inconvenient when he at least paid attention to the last thing I said. He raised his voice and called, "If you would, please go down the back hall here and leave the building by the far side hall, so you don't mess up any possible footprints up near the ladies' room."

That was the first time I ever heard a police chief worry about inconveniencing a possible murderer. But what the heck? If he was willing to let us go, who was I to argue?

I should have known it wasn't going to be that easy. As I hefted my pocketbook over one shoulder, he held up one hand. "Oh,

Judge? I'd appreciate it if you and Miss Cindy would stay behind for a minute."

# 6

All he wanted was to embarrass us in front of the others.

He took us back into the Wainwright Meeting Room and took me over my story again. What could I tell him except to repeat what I had already said: that I'd gone to the bathroom and found Willena as soon as I opened the door?

I didn't bother to add that since I had never gotten to use the bathroom, I was in serious discomfort by now. The office of judge requires a certain bit of decorum. Still, I hoped he'd finish with us soon and let us go.

Instead, he turned to Cindy and started questioning her again. "Don't you think it's a little odd for somebody to stand for thirty minutes out in the rain trying to call kids?"

"I had an umbrella," she repeated. "If you'll go check, you'll see it's sopping wet. My daughter was on the phone — she's thirteen — and I couldn't get through for a while."

"Don't you folks have call waiting?"

"Yes, but she didn't pick up."

I could have told him that when Cindy is trying to reach her children when they're at home alone, a hurricane or tornado wouldn't deter her, but I decided to keep my mouth shut. The sooner they finished, the sooner we could go.

As Robert Burns once remarked, however, the best-laid plans of mice and men go "aft agley." A deputy foiled our escape by coming in to announce, "We found a raincoat, Chief, spattered with something that looks like blood."

Chief Muggins turned with the eagerness of a bantam rooster eyeing dinner. "Where was it?"

"In a trash can at the back of the building, balled up and shoved in. It's a kind of brown-red color, so it's hard to tell what has spattered it."

Cindy caught a quick, short breath.

Chief Muggins heard and whirled in our direction. "One of yours?"

I shook my head. "Neither of us brought a raincoat. Cindy brought an umbrella and came into our garage to get me, so I didn't think to bring anything. But I'd bet that's the one MayBelle was asking about before she left. Sounds like hers."

"Could you identify it?" Chief Muggins asked us.

I hesitated, but Cindy nodded. "I think so."

"Bring it in," he commanded the deputy. The deputy returned carrying the coat in gloved hands. It was a gory sight, the front covered with spatters and one wide stream of dark brown.

I've seen gruesome things in my day, but they always make me queasy. I swallowed hard. Cindy turned green. "Yeah, that's hers." She clutched her mouth and headed for the kitchen. We heard her being violently ill, then water running in the sink.

"Don't mess up evidence," the chief shouted in to her.

"You were the one who insisted she look at the coat," I reminded him. "Willena was a friend of hers."

As soon as I'd said it, a chill rose from my feet toward my heart. Cindy and Willena were in a lot of clubs and organizations together, but they were anything but friends.

Willena had disliked Cindy ever since Cindy joined our local Daughters of the American Revolution chapter. Willena and Wilma, as chapter members with the most confirmed ancestors who had fought in the Revolution, had pretty much run things their way until then, but Cindy's family had been active in the DAR for generations, and she had started attending DAR meetings and conventions with her mother and grandmother before she could walk. When Willena asked the Hopemore chapter to provide funds for a memorial marker and stone for her maternal many-times-great-grandfather to replace a stone that had been vandalized, Cindy asked for verification that he had fought in the Revolution. Willena brushed that off, pointing out that while there was some doubt that he had actually fought, he had lived in Georgia during that period and supported the cause of freedom. Cindy then reminded her that DAR chapter funds can be used only for markers on the graves of actual Revolutionary soldiers.

She wasn't casting aspersions on Willena's membership. Willena had plenty of qualifying ancestors. Nevertheless, Willena got furious. Especially when they checked the by-laws and she was forced to admit that Cindy was right. Ever since then, Willena had smiled and said sweet things to Cindy in public, but she carried daggers behind her eyes and fought Cindy tooth and nail over points that would never have mattered to anybody else.

Tonight, after Grover had given his presentation and Nancy had given the treasurer's report, Cindy got a puzzled wrinkle between her brows. "Why do we have so much money in the treasury? Didn't we vote last month to spend four thousand dollars?"

Gusta had leaned over to me and said in what I guess she thought was an inaudible murmur, "We voted to buy stock in the insurance company Walker works for. Good buy, too. It's gone up two dollars a share this month."

I knew that. I own some, not only because it shows confidence in our son to own stock in the company he represents, but because insurance companies these days are run largely for the benefit of shareholders instead of the insured, so I figure that owning stock is the only way to recoup some of my overpriced premiums.

After Gusta spoke, the room had grown still. Nancy looked toward Willena, and Willena stood behind the table watching her hands fiddle with her pen. Finally she looked up with an apologetic little smile that was about as sincere as a car salesman's handshake. "I told Nancy to hold off on that purchase until we could discuss it further. We have never had a policy about investing in companies for which our members or their husbands work, but I think we ought to. We don't want to get into the problem of conflict of interest."

I had taken a quick mental poll. Gusta, Willena, Wilma, Rachel, and Sadie Lowe were not married. Gusta, Willena, Wilma, and Sadie Lowe were not employed. Rachel was a lawyer, as was Meriwether's husband. Meriwether, MayBelle, Nancy's husband, and I all owned businesses, but they were privately held, so none of them had stock for sale. Cindy was the only person there whose husband worked for a company that traded on the stock exchange.

Cindy must have been doing the same calculations I was, because she objected, "You've bought stock over the years in Du-Bose Trucking, Wainwright Textile Mills, and Kenan Cotton Factors. Has this ever been an issue before?" Her eyes were flashing, her cheeks pink. She was no longer addressing Willena but the whole group, a new member asking to know the group's history. Most of the members were already shaking their heads.

That was when we reached the place where the magnolias met the manure. Willena waved one hand to dismiss Cindy's objection. "Of course not, honey, but Gusta,

Wilma, and I don't any of us *work* for those companies. Neither did Pooh."

It was the first time I ever heard *work* sound like a four-letter word.

"If we had invested four thousand dollars in Walker's company last month, as we voted, we'd be a good bit richer now," Gusta snapped. That was a typical Gusta exaggeration. Four thousand dollars invested in that particular stock a month ago would be worth forty-two hundred and ninety by now. Even if Gusta held twenty-five percent of the total investment (the most permitted by the bylaws), she would have made around seventy dollars. Still, to Gusta, any money she could have earned and didn't was a fortune lost.

Willena shrugged. "I know we lost a little money, Miss Gusta, but that's how the market is. We win some and we lose some. I feel we need to have a discussion on this matter after Wilma takes the helm, when I can speak freely."

Cindy didn't say a word, but she breathed heavily beside me and her eyes glistened with tears. If looks could kill, Willena would have lain dead on the floor.

Now she rejoined Chief Muggins and me, pale but composed. With the chief's permission we headed to her silver Lexus SUV.

The only other car in the parking lot, except for police vehicles, was Willena's white Jaguar convertible. I wondered who would come to take it home.

When we got out on the front porch, I steered Cindy over to the far side, where it was dark. "Do you see any cigarette butts?" She peered at the porch floor, which was littered with a few dead leaves.

"Not a one. I never saw Sadie Lowe, either, or smelled smoke when I came in. But why should she lie?"

"Maybe she dropped them off the edge." I drew her in that direction by the elbow. We peered down into streaming darkness but didn't see a single butt. I gave the door a worried look. "I hope the chief will think to check for them." Charlie wasn't known for his thoroughness in investigating statements.

"Leave it alone, Mac," Cindy advised. "You know Pop doesn't like you getting involved in things like this. Chief Muggins can find out what happened to Willena." She gave a short little laugh. "And if he doesn't, do we really care?"

She had a point. I was tired, I had enough on my plate already, and I didn't know Willena Kenan well enough to have any of the insider knowledge that in the past had

79

helped me find a solution to a case. Furthermore, while I firmly believe in justice for all persons, I hadn't liked Willena enough to expend much energy in doing Charlie's job for him.

With relief, I realized that this time there wasn't a single reason for me to do what my boys call "meddling in murder."

"It's all Charlie's," I said cheerfully, following Cindy out into the rain.

We shared her umbrella as we wended our way through the parking lot. It wasn't a great distance to her SUV, but since she is five-eight to my five-two, I got pretty damp. Especially since, on the way, she fumbled and fumbled in her purse, turning the umbrella this way and that until it occasionally dumped rain down my neck or on my shoulder. Although the air was warm, the rain had fallen from a great height and was chilly. I shivered and looked forward to getting into the car.

"I can't find my keys," she confessed when we stood dripping beside the big vehicle. She peered down at our feet. "You don't see them, do you?"

Siamese twins joined at the umbrella handle, we circled her car. No keys gleamed on the wet gravel. She gave a huff of disgust. "I must have dropped them somewhere inside. Here, you keep the umbrella, and I'll dash —"

"Don't be ridiculous." I took a firm hold of her arm. "You'll get soaked and probably die of pneumonia. Then I'll have to raise your kids. I'd rather come with you."

By the time we got to the door, I was soggy from shoes to knees and my hair was plastered to my forehead. "The investment club may have had richer new members," I quipped as she held the heavy front door for me, "but it has never had a wetter one."

We were laughing together — and I was thinking how good it felt to finally be getting to know this daughter-in-law well enough to laugh with her — when we entered the hall and saw Chief Muggins standing there, glaring at us.

We stopped laughing at once, embarrassed to be caught carrying on while Willena lay dead down the hall. On the other hand, anybody who has been through a trauma knows that without laughter, you lose your mind.

Cindy stammered, "I-I'm sorry I . . . I-I've left my keys somewhere."

The chief's eyes narrowed. He went to the door of the ladies' room and called, "Hey, Hank, you still got those keys you found?"

"Right here." A deputy handed them out,

encased in a plastic bag.

"Are these them?" The chief knew no more about grammar than he did about criminal investigation.

I caught Cindy's elbow, willing her not to say a word, but she'd already exclaimed, "Yes!" and reached for them. When he pulled them back so she couldn't touch them, with a gleam in his eye, her voice dropped to a hoarse whisper. "Where did you find them?"

"Right where you left them," Chief Muggins said with satisfaction. "Under Miss Kenan's body."

# 7

Cindy's eyes widened and her face turned white as chalk. I felt the world start a slow spin, and wasn't sure I could keep my balance.

"You can go on home now, Judge," the chief said to me, jerking his head toward the door. "Mrs. Yarbrough and I need to chat a little longer."

"I'm not leaving until her lawyer gets here." I planted my unsteady feet as firmly as I could on the community center floor.

"So how'd your keys get under Miss Kenan?" the chief asked in a jocular voice, as if he were asking how she'd done in a tennis match.

Cindy shook her head. "I have no idea. I thought they were in my purse." She held it up helplessly. "I did run into the bathroom to blow my nose before I went out to call our kids — I didn't have any tissues —"

"You told me you didn't go into the

bathroom," the chief reminded her.

"I did not!" she replied hotly. "You asked whether I *went* to the bathroom. I didn't go. All I did was blow my nose and come straight back out."

Ah, the English language can be so confusing sometimes.

Remembering the urgency with which she had left the meeting, I suspected Cindy had also needed a moment to cry out her fury at Willena before talking with the children.

"So how did your keys get under Miss Kenan?" The chief repeated his question in a voice like warm oil.

"Don't answer," I warned. "Don't say a word until you've called your lawyer."

Cindy was too upset to pay me any attention. "I told you, I don't know. Willena wasn't even in there. But wait! I got the keys out of my purse because I thought I might get in the car to make my call. While I was blowing my nose, I put them down on the counter. But Willena wasn't there. Nobody was. They were still in the meeting."

"Willena left several minutes after Cindy," I contributed.

The chief ignored me. "May I see your cell phone?" he asked her, holding out one hand.

"Wait!" I cautioned. "Call your lawyer."

But with what some call the frankness and others the naïveté of the innocent, Cindy had already fumbled in her purse and held it out. He snatched it, turned it on, and pushed the redial button. In a second I heard my son's voice. "Hey, hon. You feelin' better, or is that Kenan bitch still gettin' you down?"

Chief Muggins closed the phone and palmed it. "I'll need to keep this for evidence. I'm taking you down to the station, Mrs. Yarbrough. You can call your lawyer from there. You go on home, Judge. If I need a magistrate, I'll have to call another one."

Cindy's phone began to ring — no doubt Walker wanting to know why they had been cut off. The chief ignored it.

Cindy reached back into her purse.

Faster than I knew he could move, he pulled his gun and aimed it straight at her. "Freeze!"

My heart thudded in double time. Cindy dropped her purse, shaking all over, and lifted her hands. "I was getting my keys for Mac." Then she remembered that her keys were still in the chief's hand. Her eyes locked on them as she added in a an unsteady voice, "She came with me."

I gave the chief the look my sons call Mama's Freezing Look. "You can put that gun away now."

He lowered it and returned it to his holster, but I could tell he'd enjoyed that little display of strength and power. I've always thought that the biggest problem with guns is that so many of the people who carry them are the kind to act first and think later. "You'll have to come with me," he told Cindy.

"But Mac . . ." She turned to me, her eyes huge and full of all sorts of messages: *I'm sorry I can't take you home. I'm scared to death. What about my children? Do something, please!*

"I'll call Joe Riddley to come get me," I told Cindy, willing my voice to sound steady and calm. "He owes me a ride or two. And I'll go stay with the kids until you get home."

"Don't tell them about this, please?" Her face was so white I was afraid she was about to faint.

"I won't. I'll send them to bed, shall I?" I tried to sound like this was a normal delay in her schedule.

"Please."

"Then I'll send Joe Riddley back over here."

At that point the chief decided to be magnanimous. He held up the bag of keys. There were several on the ring, plus a silver disk engraved with Cindy's name and her cell phone number. "Do you agree that you left these keys in the ladies' room?"

Cindy nodded. "Yes." Her voice was barely a whisper.

"Judge, if necessary, are you ready to testify to what she said?"

"If I have to." I felt like I was cutting my daughter-in-law's throat, but I have sworn to uphold the courts.

"What keys are on the ring besides your car keys?"

"Our house keys, my parents' house key, and a key to Walker's office."

He called to one of the deputies. "You still got on gloves? Come here a minute." He instructed the deputy to open the bag and remove the car key and the gizmo that unlocks the doors from the ring. "You can have these, Judge. The rest ought to be sufficient to establish they are Mrs. Yarbrough's keys. We'll bring her home after I've talked to her some more."

"I'm gonna call Walker to come home," I promised Cindy before I headed out.

Walker was somewhere in the wilds of North Carolina at the moment, on something called a Corvette cruise. I knew that because the previous Friday I had come back from making our deposit at the bank across the street to find Walker's whole family inside my office. Tad and Jessica were still in their private school uniforms, but Walker and Cindy wore matching yellow polo shirts and khaki slacks. Matching outfits is one of those things Cindy likes that used to drive me crazy.

At thirteen, Jessica was already taller than I am. Tad, at eleven, was up to my eyebrows. Both Cindy and Walker are tall, so I figure there will come a day when I'll have to look up at all of them. The trick will be to make sure none of them ever looks down on me.

"What's happening?" I had asked. They were all bouncing on the balls of their feet like they would burst from holding something in.

"Come see!" Tad shouted. "Come see what Daddy's got!"

I followed them out to the parking lot. A bright blue Corvette gleamed in the sunlight. "Electron blue!" My son stroked the top like it was a new wife. "They only made this color a couple of years. I was lucky to find one."

Two years before, Walker had bought a guitar and gone so far overboard with country music that he neglected his whole family. Cindy finally took their kids and went to her mother's for several months, which nearly scared me to death. I could not bear to think those children might grow up without their father and away from us, but Joe Riddley had assured me, "Walker's just having his midlife crisis a tad early. He'll come around." Sure enough, Walker had come to his senses, settled down, and been a real good husband and father ever since.

Does a man get to have two midlife crises?

I couldn't help a shiver of worry as I stood there looking at that car. Then Walker put his arm around his wife and squeezed her good. "Cindy bought it for me. We're going to join a Corvette club and go on cruises all over the country. If you and Daddy will babysit, that is."

"We want to go! We want to go!" his children objected in unison.

"You all can go sometimes," he relented, "but the first few times your mama and I want to be alone."

"So they can smooch," Jessica told Tad.

He screwed up his face and made gagging sounds.

I was still trying to get my mind around the idea of a car cruise. "You take the cars on boats?" I could picture one of those huge cruise ships with a hold full of Corvettes, but I couldn't see the sense of it.

Walker laughed. He must have been seeing the same picture I was. We do that sometimes. "No, Mama, we cruise the highways. We meet up someplace and all drive together for a few days. Doesn't that sound great? I'm going on one up in North Carolina next week to get the hang of this baby, but I'm going alone. Cindy won't come."

"I have to be here for the investment club," Cindy reminded him.

"I'll only be gone three days, though," Walker added, "testing her out."

Have you ever noticed how men call their favorite cars "her"? And then get upset when their wives and girlfriends claim that the cars have become competition?

"Looks like a 'him' to me," I said. "I'd name him Roger."

"Roger?" Tad's nose wrinkled in disgust. "Mighty Motor would be more like it."

"Mighty Motor will do," I agreed.

Jessica stroked the shiny hood. "Hey, Mighty Motor. I'll be able to drive you in a couple of years."

"Dream on," her father told her. "You're not driving this baby until you are sixty."

"So when do I get to drive it?" I teased. "I'm past sixty."

He gave me a long, level look, then handed me the keys. "Take her for a spin, Mama. Go on. I dare you."

I have never yet refused a dare from one of my sons. Besides, I was itching to get behind that wheel. I slid across a leather seat soft as butter and started a motor that sounded like we could lift off into the stratosphere. Knowing they were all watching me, I made sure to shift smoothly as I pulled out of the parking lot. Even with my sore hand, that car handled like a dream. I tooled through town and waved to several startled friends, then went down through the sheriff's detention center parking lot to show off to any deputies who might be around. I saw a couple and gave them a wave, sure they'd report back to their friends. I considered taking off for Dublin or even Macon — spending the whole afternoon cruising up and down country roads. Never before had I coveted anything either of my sons ever had, and I was generally content to live pretty simply, but I could get used to a Corvette.

Reluctantly I headed back to the store. They were all lined up in the parking lot, waiting for me. "Thought you'd gotten lost," Walker greeted me, opening the door.

"It's a great drive," I admitted. "Leave it

to me in your will, okay?"

"No, leave it to me!" Tad insisted, grabbing his daddy's arm. "Me-Mama will be dead before you are. She's old!"

Cindy frowned at her son. "Old, is she? Too old to buy birthday presents in a couple of weeks for grandsons who insult her?"

"Almost," I agreed, giving Tad a considering look.

"You're not old," he had conceded. "Just too old for a Corvette."

"So help me," I muttered as they drove away, "I will join that investment club and we will make lots of money. I will get so rich I can buy my own Corvette. I'll get a red one."

Instead, here I was, dripping wet, climbing up into Cindy's huge SUV while she was being questioned about her activities during the time a murder was being committed.

"Walker, come home quick," I begged as I hoisted myself up onto the seat. I had reached for my cell phone to punch autodial when I decided I'd let his daddy explain what was going on. Walker was sure to think it was my fault Cindy was in this predicament, and he tends to pound things when he's upset. Not people, but walls and doors. I didn't want him damaging a perfectly good motel. Besides, it was Joe Riddley I wanted to talk to.

The air inside the vehicle was hot and muggy and the windows were steamed, but it was raining too hard to open a window. I started the engine and figured out the windshield defroster, then called home. "I've got to go over to Walker and Cindy's, honey. Willena Kenan got herself killed tonight. Somebody screwed a corkscrew into her throat. And Charlie is honing in on Cindy as a suspect."

"Cindy?" His astonishment mirrored what I was feeling. The idea of our chic daughter-in-law committing murder was about as credible as Laura Bush participating in mud wrestling.

"Yeah. You know Charlie — six cents short of a dime. I'm going over to Cindy's while he questions her some more. Could you call their lawyer, then come over to the community center and stick with her until her lawyer arrives? I don't want Charlie leaning on her too hard. And call Walker. He's on that Corvette cruise in North Carolina somewhere, but his cell phone is on."

"I'm on my way. You get over to the kids." Joe Riddley hung up without asking a thing about Willena.

I sat and counted to thirty.

My phone rang. "How are *you* mixed up with Willena's death?" he demanded without preamble.

"I'm not," I assured him. "I didn't know her well enough to kill her."

"You didn't stumble over her body, or see anything suspicious?"

Oh, that man knows me as well as I know him.

"I happened to find Willena when I went to the bathroom —"

He made a sound somewhere between a growl and a bark.

"You got me into this," I reminded him. "And you can't fault a body for needing what Cindy currently calls 'a lipstick break.' Which I never did get, by the way, so I need to get off the phone and over to Cindy's as fast as possible. I can't leave the kids until she comes back, so do your best to get her home soon. Bye."

I hung up and checked out where to find essentials like wipers and lights and moved the seat up until my knees hit the dashboard and I could reach the pedals. I told myself that driving an SUV couldn't be any harder than driving one of our company trucks.

It wasn't driving that was hard, it was behaving myself. I have always called SUVs "bully cars," because their drivers so often bully everybody else on the road. Once I had backed out of my parking space, I realized why. Away up there in the air, I felt like I had joined the elite who rule the world. "Look out, lesser mortals!" I muttered. "I can mow you down and never feel it." As I headed through the parking lot, all those TV commercials about SUVs climbing rugged mountains and taking on marshy swamps made me want to do something daring. I pictured myself running up over Charlie Muggins's new cruiser, leaving a stripe of tire tracks up his trunk, across the top, and down his hood.

I resisted that temptation, but the size and power at my command fueled my fury at Charlie and released all my basest instincts. I have always contended that our true selves come out when we are behind the wheel. The self I became while driving Cindy's SUV was not a nice person at all. At the street, a car was heading my way. I pulled right out in front of it. "If you hit me, bub, you'll get the worst of it," I warned.

Traffic is light in Hopemore at that hour of the evening — mostly teenagers or people going home from meetings. Comfortable in the knowledge that between the tinted windows and the rain, nobody could see who was driving, I roared down Oglethorpe

Street with the sensation that I had the only real vehicle, and was surrounded by little bumper cars.

Only when I turned onto Walker's street did common sense finally return. I rolled down that tree-lined avenue like the grandmother I am, thinking maybe I'd better not buy a Corvette. I wondered why all those people who buy SUVs to protect their children don't think about other people they endanger in the process, or worry about the trashed atmosphere their SUV fuel emissions will bequeath their grandchildren. I read somewhere that one American Indian tribe never makes a decision without asking the grandmothers, "How will this affect the seventh generation?" As I pulled into Walker and Cindy's drive, I wished somebody would ask that question in Detroit and Japan. Historians will probably cite SUVs as the quintessential symbol of the Me-First generation.

Tad and Jessica were amicably watching television when I got there, snuggled up with the dog, two cats, and Tad's new rabbit. Tad, like his mother, thinks a house isn't complete unless it resembles a zoo.

The kids fetched me a thick towel to dry off and asked where Cindy was, but accepted my explanation that she'd gotten tied up after the meeting and had sent me to put them to bed. They are good kids. They went without grumbling. Only when I was tucking Jessica in did she ask, her hair dark on her pillow and her eyes heavy with sleep, "But why did Mama let you drive her car? How is she going to get home?"

"Pop is bringing her," I replied. "He's with her." I bent to kiss her cheek.

"Is it something for Tad's birthday?" Her voice was drowsy.

"It's a surprise." That was as close as I could get to the truth and still answer.

She smiled. "That's nice." She was already drifting into sleep. I stood by her bed for a minute asking God to bless this serious, quiet child and her family. Her parents weren't praying people at the time, but I had a suspicion they were about to be.

An hour later, Joe Riddley took the steaming cup of coffee I handed him and sat down at our dining room table. "Charlie was within his rights to question her," he repeated, then heaved a sigh that let me know how worried he was. "Her keys were found under the body when she'd told him she hadn't been in the bathroom."

"That's not what he asked or she answered," I reminded him. "He asked her,

'Did you *go* to the bathroom?' and —" I stopped. We'd been over that already and had agreed that Charlie would never admit he had asked a sloppy question and gotten an exact answer.

I collapsed into the chair across the table and sipped my own coffee, but continued to shiver. I'd been shaking off and on since Charlie pulled that gun. Joe Riddley fetched Mama's old afghan, which we keep folded over the sofa, and draped it over my shoulders. Then he stood behind me and massaged my shoulders with his long fingers. I put up a hand and covered his.

"It's gonna be all right, Little Bit," he promised. "Stop shaking. At least Charlie didn't try to hold her." I hadn't told him about Charlie's gun. I didn't want him going to jail for policide.

"None of the other women saw her in the bathroom, so she must have been outside by the time they saw Willena alive and well, and she didn't come in until right after I found Willena. Can't they check her cell phone records to see how long she was talking?"

"Maybe so." His fingers worked deep into my muscles. I hadn't realized how tight they were. I squirmed with pain, but it felt good. "They found a footprint in the blood, too.

It doesn't match Willena's shoes and it doesn't match Cindy's."

I drew the afghan tighter around me and heaved a sigh of relief. "You know what I think? I think Charlie is hassling Cindy to needle me."

"Could be," Joe Riddley agreed. "I've been thinkin,' Little Bit. You know in the Bible where it says we are to do all in our power to live at peace with other people? I think you need to take that to heart where Charlie is concerned. Be nicer to him. Cut him a little slack."

"I'm gonna cut something," I warned, "if he goes after Cindy. What about Walker? Did you call him?"

His fingers continued to knead my shoulders, bringing me back to life. "He was on his way back home already when I got him. He said Cindy called him earlier to complain about Willena's high-handed decision not to invest in his company. She said Willena made her feel like dirt, and they talked nearly twenty minutes while he tried to calm her down. After they hung up, he decided to come on home and not finish the cruise."

Walker's concern for his wife was heartening. I took another sip of coffee and finally began to feel warm. "Good. She couldn't have been talking on the phone and killing

Willena at the same time. Right?"

"I doubt it. All we've got to do now is convince Charlie."

# 8

Early Tuesday morning, I discovered we had to convince other folks, as well.

Around nine thirty, Slade Rutherford ambled in. Tall, dark, and far too handsome for his own good, Slade edits the *Hopemore Statesman,* our weekly paper. Real smart except in the matter of romance, he had three criteria for the only woman he could love: She needed to be rich, almost as smart as he was, and beautiful.

I had tried to steer him toward a couple of teachers I knew who were cute and at least as smart and well-off as he, but each time he had shrugged and said, "Sorry, not my type." Since then I had concentrated on writing my monthly garden column and had let Slade find his own romance. Gradually we had become friends. Cindy had also tried to fix him up with a few of her friends who met some of his three criteria, but she and her circle had finally dubbed him "Mr.

Impervious" because, they said, "Romance can't penetrate his hide."

When Sadie Lowe had first moved back to town, Slade went after her in a big way. They had a lot in common — both had come up poor and liked money, and both had figured out that their best bet was to marry it. However, now that Sadie Lowe had her bundle, she had no interest in men who wanted to share it. After they'd been seen together around town for a few weeks, making a striking couple, Slade confided to me, "She says I might as well buzz off, because we have no future together." He didn't seem heartbroken, I had been glad to see.

That morning he sank into our wing chair and slid down so his long legs stretched almost to my desk. "What's this I hear about you finding the body last night? Care to give me a story?"

"There's no story. I went to the ladies' room and found Willena lying on the floor. I backed out and called the police. End of my involvement. You probably know a lot more than I do if you went over there. Did you?" Slade had a police-band radio in his car and often made it to a crime scene within minutes of the police.

"Yeah. I arrived about the time you were

leaving, if you were driving that big silver SUV that nearly ran me down. It came barreling out of the community center driveway like the proverbial bat out of hell, and Cindy said it was probably you."

"Don't blame me, blame that monster car. It inspires other-wise nice people to do rude things. Did you see Willena?"

He nodded and reached up to touch the knot of his tie. When he realized what he was doing, he grimaced. "I've been doing that ever since I saw her."

"Me too." My fingers found the soft spot at the base of my throat.

"But the corkscrew wasn't what killed her. Did you know that?"

I stared at him in astonishment. "Are they sure?" When he nodded, I demanded, "Did they look for poison? She was mighty sick just before she died."

"I don't know. The only word I got is, she would have taken a while to bleed to death from that wound, and she was seen by several folks not too long before you found her. That means the corkscrew hadn't been in long — probably about as long as it took her to get to the bathroom door and collapse. You reckon she was chasing her killer?"

"Or looking for help. There are two doors

to that ladies' room, you know. One goes into the hall and another into the ballroom on the other side. Somebody could have gotten out that way."

"You could be right about the poison," he said thoughtfully. "She wasn't shot, strangled, or stabbed. The chief said he's waiting for the autopsy to figure out the cause of death. You don't have any theories about the corkscrew and its significance, do you?"

I shuddered. "No, but it was one of the most gruesome things I ever hope to see."

"What can you tell me about Cindy and why the police chief thinks she might be involved?"

I would like to have said, *Because the police chief has spaghetti for brains,* but a judge can't go around talking like that. "He found her keys under the body. That's all." That would soon be common knowledge anyway. "Cindy went in to blow her nose and left her keys there — but that was before Willena arrived. We don't know how the keys wound up on the floor under the body."

I plumb hated calling somebody I had known and talked with less than twenty-four hours before "the body."

Slade must have felt the same way, because

he was silent a moment before he asked, "Was anybody else in the ladies' room when Cindy was there? Besides Willena, I mean?" He had pulled out a notebook and was taking notes.

I wanted to make sure he got as clear a story from me as I could give. "I told you, Willena wasn't there when Cindy was. She was still in the meeting, turning the club over to Wilma. The position of senior partner rotates alphabetically, so Wilma inherited it from Willena."

"Along with all her money, I'd guess." He sounded gloomy. I wondered if he had ever dated Willena. She was a few years older than he, but what would that matter to Slade? He wouldn't be marrying her for love. On the other hand, I couldn't see him marrying Wilma for all the money in Georgia. Rich isn't everything.

"I guess," I agreed. "They're only third cousins once removed and have been known to battle it out from time to time, but I would guess they've made their wills in each other's favor. Can't have those Kenan dollars going anywhere else. On the other hand, given that neither of them has ever been down to her last ten million, I doubt that money would be sufficient cause for either to murder the other."

Slade wrinkled his brow in a puzzled frown. "I thought they were first cousins. I've heard them both refer to Granddaddy Will."

"Yeah, but that was old William Robison Kenan, who made the family fortune. He was Wilma's great-granddaddy and Willena's great-great-granddaddy."

"Is there anything in the family story to make a good human-interest piece to go with the murder? The big boys will descend from Atlanta, New York, and who knows where to cover the murder, but I might get a wire story with a human-interest angle. This thing is going to be big for several days, given who Willena was."

Did he hope this would be his chance to move on to a bigger paper? He had seemed happy in Hopemore, but maybe he yearned for city life. I would hate to see him leave, but I liked him enough to help him if I could. "You can read all about the Kenans in a book Wilma wrote and printed up a few years back for friends, relations, and the public library, but here's the gist.

"The first Kenan came to Hopemore around 1820 with three sons and built a cotton gin. They drove around in mule-drawn wagons, buying cotton from farmers; then they ginned out the seeds and sold the cotton to textile mills. Within thirty years they had expanded the business and built gins all over Georgia. I think they had some in Alabama and South Carolina, too. When the war came, Will was still a little boy, but he's reputed to have said, 'Oh, boy! All those soldiers are gonna need clothes and bandages. We can sell *lots* of cotton!' The family claims that was his first flash of brilliance. So while all the other families sent their men to fight, the Kenans sent their men around buying cotton from anybody who could still grow an acre or two. Will apparently rode with his granddaddy, daddy, and uncles on the wagons, and the family swears he drove wagons himself through enemy lines, telling each army that the cotton was going to make their uniforms. It is historical fact that the Kenans sold cotton to factories on both sides of the conflict — which didn't make them real popular around here for a while. Especially since they did real well while other people were losing everything."

I lowered my voice to a whisper. "You won't read that in Wilma's book." I resumed in a normal tone. "After the war, though, most farmers swallowed their anger and their pride when the Kenans offered to sell cotton seed cheap and buy the crop at a fair price. Folks were too poor and hungry to quibble. Still, you'll sometimes hear somebody mutter even now" — I cupped my hands and spoke softly — " 'You know their money came from selling *our* cotton to the Yankees.' "

Slade laughed. He grew up in the South, too. He knew as well as I did that old perceived wrongs still rankle.

"I'd never have guessed that Granddaddy Will lived so long ago. The way Wilma and Willena talk about him, I thought they'd known him."

"No, but he died only a few years before Wilma was born. He lived to be ninety-seven. And for the Kenans, he was right up there next to God. He was the one who transformed the family from prosperous to filthy rich. When he grew up, he bought out his brothers, uncles, and cousins and consolidated the business into his own hands. He seems to have had a magic touch, too. In the Reconstruction South, he made enormous amounts of money. By the time he was thirty, he had enough to build the old home place where Wilma now lives. Around 1900 he bought a small shipping line. Up until then, Kenans had bought only U.S. cotton and sold only in the United States and England. With that shipping line,

Will started buying wherever cotton is grown in the world and shipping —"

" 'We cotton to the whole world,' " Slade quoted the business motto. He poised his pen. "So make it clear again how he was related to Wilma and Willena?"

"He was Wilma's great-granddaddy and Willena's great-great-granddaddy." I settled back in my chair. We Southerners love to trace a family history, even if it's not our own. "Will had two sons, Will Junior and Frank. They each had a son, Billy and Robison. They had other children, too, but none of them lived to adulthood except, I think, a sister of Robison's. When Billy and Robison grew up, they went into business with their daddies and granddaddy. During World War Two there was again a rumor that Kenans sold cotton to both sides of the conflict, but nobody ever proved it. Anyway, after the war — about the time old Will was dying — his sons and grandsons took the company public and it began to grow into the multinational corporation it is today."

Slade gave me a penetrating look. "You reckon they went public because they didn't have sons themselves?"

"Your guess is as good as mine, but actually, Robison did have a son, John. He was a little older than me, and a talented photographer. He wasn't the least bit interested in cotton, but he went into the business to please his dad. He left any chance he got, though, to travel to faraway places and take pictures. He photographed several articles for *National Geographic*."

Slade was drawing lines. I figured he was working out the generations. He confirmed that when he looked up and asked, "So how did the generations get uneven?"

"Billy didn't marry until he was forty, and he was heading for fifty before Wilma was born. Meanwhile, Robison had had John when he was thirty, and John had Willena when he was in his midtwenties, so the girls were ten years but a whole generation apart."

"Did you mention a sister in there somewhere?"

"I think Robison had a sister, but I don't know what happened to her. Why don't you try to track her down?" That might keep him too busy to pay any attention to Cindy.

No such luck. He pulled himself to his feet. "Maybe later. First I want to talk to Cindy and at least one more member of the investment club." He rose and stood jingling the coins in his pocket. "MayBelle Brandison might be good for a quick interview, if I mention Brandison Builders. Would you

110

save me a trip back to my office and remind me who else belongs to the Moneyed Ladies?"

I blushed to realize that nickname was so well-known. "You'd better not call them that. Gusta, Meriwether, Sadie Lowe, Nancy Jensen, and Rachel Ford all belong."

"Is Rachel that scrawny lawyer with the messy hair?"

"It's curly and she doesn't straighten it, if that's what you mean. I think it's attractive."

He snorted. "Looks like she climbed out of bed and discovered her brush had been stolen. And it would be a waste of time talking to her. She's first cousin to the clam. I tried to interview her right after she came to town, but all she'd talk about was the law center and its work. What I wanted was something personal." He sketched quotation marks with his fingers. " 'International lawyer descends to head small-town Poverty Law Center,' that sort of thing. Her only response to every question was 'No comment,' 'No comment.' " He did a fair job of mimicking Rachel's New York accent. "Last winter I tried to get the full story behind that big drug case they were involved in, and again, 'No comment.' I won't waste time on her. I'm already past deadline. You sure you don't have anything else you can tell me?"

"I could tell you Cindy had nothing to do with it, but I doubt you'd print that," I retorted.

"Have to print what people want to read," he reminded me.

"Just don't go putting my name in the first paragraph."

He laughed. "Read it and weep, Judge." He gave me a mock salute and slouched out.

I planned to start sending out invoices after he left, but he hadn't been gone five minutes when I heard a crash in the parking lot, then voices raised and shouting. I slipped my feet into my shoes and dashed out to see what was going on.

Slade stood at the rear fender of his black Lexus waving his arms. Rachel Ford stood at the side of an elderly blue BMW sports car, rubbing the back door and breathing fire.

"Why didn't you look before you backed?" she demanded as I came down the side steps from our store to the parking lot. I was surprised to see that she had tears in her eyes.

Slade jerked his head toward a white van parked beside him. "I couldn't see around that van. If you hadn't come barreling in here like this was a NASCAR track . . ." He slapped his fender with his fist. "Look at that! The taillight is demolished. They'll probably want to put on a whole new fender. I wouldn't be surprised if the frame isn't bent, too."

"You were clearly at fault," she replied in an imperious tone. "And my poor baby will have to have a new back door. I need the name of your insurer."

"The hell you do. I wasn't at fault! I was barely moving. You were going at least fifty."

"I couldn't have been going fifty. I had just turned in and was looking for a parking space."

I went to join them. "I see you two have met."

They both stopped shouting, but each put hands on hips and stood glaring at the other, breathing heavily, like some well-choreographed ballet. I sidled around both cars, inspecting the damage.

"Doesn't look too bad to me," I reported. "I can give you the name of a good body shop, Rachel. They can take that dent out so you'll never know you got it. And it looks to me like all you need, Slade, is a new back light."

They each sullenly inspected the damage again.

"You are both in shock," I went on. "That's why you are yelling. It's scary to hit somebody or get hit. Why don't you leave both cars here and go down to Myrtle's for a cup of coffee and some pie while you talk things over?"

Slade looked at me through narrowed eyes. I could tell he thought I was trying to fix him up again, but nothing was farther from my mind. Rachel had too many brains and too few dollars to attract Slade, and with those tempers, putting the two of them together would ensure that sparks were going to fly. I didn't want Hopemore going up in flames.

Emeralds flashed in Rachel's ears as she turned her head. I wondered again how she had gotten into the investment club. Were the jewels a sign of hidden wealth, as Joe Riddley suspected, or merely the only thing of value she owned?

The important thing now was to get them out of my parking lot, where they were attracting the wrong kind of attention. I told Slade with a clear conscience, "I thought you all might like to talk about this at civilized decibels. I'm busy, so I can't invite you into my office, but Myrtle's isn't full at this time of day. Go over there to discuss what you want to do."

Rachel exhaled a puff of frustration. "There's nothing to discuss. I know where to find him and he knows where to find me. If you'll give me the name of that body shop, Mac, I'll see what their estimate is. If it's not exorbitant, I'll pay my part of the bill." Her generosity was canceled by her begrudging tone.

I gave her the name and she tapped it into one of those little handheld gizmos modern women seem to use so much nowadays. You have to be below a certain age to appreciate them. I bought one, but never had four free days to sit down and read the manual.

As she climbed back in her car, Rachel snapped, "You, Mr. Editor, can buy your own taillight. And next time you back up, if you can't see, then pull out real slow." With a toss of her head and one last flash of her eyes, she started her engine and drove away.

Slade rubbed his broken light like a mother rubs a scratch on a beloved child's face. "That woman is a menace, Mac. Can't we send her back to wherever she came from?"

When the *Statesman* arrived at my desk Wednesday morning, Willena's murder filled half the front page, and I could cheerfully have throttled Slade. He had managed to

115

unearth head shots of each member of the Magnolia Ladies' Investment Club, had cut them into ovals, and arranged everybody but me at the top of the article like a group of middle-aged debutantes. Willena's picture was largest and occupied the position of honor, top and center under the headline: "Local Woman Mysteriously Murdered." My picture was down at the bottom of the article, and the cutline read, "Judge Yarbrough does it again! The newest member of the illustrious Magnolia Ladies' Investment Club found the body of outgoing senior partner Willena Kenan."

If Slade had been in my office, he'd have sizzled from the steam pouring from my nostrils. The volume of steam increased as I read.

Judge MacLaren Yarbrough got a jolt Monday evening when she opened a door at the Hopemore Community Center and found the body of Willena Kenan, outgoing senior partner (president) of the club and one of the heirs to the Kenan Cotton Factors fortune. The method of murder has yet to be determined by autopsy, but in a bizarre twist, a silver corkscrew was twisted into the victim's throat. "That

116

was one of the most gruesome sights I ever hope to see," exclaimed Judge Yarbrough, although she has seen many. The judge has been active in the investigation of a number of murders in Hopemore in recent years.

The corkscrew was part of a boxed silver bar set presented to Ms. Willena Kenan as the outgoing senior partner of the Magnolia Ladies' Investment Club (members pictured above). The murder took place at the regular monthly meeting of the club, during a break for refreshments prepared by Ms. Wilma Kenan, cousin of the deceased and her successor as the leader of the club.

According to Police Chief Charles Muggins, no arrest has been made, but Cynthia Yarbrough is being questioned in connection with the murder. According to another club member, MayBelle Brandison of Brandison Builders, Cynthia Yarbrough and Willena Kenan frequently clashed in various civic organizations. Their latest dispute took place during the meeting prior to the murder, Ms. Brandison reports, because Willena Kenan, in her role as senior partner, deferred a decision made last month to purchase stock in the insurance company

Mr. Yarbrough represents until the matter of conflict of interest could be discussed. Mrs. Yarbrough pointed out that the investment club portfolio includes stocks from businesses connected with other members, "and then stomped out, furious," said Ms. Brandison. Mrs. Yarbrough's keys were subsequently discovered under the body of Ms. Kenan.

"I am confident we will solve this murder efficiently and speedily," declares Police Chief Muggins.

I sat there glaring at that story for a long time, thinking of appropriate ways to wreak vengeance on Slade. I rejected boiling oil as too messy and tar and feathers as too hard to come by. I was in the process of considering resurrecting the stocks so I could encourage people to throw cabbages at him when the phone rang.

"MacLaren, did you see this morning's paper yet?"

"I saw it, Gusta."

"I don't know where Slade unearthed that picture of me. He must have taken it at last month's Little Bookclub luncheon, since that's the last time I wore that dress. I've never particularly liked it. It makes my neck look scrawny. Still, the picture wasn't bad, considering." Gusta always liked getting her picture in the paper.

I knew good and well she hadn't called me simply to preen, though. Sure enough . . .

"I do think you might have exercised a little restraint. You didn't need to boast about finding the body and worm your name into the first paragraph twice! And why MayBelle had to bring up that little disagreement Willena and Cindy had at the meeting . . . All I can think is that Slade charmed it out of her."

"No doubt," I agreed. "Just like he charmed me into confessing I found the body."

"Well, please remember in the future that the club does not need this kind of notoriety." Before I could reply, she added, "I have to go now. I don't have time to gab all day. Meriwether and I are going down to Hilton Head for the rest of the week, to let this blow over and give little Zachary a look at the ocean."

"Chief Muggins told us not to leave town," I reminded her.

"Oh, I had a little talk with him. He knows Meriwether and I didn't have a thing to do with that mess." I could almost see her little wave of dismissal. Queens don't have to obey the same rules we common folks do.

As I hung up, I looked out my window. A CNN van was turning around in our parking lot. The national networks had arrived. Where could we send Tad and Jessica until all this "blew over"?

# 9

I wasn't the only one worried about Cindy's children. When Joe Riddley and I got home that evening — having spent the day holed up in our office to avoid reporters — Walker had left a message on our voice mail. "This is for Daddy, Mama. Don't listen. Please!"

I handed the phone to Joe Riddley and watched his face turn to stone as he pressed the receiver too close to his ear for me to hear a word. Lulu, our three-legged beagle, sensed that something was wrong. She inched up against my ankles and whined, a wriggling mass of anxiety.

"What is it?" I demanded. "What's he saying?"

Without a word, Joe Riddley pressed a button to delete the message, and hung up.

"What was it?" I demanded again. "What was Walker saying?"

"You don't want to know." He headed for

the cabinet where we keep animal feed. "I need to feed Bo." Bo was a scarlet macaw we had gotten stuck with a couple of years before when his owner turned up dead at Joe Riddley's birthday party.[3] Joe Riddley dotes on the creature. I tolerate him because Bo was helpful in Joe Riddley's recovery after he got shot. However, I know Joe Riddley as well as he knows me. If he was trying to divert me from asking questions about one of our sons, things were serious. A chill started in my feet and rose up my entire skeleton.

I grabbed his arm. "You know as well as I do that Bo won't starve if you wait a few minutes to feed him. What did Walker say?"

Joe Riddley gave a huff that means he is plumb fed up with my contrariness. "You don't want to know, Little Bit. You are an officer of the court." He grabbed up the bag of feed and strode onto our back porch, which we had glassed in and converted into a glorified birdcage.

I followed him to the door and could hardly speak the words. "You mean he's done something illegal?" Walker was our impulsive son, the one who raced off on tangents without thinking things through.

[3] *Who Invited the Dead Man?*

Bo flew to Joe Riddley's shoulder. Joe Riddley stroked the scarlet breast with one forefinger while a vivid rainbow of tail feathers spilled down his back. "Let it go, Little Bit."

I dismissed the notion that Walker had shot Slade over the article, but what else had he done to upset his daddy enough for Joe Riddley to be curt with me?

I knew in an instant. "He hasn't taken Cindy out of town, has he? She can't leave while she's under suspicion of murder."

Joe Riddley turned without a word and carried Bo past me into the house. "I gotta run an errand. I'll be back for supper." He slammed the door behind him. I could still hear Bo squawking on his shoulder. "Little Bit? Little Bit! Back off! Give me space."

I am never sure whether that bird knows what he's saying or whether he's real good at picking up on Joe Riddley's moods.

As soon as I heard the automatic garage door shut, I tried Walker's cell phone. I got voice mail. I tried Cindy's and got voice mail, as well. This was serious, if they had turned the telephones off. They never turned their cell phones off. Joe Riddley and I suspected they slept with them on under their pillows. Each of their children has a phone, since Cindy likes to stay in touch, but those phones were off, too. Walker must have taken the children, wherever they'd gone.

In that Corvette, they could be in Alaska pretty soon. Walker often fails to demonstrate what I would call good sense, but if he had whisked Cindy out of the county while she was a suspect in a murder case, this was the dumbest thing he had ever done, and the most potentially dangerous.

I couldn't talk about it with a living soul, even Joe Riddley, because as an officer of the court, I was under oath to report any infraction of the law I even suspected had been committed. That was why Joe Riddley had stomped out. He was a magistrate for thirty years and has more integrity than any man I know. If he so much as hinted to me what Walker had done, he'd insist that we report Walker and Cindy so Chief Muggins could alert authorities to pick them up. In all probability, they'd be tried. And while Joe Riddley and I trust the courts to execute justice in most cases, we also know that courts can be fallible. This was our son and his family in jeopardy. Their marriage had nearly fallen apart two summers ago, and they were working hard to rebuild it. Walker's parents couldn't fault Walker for wanting to take care of and protect his family. Still, if I'd had him in grabbing range right that minute, I'd have shaken him until his teeth rattled and fell out one at a time.

I settled into one of the two recliners in the living room and sent up wordless prayers which, if translated, would have been something really profound like, *Help! Help! Help!*

As I reached for the remote my finger caught in a small tear in the upholstery, reminding me that I needed to go up to Augusta soon and look for new recliners. Those had been all right in the big house, where we had both a living room and a casual den, but they looked tacky in our new living room. Joe Riddley had agreed I could get new ones if he didn't have to help pick them out.

Lulu scrambled up and settled on my lap. I don't know how people survive problems without prayer and a lapful of dog.

When I switched on the national television news, I saw a reporter in front of the Hope County Courthouse interviewing Chief Muggins. I'd never realized before how aptly Charlie was named until he mugged for the camera while assuring the world, "We got things under control down here. We are confident of making an arrest soon."

"She was killed by a corkscrew twisted

through her throat — isn't that right?" the reporter asked. Why are reporters so avid for bloody details? I touched my throat and closed my eyes, but that image of Willena was branded on the inside of my eyelids. I groaned. Lulu gave me a comforting lick.

Chief Muggins touched the knot of his tie. "I cannot comment on that at this time, but it was a gruesome way to die." He grinned like a polecat, but the camera shifted to the reporter's bland face.

"Chief Muggins indicates that the primary suspect at this moment is a member of the ladies' investment club who had quarreled with the deceased over the use of club funds. He is not releasing the name at this time."

I knew full well that the only thing muzzling Charlie was his desire to be in the news again. He wouldn't hesitate to reveal Cindy's name if he could avoid a lawsuit and still get his pointy nose on television, but he'd drag the story out as long as he could.

Cindy's desperate eyes floated between me and the screen. I laid my head back and asked the Boss upstairs, "Please, is there something I can do?" This was the first time my daughter-in-law had ever needed my help. I didn't want to let her down.

A voice from heaven would have been good.

I'd have settled for one good idea of how to proceed.

Instead, my first impulse was, "Call Martha!" My other daughter-in-law, Ridd's wife, is an emergency room nurse, Bible scholar, avid gardener who supplies us with canned goods each winter, and somebody I would unhesitatingly nominate for Wise Woman of the Year. She is my rock in times of storm. But she was not only in the middle of getting her daughter through her final weeks of high school and her little boy through his final weeks of pre-K, she was also "another person." If I so much as hinted to Martha that Walker had taken Cindy out of state, I'd have to tell Charlie what I suspected. Reluctantly, I pushed the idea of Martha down where it belonged and tried to think of what else I could do.

I wished I were smart like Sherlock Holmes, with all sorts of knowledge at my fingertips, so I could sweep into the community center ladies' room, take one gander at the site, and say, "The murderer was XYZ. I once wrote a monograph on the subject."

Instead, I couldn't even get into the community center, and wouldn't if I could. I didn't want another visit to the site. One look at Willena had been enough for my lifetime. The only other thing I could think to do was talk to the other members of the club. One of them might remember something that could clear Cindy. That's all I asked. If they could also provide Charlie with another suspect, that would be a bonus, but I wasn't asking for a major miracle, just a little one to demonstrate what I knew: Cindy never killed anybody.

How long did I have before people began to wonder if the younger Yarbroughs were still in town? I didn't dare let myself think about that for long, or I'd want to know for sure where they were. If I found out, I'd have to report them. Better to talk to people about the murder.

I'd have to act casual, though, so Joe Riddley wouldn't suspect. He pure-tee hates it when I get involved in asking questions about a murder case. Especially since I've gotten myself in sticky situations a time or two. And while he had almost fully recovered from the traumatic head injury he'd gotten when he was shot, his emotions were still a tad unpredictable. He snapped at me once in a while, which he never used to do. And he'd gotten more protective.

On the other hand, waiting for the police

to find Walker and Cindy would nearly drive him crazy. It wasn't good for him to get upset, and from the way he had slammed our back door when he went out, he'd be doing a lot of damage to the property if I didn't do something.

Having rationalized my determination to look into things, I fetched paper and a pen and jotted down ideas as they occurred to me.

*1.*
Did anybody else come in while we were there? Why was door unlocked?
*2.*
Nancy: What got her so upset?
*3.*
Grover: Did he see Cindy talking on her phone? (could provide alibi)
*4.*
Wilma: Would she have had time to kill Willena and still do refreshments? Why should she?
*5.*
Sadie Lowe:

I got stuck at that point. I disliked Sadie Lowe, but I couldn't imagine a single motive she could have for murdering Willena. In fact, I couldn't think of a single motive *anybody* could have for murdering her. A lot of women had felt the rough side of her sweet-talking tongue and might want to smack her. But murder?

Murder, I had heard, generally springs from three motives: love, lucre, and . . . what was the other one? I was having a middle-aged moment and couldn't remember. But neither of the other two seemed applicable here. Willena and Grover, if they were in love, showed no signs of quarreling. They'd been laughing together over some private joke before the meeting started. And Wilma, her presumptive heir, was well fixed in her own right. I had no idea how the two fortunes compared, but doubted that Wilma would have killed Willena for money — especially at a public meeting. She had weed killer and other yard chemicals at home she could have used privately. Besides, for all I knew, Willena had left her money to the Sierra Club. There went Wilma's only motive. But I reached for my pen and added two additional notes:

6.
Find out how Willena left her money.
7.
Figure out who had the corkscrew last. Who was sitting at the back? Where did

they put the box after they looked at it?

After Wilma presented it to Willena, we had passed the whole set around, admiring it. It was a pretty set, and the initials on the silver shot glass were a classy touch. I could picture the little wooden box lined with royal blue velvet going up and down the rows, then . . . what? Had Willena taken the set with her to the bathroom? Or had the corkscrew been filched by whoever admired it last? Who was that?

I had no idea. Gusta had insisted that Cindy, Meriwether, and I sit with her in the third row. I hadn't looked to see who was sitting behind us.

I was cheered by having something to do besides sit and wait for Charlie to notice that Cindy was gone. I carefully put the list in my pocketbook where Joe Riddley wouldn't see it and went to see what our cook, Clarinda, had left for supper. First thing tomorrow, I'd start working down my list. Surely I would find something to clear Cindy.

# 10

Mama used to say as we dressed for our annual trip to Atlanta's smartest stores, "Gussy yourself up to intimidate them, honey, before they try to intimidate you." So although I hadn't slept at all well Wednesday night because of worrying about Walker and Cindy, I got up Thursday morning and dressed with Dexter Baxter in mind. Dexter was a snob. He strutted around Hopemore like cleaning toilets and mopping floors at the Hopemore Community Center elevated him far above folks who cleaned toilets and mopped floors in houses or offices, and he was never happier than when there was a formal do at the center and somebody rented him a tux to wear while helping the caterers.

For talking to Dexter, therefore, I put on my most expensive cream-and-green linen two-piece dress with my priciest bone pumps. I changed from my big carryall pocketbook to a small bone clutch Cindy had bought me for Christmas, because I'd heard that Dexter rated women by the maker of their shoes and purse. Halfway through breakfast Joe Riddley summoned the energy to lift his eyes from the newspaper. "You got a date for lunch? Ted Turner, maybe? Donald Trump?"

That man can go three weeks without noticing what I've got on, and then the one morning I don't want him to pay any attention, he does. I'd figured he might, so I had an answer ready.

"I'm taking Wilma a casserole, so I want to look nice." Please note that I told the absolute truth. I already had a frozen casserole in my car. If I also had a bag of frozen blueberry muffins to take to Dexter first, why mention it? Joe Riddley is all the time grumbling, "Tell it shorter, Little Bit. We don't need every detail."

We drove into work together in my Nissan, but as soon as Joe Riddley took one of the company trucks and headed down to the nursery, I picked up my clutch purse and went out to tell Evelyn, "I'm running a casserole over to poor Wilma Kenan."

As I had hoped, Evelyn was so sympathetic she didn't bother to ask when I'd return. But as I started out the door, the telephone rang and she called me back. "The sheriff for you."

Buster (christened Bailey) Gibbons and Joe Riddley had been best friends since kindergarten. He was best man at our wedding, and if anything had happened to Joe Riddley and me while our boys were minors, they'd have been raised by that sweet old bachelor. Still, when Buster and I spoke officially, we were formal.

"Judge?"

"Hello, Sheriff. How're you doin' this fine day?"

"I'm doing tolerably well for an old geezer, but I thought you'd want to know that we've detained Nancy Jensen. Judge Stedley was on the premises and held the hearing, but Nancy's asking to see you."

My heart fluttered with hope. Nancy is a sweet, competent woman whom I have enjoyed working with on several committees, but if she had been charged with Willena's murder, then Cindy was no longer a suspect.

"What's the charge?" I asked.

"Attempted murder."

Attempted?

The only murder I knew about recently had succeeded.

I decided to postpone my visits with Dexter and Wilma until after I had stopped by the detention center to find out what was what.

Poor Nancy looked like a squash in the orange prison jumpsuit — an impression enhanced by her narrow shoulders and wide bottom and the green walls of the interview room. A new hairstyle she'd gotten while I was on vacation was an improvement over the lacquered bob she'd worn as long as I'd known her. I had always considered that style too severe for her broad, plain face. However, her hair was so yellow and fluffy now that it looked like a blossom on the end of the squash.

As Nancy, her attorney, and I all took our places at the table — me across from them — I wondered why the county had decided to replace the dignified navy blue jumpsuits formerly worn by our inmates with these orange monstrosities. The only people who looked good in them were prisoners with dark brown skin. Then it occurred to me that the woman responsible for buying new jumpsuits also had dark brown skin. Maybe she hoped to give incarcerated folks a chance to feel good about themselves? If so, she had failed Nancy. I could not remember seeing a sadder, madder, drabber prisoner in my life.

Beside her, Shep Faxon looked like a magazine ad in a gray silk suit. Each silver hair was in place, and he wore the complacent look of an attorney who is going to earn lots of money no matter what happens to his client. Shep was a longtime member of the old-boy network in Hope County and the attorney for most of our aristocrats.

"Mornin', Mac," he said in his lazy drawl. Shep had never abided by the courtesy Joe Riddley established of calling law enforcement and court personnel by titles in public.

"Good morning, Counselor," I replied. "Good morning, Nancy. You wanted to see me?"

She glared at me across the table, dabbing her nose with a soggy, used tissue. Her eyes were red and soaked with tears, and her mascara had run down her cheeks, leaving little runnels in the thick layer of makeup she wore to hide the pocks from teenage acne. "I want you to get me out of here."

Shep and I exchanged glances. "I've explained the procedure and instructed her to say nothing, but she won't listen to me."

Nancy glowered at him. "Mac's my friend."

"I understand you are being charged with attempted murder." I figured we might as well get right down to business.

She flared her nostrils and narrowed her eyes until they looked like a pig's in her plump face. "I did not try to kill her. If I had, she'd be dead."

I sat there puzzled while she dabbed her nose again with a sodden tissue. Last I'd seen, Willena *was* dead. Very dead.

Shep put a hand on her arm to restrain her, but Nancy was impossible to restrain. "I shot at the ceiling," she said angrily, looking from him to me and back at him again. "Anybody can see that who bothers to look. I wanted to warn her, not kill her. How soon can you get me out of here, Mac? Shep is useless." She shifted her chair an inch or two to distance herself from him.

Shep looked at his fingernails. I stared at Nancy.

Shot? At the ceiling?

I wriggled in my chair, trying to get comfortable, but the seat was too high for anything but my toes to reach the floor. Before I asked any questions, I had to make one thing clear. "I can't get you out, honey. A charge of attempted murder means you have to go before a superior court judge. The magistrate who heard your case will send a letter to superior court, and they'll send a judge to hear the case. He ought to be here Monday or Tuesday afternoon."

"The DAR meets Tuesday morning. I have to preside."

"Somebody else may need to preside for you this month."

Every line of her face, from the drawn-together eyebrows down to the taut set of her chin, proclaimed that she thought I wasn't really trying; that if I wanted to, I could pull strings and get her out. Nancy had lived too long in a world where strings dangle for the pulling. Now she was up against the neat package of Georgia legal procedure. When it works right, there are no strings to pull.

Maybe something in my face convinced her I was telling the truth, because her eyes filled with a new cloud of tears that spilled out and ran down her cheeks. "It's all his fault. Why did he do this to me?" She flung herself on the table, head cradled on one arm, and sobbed. Her shoulders shook, and she boo-hooed loud enough to be heard uptown. The small hill of tissues she had dropped onto the table didn't have much use in them. She dragged a couple more from her pocket, but they were equally soggy. For a woman with money in the bank, she seemed remarkably short on fresh tissues.

I found a pack in my clutch and handed her a couple. "Do you want to tell me what this is about? You don't have to, but I don't have a clue."

Nancy blew her nose and wadded the tissue like she'd rather be wadding somebody's head. "Horace," she blurted. "He's having an affair." She flung that tissue on the hill, like she wished it were a grenade she was lobbing somewhere in Horace's vicinity.

Shep looked out the shatterproof window at a flock of robins that had landed on the lawn and were looking for worms the week's storm had brought to the surface. He seemed unusually embarrassed for a man known for coarse language and ribald humor in the country club locker room. I didn't know whether a crying woman made him nervous or if he'd known about the affair for a while and was embarrassed at having such a naïve client.

I did know this must be a tremendous blow for Nancy. When she'd met Horace fifteen years before, she had been a stocky high school chemistry teacher from down in Waycross who had driven up to Middle Georgia Kaolin to see if her students could visit the mine on a field trip. Meeting the heir to the company and marrying him must have seemed like a fairy tale come true, even if he did look more frog than prince. Now she stood to lose both Horace and all he represented.

For those who don't know, kaolin is a chalky substance used in a lot of products from cosmetics to the nose cones of rockets, and a good percentage of the entire world's kaolin supply is mined in central Georgia. I've never figured out what's so secret about the process, but even fifteen years ago, security was tight at Middle Georgia Kaolin. Nancy couldn't get past the receptionist. She created a ruckus, demanding to at least see somebody higher up, and Horace, who had recently graduated from college and joined his daddy's business, was sent out to deal with the troublemaker. He couldn't take her on a tour, but he took her out to dinner. Even though she was five years older than he and equally plain, they were married six months later.

When I first heard that story, I wondered if it was Nancy's spunk that had attracted him, for spunk was never Horace's strong suit. He was a big, bumbling man with thick glasses, a large nose, and a mat of dark hair with so many cowlicks that no matter who cut it, he looked like he was wearing a wig made of guinea pig fur. I don't know whom he would have married or what he would have done with his life if his family hadn't owned a company and taught him to run it, because with that abrupt, abrasive personality, he would never have found a wife or risen through the ranks of business on his charm. Even Joe Riddley, who sees the good in most folks, never found anything better to say about Horace than, "At least he has the common sense not to run his business into the ground."

Since Middle Georgia Kaolin was privately held, nobody had ever known exactly how much the Jensens were worth, but their primary clients were paper mills, which use kaolin to make paper smooth and shiny. Given how much paper is used, the Jensens had never lacked the simple necessities of life — a bed at night, running water, three square meals a day, ostentatious houses, expensive cars, and jaunts to various parts of the globe.

Soon after Horace and Nancy were married, they had built an enormous granite house out beside the country club golf course, surrounded by fifteen acres of woods. When MayBelle's subdivisions started encroaching on their borders, Horace circled the entire property with a high stone wall and Hopemore's first security gate. Nancy, who had expected to teach after she was married, found instead that Horace expected her to devote her time, as his mother and grandmother had, to committees and clubs. I'd served with her on several church committees and found her a thoughtful and creative member.

Right now, though, it looked like she'd been creative without being thoughtful.

Not that Horace had ever appreciated either her creativity or her intelligence. Nancy had confided to me once, "I would have preferred a light, airy, modern house surrounded by flower beds, but Horace wanted the fortress." I guess if your business is taking things out of the earth, it makes sense to build your house of granite, but I'd been there a couple of times and it was too dark and gloomy for me. It was also a monument to the taste of a famous Atlanta decorator. As far as I could tell, neither Nancy nor Horace had impressed their personalities on the place. In Horace's case that was a blessing, but it always made me mad to hear him say in public, with his braying laugh, "We had to hire a decorator. Nancy has no taste, you know."

They must have hoped for lots of children, because the house had eight bedrooms, but only one son ever arrived: Horace Junior, known as Race. He was a good student, a good athlete, and looked like his mother. On a boy, though, the round face, wheat blond hair, eyes like chips of sapphire, and wide, engaging grin looked cute. He had Nancy's personality, too — calm, thoughtful, helpful, and generous. The only thing Horace seemed to have contributed to his breeding were cowlicks. Race had a number of those, which may be why he generally kept his hair cut to less than an inch. Now a freshman in high school, he said he wanted to study business at the University of Georgia. He ought to be an asset to Middle Georgia Kaolin one day.

Unlike his father, who had matured into a stingy, crabby man who confused his ability to grab kaolin from the ground with a right to grab anything he wanted. If he had decided to run around on Nancy and replace her with a younger trophy wife, Nancy would have a hard time getting much recompense from those tight, furry fists.

Now you know as much as I did about Nancy Jensen's married life the morning I visited her in jail.

"How could he?" she finally wailed, dabbing her nose with one of her well-used tissues. I handed over a couple more, reflecting that at this rate, the investment club had better buy stock in Scott paper or Kimberly-

Clark. Nancy looked up at me through tear-drenched eyes. "Why would *she* do that to me?" she wailed. "And all this time I thought it was Willena. I thought Grover was camouflage."

Shep grabbed her shoulder. "Don't you say another word. I warn you, if we don't end this conversation right now, you can find yourself another attorney."

He obviously didn't want Nancy saying outright that she'd killed Willena. He could defend her a lot easier if I hadn't heard a confession of guilt.

Nancy sniffed and waved at him with one large hand. Her hair was damp and plastered to her forehead in front, but she didn't seem to care. "Go on, leave. You're Horace's lawyer, anyway. You don't care one bit what happens to me."

"It's your funeral." Shep exuded relief as he shoved back his chair, strode out of the interview room, and slammed the door behind him.

# 11

Nancy dabbed her nose with a handful of used tissues. "Oh, great. Now I don't have a husband and I don't have a lawyer."

I handed her another clean tissue. "Call Jed DuBose. He's a better lawyer, anyway, and if you are thinking of divorce, the worst thing you can do in the world is be represented by somebody with Horace's interests at heart."

Both of her chins quivered. "I don't want a divorce. Horace needs me!" She laid her head on her arms and sobbed some more.

I couldn't sit there all morning watching her cry. Any minute a deputy would step in to tell us our time was up. I couldn't in good conscience ask her if she'd killed Willena, either, but maybe I could ask it another way. "Why did you leave the meeting early Monday night? Wilma said you got sick?" I made it a question, hoping she'd elaborate.

She jerked erect, her face flushed. "I

didn't get sick, I got mad. I knew good and well Willena wasn't gone all that time to wash off a little mascara. I figured she'd gone to meet Horace while I was talking to the others, so I went looking for them. I looked everywhere — on the porch, in the big ballroom and all the little rooms, even in the kitchen and the broom closet — but I didn't see a soul."

"You didn't see Cindy outside?" I slid in the question like butter on a hot biscuit.

She shook her head. "I didn't see anybody. I thought he might have driven her off somewhere and that upset me so much, I got a migraine. I could hardly stand up." Nancy rubbed one hand over her eyes at the memory. "I went back and told May-Belle I was leaving; then I went out to my car and started driving. I planned to drive around town looking for them, but next thing I knew, it was morning and I was in the parking lot of our condo down at Hilton Head. I guess I drove down there without thinking and slept in the car. As long as I was there, I figured I might as well stay a day or two to get my head together, but you know what I did instead?" She hung her head like a misbehaving child. "I drank a fifth of Horace's scotch two days in a row. I never did that in my life. Last night I ran out of scotch, threw up a lot, and finally came to my senses. I decided I might as well come on back here and face the music."

I wanted to ask, *Music for what?* but she didn't pause for breath.

"I left at midnight and drove back. But then —" She stopped, quivering. I waited while she took a couple of deep breaths, then plunged on. "When I got home Horace wasn't there, and I went crazy again. I got back in my car and drove all over, looking for him. And when I found him this morning" — she gasped for air — "with *her*" — she gasped again.

I considered carefully what to say next. "Not Willena . . ."

She shook her head again. "I thought the car was hers, but maybe it wasn't. Or maybe it was then and isn't now. He's making me crazy, Mac! Plumb crazy. That's why I fired the gun. To show Horace how crazy he's making me. I wasn't aiming at anybody, but the stupid maid who was cleaning the room next door called the police, and —"

A guard rapped at the door. "Time's up, Judge."

"— and now they say I have to stay here!" Nancy wailed desperately. "Do something, Mac. Get me out of here." Her eyes were terrified.

I stood. "I wish I could, hon, but I can't. I'm sorry. But you'll be in good hands with Jed."

She was sobbing when I left, and I was no more enlightened than when I'd come in.

I went to see Sheriff Gibbons again. "Would you mind telling me what Nancy Jensen is accused of doing? In words I can understand, without tears or sniffles?"

He grinned. "Same thing you'd do if you caught Joe Riddley cattin' around. She saw Horace's car at a motel, parked to block him in, and pounded on the door. When he opened it, she fired a pistol. Fortunately, she missed."

"She says she fired at the ceiling."

"That's what she claims now, since the bullet hit the ceiling."

I shook my head. I had remembered something else I knew about Nancy. "She's one of the Three-Ds. She wouldn't have missed."

The Three-Ds — officially the Dangerous Dixie Dames — were Hope County women who competed successfully in shooting events across the Southeast. Cindy, who grew up hunting, had joined them soon after she married Walker and moved to Hopemore. MayBelle was in the group, too.

Cindy had urged me several times to join, but while I can shoot, I hate guns and don't have time for another club.

It occurred to me now that if I had joined the Three-Ds, I could have spent time with Cindy without joining the investment club. Then I wouldn't be involved with Willena's murder.

Everything in life hinges on something else.

I pulled my thoughts back to the matter at hand and spoke slowly, feeling my way. "Nancy said she thought it was Willena with Horace. Something about cars."

"A white Jag convertible like Willena's was parked next to Horace's car at the motel."

"Oh. Nancy also says she's been down at their beach place since Monday night. Do you reckon she doesn't know Willena is dead?"

He rolled a pen between his palms. "That's what she wants us to think."

I mulled that over. "She could have killed Willena and driven down to her beach place afterwards. That would make sense of why she drank herself into a two-day stupor — to keep from thinking about it. But even if she did, that doesn't answer the question I asked you first. Who did she shoot at this time? Do I know her?"

"Sadie Lowe Harnett." He brushed back his hair with one hand.

"Sadie Lowe and Horace?" That took some getting used to. Beauty and the beast. "Why on earth, with all the men in town panting after her, would she choose Horace?"

"Not all the men," he objected. "Not Joe Riddley and me."

"Ha. Even you two can't say her name without getting a silly grin on your faces, slicking back your hair, or fiddling with something."

I said that because the sheriff was fiddling with his pen again. He dropped it into a lopsided blue clay mug Ridd had made for him in third grade. "I'd guess the reason she hangs out with Horace has to do with the color green, and I don't mean jealousy."

"I'd think she has enough of the green stuff already," I said grumpily. Adultery is a sin that makes me sick to my stomach, since it killed a dear friend of mine. Before I left, I had one more question. "So is Nancy a serious suspect for Willena Kenan's murder?"

"That's for Chief Muggins to decide. He's coming to talk to her." He added, sliding a look my way, "Joe Riddley says you've joined that highfalutin investment club."

"Joe Riddley got me into it," I corrected him. "I never plan to let him forget it."

# 12

On my way to the community center, I tried to get myself in a charitable frame of mind. As you may have guessed, I did not like Dexter. He was not only a snob, he was also a racist. He bowed and scraped to black doctors, lawyers, funeral directors, businessmen, and preachers if there were poorer black people present, but I had watched him steer a black surgeon to one side so a white one could get to the hors d'oeuvres first. That sort of thing sticks in my craw.

However, Mama used to say, "When you need something from somebody, you don't start out by kicking them in the knee," so as I turned into the community center drive, I took a so-help-me-God breath and put on a be-sweet-now face.

I could have spared myself the effort. The center was still a crime scene, with yellow tape blocking entry and nobody there. I parked by the front steps and prowled around in the bushes looking for cigarette butts, but didn't find any. In the best-case scenario, Charlie had them in a little plastic evidence bag. I figured the odds on that were about a thousand to one. If Sadie Lowe hadn't been smoking, where had she been?

I drove around back, but Dexter's old black Ford wasn't in the parking lot. I would need to drive over to his house if I wanted to talk with him. The problem was, I had no idea where Dexter lived.

That may seem strange to you, since greater metropolitan Hopemore contains only thirteen thousand people. However, like you, I tend to spend most of my time with a fairly limited circle of friends. Dexter and I had never been friends.

The best place to get information in the South is a convenience store, if you have the patience and know the rules. I stopped at the Handi-Stop down the street from the center and went in. The girl at the counter had long stringy hair, eyes lined to make her look like a raccoon, and skin the color and texture of dough that's been kneaded too long. Still, she had made an effort. Her nails were painted bright purple to match the skintight magenta top she wore with her jeans.

"Kin I hep you?" she asked in a high, nasal whine.

"I hope so. I'm trying to find out where Dexter Baxter lives. The custodian down at the community center?"

"I know Dexter," she allowed. "He comes in here all the time to buy stuff. But I don't know where he lives." She turned and started putting cigarettes on the shelves.

*Rule One: Don't give up yet.*

"Anybody here who might know?" I inquired.

"Purvy might. Hey, Purvy?" She raised her voice from where she stood and called to somebody in the back. "You know where Dexter Baxter lives?" The last word was drawn out to two syllables.

"Who wants to know?" Purvy Wilson came to the door of the stockroom, a burly man with skin like burnished walnut. I'd had to fine him a couple of times for dumping litter instead of paying to have his Dumpster emptied properly, but he seemed to bear me no malice, for he greeted me amiably enough. "Oh, hey, Judge. You needin' Dexter?"

*Rule Two: Act casual. Don't let anybody know it matters.*

"Needin' to talk to him," I agreed, dropping my own *G*s and leaning up against the counter like I wasn't in any particular hurry.

His eyes were watchful. "What's he done?"

*Rule Three: Expect resistance. Be reassuring.*

"Nothin'. I need to ask him if I left somethin' at the center Monday night at a meetin', and the place is still shut up until the police are finished with it." I don't normally use phrases like *shut up* for *closed,* but I have them in my repertoire if I need them.

"Understand they had a little trouble over there. You know anything about it?"

*Rule Four: If you want information, you'd better give information.*

"Willena Kenan got murdered, is all I know. We were meeting there at the time, but we didn't see anybody. Now the police have the center closed, but I want to find Dexter and see if he saw my notebook. It's not valuable, but it's something I'm needin' to get on with my day's business." I stopped short of pronouncing the word *bidness,* like my daddy used to. I also stopped short of saying I left the notebook at the center, since it was locked in my trunk.

Purvy scratched one cheek with his fingernail. "I understand he stays over in Pleasantville 'bout the middle of Good Hope Lane. Ask somebody there. They can point you to the house."

155

*Rule Five: A crooked statement will get you farther than a straight question.*

I wrinkled my forehead like I was trying to figure that out. "Good Hope Lane runs off Adams Street, right?"

"No, it's off South Jefferson, but you have to use Wilford to get there from here. You know Wilford?"

"Slightly." I seldom drove it, but a lot of the men I met through drunk-and-disorderly charges gave addresses on Wilford Road.

Purvy went to the door to point, the better to direct me. As he talked, he gestured with each hand, so he looked like he was swimming in air. "Go down to the red light and make a right. Then you go three–four blocks to Wilford. They's a blue house on the corner. You can't miss it. Turn left on Wilford, follow it two or three blocks, and make a right at Mad Mooney's Bar. That's South Jefferson. Go on to the Good Hope Church of God Appearing and turn left just past the church. That's Good Hope Lane. Dexter lives about half-way down."

At that point a Yankee might have thanked Purvy and gone on her way. They don't know *Rule Six: Why are you in such a hurry?*

I stayed a few minutes more, thanking him and chatting about car races over in Dublin. I don't know much about car races, but any woman worth her salt can discuss car races in the South. All you have to do is keep nodding and agree with whatever a man says.

As I headed back to my car, I wondered why directions in the South invariably include "go to the red light." You'd think our stoplights never turn green.

At a house that was more green than blue, I turned onto what I presumed was Wilford Road, although the sign was missing. It led me straight into one of the sorriest parts of our little town.

Hope County, like most counties in the South, has a lot of poverty. Most of our small cotton farms have been swallowed up by conglomerates, and we have lost so much industry, there's not enough left to employ our people. Caught in a cycle of illiteracy and poverty, too many people have few job skills, but find unskilled jobs harder and harder to come by. The ones they can find don't pay enough to live on, given that the national minimum wage has been raised by only one administration in the past twenty-five years. I wonder sometimes which of our elected officials would be willing to live today on what he or she made twenty-five years ago, and why they think poor folks ought to be smart enough to do it when they can't.

The good news is that we no longer have the unpainted shanties that dotted the South when I grew up. The bad news is that Hopemore, like many other small towns, has large pockets of substandard housing, poverty, drugs, and crime. The only difference between a small town and a big city in that respect is that in a small town, poor people live closer to the rest of us and are generally related to somebody else we know.

As I drove down Wilford Road, I remembered a Sunday school lesson that Martha, Ridd's wife, had taught recently on Deuteronomy 15: 4–11, which she called "God's solution to poverty." She said that God knows that people will sometimes, from their own foolishness or misfortune, hit a rough patch and become poor, so God commands those of us with more than enough to take care of them during those times and help restore them to prosperity. Martha pointed out that Deureronomy 15:4 makes an amazing pronouncement: *There will be no poor among you if you obey God's commandment.* But verse eleven ends the passage with an indictment of us all: *The poor will always be with you, so open your hands and be generous.* I will never again look at people living in second-, third-, and fourth-generation poverty without knowing that it is, in some sense, my own fault.

The fact that Dexter lived in Pleasantville (which wasn't pleasant at all) surprised me. I had pictured him in a neat brick house like Clarinda owns. I wondered whether the Hopemore Community Center job was paying him a fair wage, and knew that was something I'd need to look into.

I was so lost in those thoughts that I almost missed Mad Mooney's Bar. It was easy to miss, not more than fifteen feet wide with a faded sign over the small screened door. My sudden right turn caused the driver behind me to lay on his horn and a teenager beside the fire hydrant to give me a thumbs-up and a grin.

When I found Good Hope Lane, I wondered whether the person who named it had been drunk or facetious. Hope didn't live on that lane. Porches sagged. Screens hung in tatters. Lawns were decorated with appliances and rusting cars. A toddler in paper diapers and a red shirt explored the debris in her yard, while two apathetic women sat on the front porch waving away flies and talking, paying her no attention whatsoever. When a rat the size of a small cat dashed across the road in front of my car, I made a mental note to ask Chief Muggins to send some deputies around to check on code violations and force the owners to clean up the worst of the trash. We'd be real busy in magistrate courts in coming weeks, if I got my way.

I thought maybe Dexter's house would stand out as clean and well kept, but no house looked better than the others. Spying two boys hanging around a souped-up yellow Mustang down the street, I pulled up and asked, "Do you all know where Dexter Baxter lives?"

They shuffled a bit, aware they ought to be in school. From the way the bigger one flicked his eyes toward me and then away, he knew who I was.

He looked about twelve but outweighed me by several pounds. "He lives over there," he volunteered in a husky voice, jerking his thumb toward a house that had been painted white so long ago that the color was mostly memory. Down behind it I saw Dexter's Ford under a carport made from rusty pipes and a corrugated green fiberglass roof.

"You all need to get on to school," I pointed out. "It's already past ten."

"Yeah, we was just goin'." The smaller boy, who looked like he might be ten and was as skinny as the other was fat, gave me a saucy grin and jerked his head toward his partner. "Come on, dude, we're late."

They strutted down the street like I had been detaining them. Yet I suspected that, if I checked with the school later, neither would have shown up. Those boys were neither dumb nor lacking in interests, they simply found the schooling we offered them boring and unrelated to their lives. As I turned and parked in front of Dexter's, I wondered what kind of education those boys could get excited about, and what it would take to convince our school board to provide it for them. We are so caught up in schools looking good, teaching arcane literature and complicated math, we tend to forget that the point of education ought to be to help children learn what they will need to get on in their actual lives.

I am used to carrying my pocketbook over my shoulder. Keeping up with that clutch was troublesome, especially since I couldn't carry it in my wounded left hand. I settled for tucking it under my left elbow and carrying the bag of frozen blueberry muffins with my right hand as I headed up the cracked cement walk leading to Dexter's house.

It had no screened porch, only a little cement stoop, but the peeling gray front door sported a shiny brass dead-bolt lock that looked sturdier than the door itself. Seeing no doorbell, I shifted the muffins to my other hand and knocked.

No answer.

I knocked again. "Dexter? It's Judge Yarbrough."

No answer.

I pounded the door so hard, I skinned my knuckles.

As I paused to listen for sounds inside, I sensed somebody watching me from behind.

I turned. Three feral dogs stood stiff-legged beyond the bottom step, regarding me like they had spotted dinner. When the nearest one growled low in his throat, I felt the hair on the back of my own neck tingle.

I like dogs. Lulu is the light of my life. But these dogs were no more like my friendly little beagle than a drug-crazed addict is like a kindergarten teacher. The leader was lean and mean, built like a German shepherd, with a coat so dirty and neglected, it was gray. The others were of no recognizable breed and equally dirty and scrawny. None wore a collar or tag.

All three stood with teeth bared, front feet braced. The leader took a step toward me. The other two followed. They growled in evil three-part harmony.

I darted a glance across the street, hoping the two women on the porch might be of help. They were no longer there. I didn't blame them. If I had a child on that street and those dogs came down it, I'd go inside, too. But I sure could use some help here.

I turned and pounded on the door. "Dexter? Dexter!"

The lead dog put one foot on the bottom step.

One of his followers inched forward and bumped the leader's lean haunches. The leader turned with a snarl and snapped at him. He backed up.

That gave me a second to act.

Years ago Mama taught me that if a dog approached and scared me, I should bend down, pretend to pick up a rock, and hurl it toward the animal. I'd done that a time or two, and it works. I didn't dare bend down with those dogs so close, and imaginary rocks wouldn't keep them at bay long enough for me to reach the street, but I had something better. I awkwardly pulled one of the semithawed muffins from my zipped plastic bag and pitched it with a yell. "Git! You hear me? Git!"

The lead dog was so close, I hit him smack between the eyes. He yelped and swerved into the yard, where he stood barking furiously.

I pitched two more muffins in rapid succession and hit each of the other dogs. At that range it would have been almost impossible to miss. Both joined their leader, snarling and barking. None looked like they were planning to leave anytime soon.

"Git! Git on now!" I took a cautious step down the steps, holding a muffin above my head. I hoped I looked more confident than I felt. It's hard to walk on jelly knees, and any minute my purse was going to slip from under my elbow.

Frantically I tried to remember whether you are supposed to maintain eye contact with a vicious animal or avoid looking it straight in the eye. It was a moot question. I couldn't drag my eyes from those brutes.

I edged down the walk, another muffin at the ready. When one cur started sidling my way, I pitched the muffin with all my strength and hit him in the side. He yelped and darted toward the back yard, tail between his legs. I pitched two more muffins for good measure, but missed. Why hadn't I been more willing to play catch with my little brother years ago?

The lead dog edged over to sniff the useless weapon. Next thing I knew, two dogs were wolfing down the fallen muffins. In a minute, would they come after the rest?

I pitched four or five for good measure, then covered the rest of the distance to my car at a fast walk. Later I would tell the story and make people laugh at the picture of me fending off feral dogs with deadly muffins, but at the time I simply hoped to live long enough to reach my front seat.

I had an anxious few seconds when I had to stop firing muffins long enough to find my keys, but I kept one ready on top of the car and was relieved that keys were easier to find in a clutch than in my big pocketbook. The dogs finished gulping down all the muffins I'd pitched so far and stood staring at me, like they were calculating the best plan of attack.

I jumped in and slammed the door, then sat there trying to remember how to breathe. My hands were shaking so badly, I could not hold my keys, so I dropped them onto the passenger seat and laid my head on the steering wheel. I was shaking from head to toe.

Slowly my body recovered from terror. I found my cell phone, called the police station, and told one of the deputies, "Send a dogcatcher out to Good Hope Lane. Pronto!"

I stayed until the truck arrived, pitching an occasional muffin through my window to keep the dogs in Dexter's yard. Not until they were safely locked in the animal control truck did I breathe easy.

One of the women from across the street came out on her porch to watch the process. As the truck drove away and I prepared to follow, she yelled a stream of profanity after me. The only part I clearly heard was, "You got no call to sic the cops on Dexter's dogs. Them is his babies."

# 13

After all that squalor, it was a treat to head out to Wilma's. Although few Georgia planters ever lived in big plantation houses, and the Kenans bought cotton instead of growing it, William Robison Kenan had built himself an enormous Southern plantation home. White with black shutters at each tall window, the house had massive square columns supporting both a downstairs and an upstairs front porch. The upstairs porch had intricate crisscross banisters that gave an airy effect to the weighty house. Oaks, hickories, maples, magnolias, and poplars provided shade in summer and a gracious setting year-round.

As I turned into the long curved drive, lined with crape myrtles so old, they had become trees, I couldn't help thinking what a shame it was that one single woman owned all that. Knowing Wilma, she'd will it to the county for a museum without leaving enough money to maintain it, for keeping up a house that big and old is like trying to stop a waterfall with your bare hands. I wondered whether the county commission would sell it to some Yankee with more money than sense, or tear it down and sell the land for development.

Of course, MayBelle Brandison might buy it and make it the elegant clubhouse for a new subdivision, but as I looked at the wooded acres leading to the house, that idea was so distressing that I pushed it out of my mind. I rounded the last curve and saw Wilma bent over, pulling weeds and tossing them into a four-wheeled rubber wheelbarrow she had positioned nearby. She stood and looked to see who I was.

I parked on a patch of gravel near the house and waved. "Good morning!" I called as I walked back toward her.

She'd been working in her herb garden that morning, one of several theme gardens that dotted her yard. From the drive I could see her Shakespeare garden, her Bible plants garden, and her formal English garden. Over in the side yard were her rose garden, her lily bed, and a Japanese garden, complete with raked sand, a small water feature, and a tiny humpbacked bridge. Each of the gardens was lovely in itself, but taken together, I found them a tad overwhelming.

She wiped her forehead with one arm. "Why, hello, MacLaren."

For gardening, Wilma wore a pair of pressed khaki slacks, a white cotton shirt with the cuffs neatly buttoned, a straw hat, and black rubber Wellington boots that she reordered every time a pair wore out. I wear rubber clogs in the garden, but Wilma lived in terror of snakes, so she preferred boots that came to her knees.

She pulled off her gloves and threw them on top of her weeds, then clomped across the grass in my direction, talking as she came. "The weeds are growing like wildfire with all the rain we've been having, so I thought I'd pull some while the ground is soft. My grounds are sorely neglected. The trees need pruning, the borders need edging, and the liriope is taking over my lawn." As she reached me, she took off her hat and held it loosely at her side. "I'm needing to get somebody out here to help me, but you know as well as I do that you can't get anybody to work anymore."

What she meant was, she was reaching the limits of Hopemore's available gardeners. No wonder. She worked her yard men like slaves, paid them as little as she could get away with, and insisted on supervising and criticizing every blessed thing they did. I suspected she was hinting that it would be neighborly of me to send one of our landscaping crews out for a day or two as my contribution to alleviating her sorrow, but I couldn't. Most of our lawn service staff had worked for Wilma at one time or another, and they had all nodded when one of them begged me, "Doan ever send me out to her place to work, Miss Mac. There's not a man God ever made who can dig or prune to suit that woman."

When I hadn't said what she expected, she added, "Lincoln can mow, but that's about all he's good for in the yard."

I felt a spurt of resentment on Lincoln's behalf. The man kept her old Cadillac up and running and did most repairs on that huge house. When would he have time for yardwork?

I didn't know what to say, to tell the truth. She had discombobulated me by being out in the garden. I had expected to find her lying on her couch, prostrate with grief, dabbing her nose with a lace-edged cotton handkerchief, wailing about losing Willena. (Wilma, unlike Nancy, never used tissues if she could help it, and if she had to use a tissue, she never, ever used it more than once.)

Wilma must have seen my puzzlement, because she gave me a sad little smile. "I can't simply sit in the house and think about what's happened. I have to be doing something, or I'd go mad. Nothing comforts me like working in the yard." She reached into her pocket and, sure enough, brought out a white cotton handkerchief edged in an inch of lace.

I held out my dish. "I brought you some of Clarinda's chicken pecan casserole. You said you liked it at the Garden Club luncheon."

"Thank you so much. Let's go inside. I was ready to quit here, anyway."

Carrying my offering before me, I followed her up the brick walk. The paint on the house was a little dull and peeling in places, I noticed, but that wouldn't last long. Wilma might be stingy in other ways, but she never begrudged a dollar to keep up the old Kenan home place.

Near the front steps she detoured to a spigot and daintily washed the mud and yard trash off her boots. As she led me up the steps, her boots made wet footprints and some mud still clung, for the rusty water looked like Willena's blood. I shuddered.

Before we reached the front door, it was opened by Linette, Wilma's housekeeper for at least thirty years. Linette was long and lean, with a stride that let you know she knew where she was going and planned to get there. She adored Wilma and shared her dedication to perfection. Over the years she had supervised an army of young women who came in twos and threes to work for a while before throwing up their hands in despair and leaving with the cry, "They is too particular out at Miss Kenan's and don't pay you enough to live on." I didn't know what Linette and Lincoln earned, but at least they lived in.

She handed Wilma a thick white washcloth, already damp, with an equally thick white towel. Then she took my casserole with a murmured, "Thank you so much," and headed for the kitchen with a swish of starched gray uniform skirt.

While Wilma seated herself in a rocker to wipe her hands and face and exchange her boots for neat tan walking shoes that sat ready, I stood wondering how she got maids to wear starched uniforms. Clarinda has worked for me for forty years, but what it would take to get her into a starched uniform would entail more grief than I am willing to endure. Are rich girls taught at their mother's knee how to manage household help? Clarinda basically manages me.

Wilma dropped the washcloth and towel onto the porch floor and held out a foot. "Would you help me, MacLaren?" Then she noticed my bandaged hand. "Never mind. I'll do it myself." I figured Linette usually performed that service and had used my casserole as an excuse to escape.

Shod and tidy, Wilma stood. "Come on inside for a little while. Linette will bring us some tea." She left her damp boots beside the towel and washcloth on the porch floor.

Linette already had glasses of iced tea dressed with wedges of lemon sitting on silver coasters on mahogany tables in the living room. I moseyed behind Wilma into the world of high ceilings, carved woodwork, heart-pine floors covered with ancient Oriental rugs, silver and china on each available surface, and pressed-brass valances above dark green brocade drapery. An antebellum Chickering piano sat in one corner of the living room, adorned with family portraits in silver frames: Wilma's parents' wedding picture, a family picture taken when Wilma was about three, and a studio portrait of Mr. Billy, her dad, when he must have been about sixty-five. An oil painting of Granddaddy Will hung over the fireplace. He looked genial and satisfied with the house he'd created. The upholstered chair in the painting still sat beside a marble-topped table near the window, and the upholstery looked the same. Two old sofas, stiff and hard, faced each other near the fireplace.

Bookshelves built on each side of the fireplace held only leather-bound books. Wilma kept her modern hardcover or paperback books with bright covers in a sitting room–cum–office at the back of the house, where they wouldn't sully Granddaddy Will's library.

The liveliest thing in the living room were rainbows that jiggled on the stark white walls as sunbeams touched crystal prisms in the dining room chandelier next door.

Our Georgia sun can be hard on fabrics. I saw that some of the upholstery was worn on the chairs near the window, and Wilma's drapery and wallpaper had begun to fade, but she would never replace them until she could match exactly what had been there a hundred years before. It might cost her a pretty penny, but she would never think of running up to Augusta for something she liked, like the rest of us — and, probably, like the ancestress whose taste she now so slavishly followed.

She took the sofa on one side of the fireplace and nodded for me to take the one across from her. The slick seat was infernally uncomfortable, hard as a brick, and too high for me to reach the floor. Wilma valued seats more for which of her ancestors had sat on them than for the comfort they provided. I resisted an impulse to tuck my feet under me and reached for my tea.

Wilma sipped, set down her glass, and finally said what I'd expected to hear when I first arrived. "Oh, MacLaren, you are so sweet to come. Can you believe what's happened?" That was as far as she got before the composure she had found in the garden crumbled. She pulled out her wisp of a handkerchief and watered it thoroughly. When she could speak again, she wailed, "I don't know how I'm going to get on without Willena. I always thought I'd go first."

With her nose red and her eyes pink, her resemblance to a weasel was pronounced. I hoped Prince Charming didn't come riding up the drive that afternoon.

I pulled the two tissues I still had left after Nancy's crying jag out of my clutch and offered them, but Wilma waved them away. "Would you ask Linette to run up and get me a fresh hankie, please?"

Marveling that a woman could live in this day and age without fetching her own handkerchiefs, I wended my way to the kitchen. At least old Will hadn't insisted on a kitchen out behind the house, like plantations used to have, with enough space between house and kitchen for grass to grow. Wilma's kitchen was at the back of the house, largely unchanged since Wilma's daddy had remodeled it in the early fifties. I had accompanied my mama to a Garden Club meeting there as a young teen and remembered Mr. Billy taking us all back to show us what he called, proudly, "the Cadillac of kitchens." The cabinets were white enameled steel topped with stainless steel, the stove and sink both built into the countertop. The stove must have been a good one, for it was still in use.

The floor was both modern and historically accurate, for Mr. Billy's black-and-white linoleum squares had been pulled up and the heart pine floor refinished to a glossy glow.

Linette stood at an oak table in the center of the room, polishing Wilma's silver punch bowl. Silver trays and the ladle waited their turn, glinting in a ray of morning sun. The table was mighty low for somebody as tall as Linette to work at. Her back must ache at night.

A second maid in uniform stood at the sink contemplating two plastic gallon jugs of pale yellow liquid. As I came in she was asking Linette in a scandalized voice, "You want me to pour all that good juice and stuff down the sink?"

When Linette saw me, she asked, "Yes, ma'am?" instead of answering her companion.

"Wilma needs a fresh handkerchief," I told her. Seeing something glitter like silver through the window, I moseyed over to peer down a long grassy alley between two rows of Spanish oaks. "What a lovely vista. Is that the river down there?" I hadn't realized that Wilma lived so close to one of the coils of the little river that snakes through our county on its way to the Ogeechee and the sea.

"Yes, ma'am." Linette sounded as proud as if it were her own home. "I keep tellin' Miss Wilma that the best view in the house is from the kitchen."

"An' I keep tellin' you she shouldn't be cuttin' that mistletoe now. She could make a fortune selling it come Christmas," muttered the young woman at the sink.

We don't have Spanish moss this far inland, but many of our big trees are blessed with a bumper crop of mistletoe. The parasite is harvested each winter for Christmas sales.

Linette huffed. "She don't need the money, so she can cut it when she wants to. It's pesky stuff, mistletoe." She cast a worried look toward the window. "But Lincoln is too old to be up there cutting it down. She's had him at it all this past week."

I looked again and noticed a ladder propped up against one of the far trees. The branches gave an occasional quiver that couldn't be the wind.

I wouldn't be cutting it at all if it were mine. I know it's not good for trees, but they live for decades with it in their branches, and it adds a nice touch of green to the landscape in winter.

Bless her heart, I wondered whether Wilma had ever been kissed beneath the mistletoe.

Then I remembered I was here on an errand of mercy. "Handkerchiefs. Wilma needs a fresh one," I reminded Linette.

She jerked her head toward the door. "They're in the top drawer of her dresser. Shateika, run up and fetch one."

"I'll get it," I offered. "You all look busy." The way pots were bubbling on the stove, preparations for dinner were under way, and my casserole was wholly superfluous.

Linette hesitated, then nodded. "Front room on the right, up the stairs. The handkerchiefs are in the left-hand drawer. If you can't find them, ask Jackie. She's up there vacuuming."

I nodded toward the punch bowl, ladle, and trays. "When did Wilma get those back?"

Linette gave the bowl one more wipe and reached for a tarnish-proof bag. "This mornin'. She tole me to call the po-lice and ax them to bring her things. She didn't want them lying around the community center kitchen with folks tromping in and out. The chief himself brung them right before you got here."

Given that Willena had been killed far down the hall and that her murder probably had no bearing on Wilma's family silver, it made sense that the silver should have been returned already. On the other hand, from the expression of the second maid, she knew as well as I did that if it had been one of the rest of us who had left something in a building where a crime was committed, we'd have had to wait until the investigation was complete before retrieving our belongings. America may be a classless society, but like somebody said, some are more equal than others.

"We had a real tragedy that night," I allowed, propping myself against the doorjamb. "I know you've been a comfort to Wilma."

Linette pressed her lips together. "I wish I had been here when Miss Wilma got home. Miss MayBelle put her to bed and stayed until we got back, but she's not what I'd call a comforting sort."

"Not really," I agreed, mentally adding, *Not unless you prefer to be comforted by reptiles.*

"We wouldn't have gone down to Dublin that night," Linette continued, applying polish to the ladle, "but Miss Wilma insisted. She told me it had been too long since we saw our Leroy. He's got a new baby, you know. So she said she could handle things at the meeting. I wish I'd gone with her. I surely do. If I'd known . . ."

Linette sounded like she was settling in for a long chat, but Wilma needed that handkerchief, so I brought things to a close. "She's lucky to have you," I assured her. "You take good care of her, now."

"I will." Linette spoke in a docile voice to me, but her tone sharpened as she instructed the woman by the sink, "Go ahead and pour it out. I mixed that pineapple juice with real cream and other things. It's probably sour by now, and if it isn't, Miss Wilma ain't never gonna drink it. It would remind her of what happened."

"We could at least taste it," Shateika grumbled. But she reached for one jug and began to unscrew the lid. I went upstairs to the *glug-glug* of a gallon jug emptying into the sink.

I had attended meetings at Wilma's, but had never been upstairs. Oil paintings of Kenans in heavy gilt frames lined the stairwell. All of them wore sleek, satisfied looks. The men were subdued, but the women were peacocks in diamonds, sapphires, emeralds, and rubies. At the far back of the upstairs hall, lit by a small picture light like a household shrine, stood Granddaddy Will with a lady I presumed was his wife. I couldn't remember her name, but I remembered those diamond-and-emerald dangling earrings. They were the ones Willena wore the night she died. I wondered where they were now, and what happened to the matching brooch shown in the painting on the breast of a green velvet dress. The brooch was a gold square with a diamond in each corner and three matched emeralds in the center. Nobody would wear a brooch like that nowadays, so I guessed it lay in some jewelry box here upstairs, immortal and unworn.

In a dim corner of the hall I spotted a

picture I found far more charming than ancestors in oil. It was a sepia photo of a large family sitting on the front porch of an unpainted farmhouse while two black servants (slaves?) and a mule stood nearby in the yard. I wondered if one of the boys on the front steps, barefoot and in short pants, was Granddaddy Will. Probably. What else would cause Wilma to keep that humble picture among her grand ones?

Wilma's bedroom was surprising. Given the rest of her house, I expected a decor frozen around 1890. Instead, I found green wall-to-wall carpet and gold-and-white French provincial furniture that had been in style back when Wilma was a teenager. My guess was that it had been redone then and never since. Pink roses ran rampant on the wallpaper, comforter, and the canopy over the queen-sized bed, while the bed itself sported such a mound of lace-edged white pillows that I wondered how long it took the maid to remove them each night. Did a raging romantic still live underneath Wilma's frozen historical façade? Was that why she was still awaiting Prince Charming?

More silver frames gleamed from the mantelpiece, so I crossed a carpet as thick and green as grass to check them out. Wilma smiled at me from every frame. Fat pigtails on both shoulders, she grinned a gap-toothed smile from astride a glossy brown pony. At around ten she sat on the couch carefully holding a fat baby who must be Willena. At fifteen she held aloft a cake she had baked and won a prize for in home economics class. That picture, I remembered, had been in the paper, as had the next one: Wilma at eighteen in a cloud of white tulle, holding her father's arm at her pre-sentation ball. Her pointy little face looked so hopeful back then, when she had confidence her prince would soon arrive.

Mr. Billy had certainly been no prince. Little, crabby, and sharp-tongued, he couldn't have been pleasant to live with, particularly when he got old and suffered greatly from what they called "sugar di-beetees" back then. Wilma had cared for him faithfully, overseeing his diet and even giving him his shots on the nurse's night off. Maybe I ought to exercise some compassion in her direction. After all, while I couldn't imagine putting pictures of myself in my bedroom, I had pictures of children and grandchildren to scatter around.

Poor little rich woman, with nobody to love her.

# 14

I went back down to Wilma and gave her three handkerchiefs. While I was gone, Linette had refreshed my glass of tea, so I sat again, sipped tea, and chatted a few minutes longer. Eventually I managed to ask whether Wilma remembered where people were sitting during the first half of the meeting and where the little boxed gift set was during the break.

She shook her head. "I was thinking about refreshments." She gave a watery little sniff and dabbed her nose with a fresh pink handkerchief. "I couldn't tell you where anybody was sitting if my life depended on it." She stopped, then added in a voice of spite, "Except for MayBelle, of course. She was at the back, with Sadie Lowe."

That was interesting. MayBelle had been sitting on the front row after the break, but she was still standing when I first came into the room. She had come over to welcome me, then had honed right in on Grover as he arrived. Gusta had ordered Cindy and me to come sit with her and Meriwether in the third row about that time, so I hadn't noticed where MayBelle sat.

"I thought Willena was going to love her present." Wilma's voice quavered. "I spent seven hundred dollars on that set, Mac, and you know good and well they won't take it back now, with a missing corkscrew."

No, I didn't think they would. Who but Wilma would even entertain that notion?

"But you didn't see who had it last before the break?"

She shook her head. "I was thinking about refreshments," she repeated.

That reminded me of something else I wanted to ask her. "What did Willena eat that evening, do you remember? Some people said she was sick in the ladies' room."

Wilma bridled. "It certainly wasn't my food. She left before I served refreshments."

Of course she had. Why hadn't I remembered that? I was so embarrassed, I wanted to crawl out the door, but the notion of a trial — with Cindy in the defendant's seat — spurred me on. "I don't suppose you have any idea how the front door got unlocked, do you?"

She looked startled. "The door was un-locked?" She pressed one hand to her heart. "I remember now. The chief told us. I guess that explains how he got in."

Now I was the startled one. "Who?"

"The dreadful man who did this thing. I have racked my brain all week, wondering when he got in. I figured he had to have come in early that morning while Dexter was carrying out the trash, and hidden in the building all day long."

I tried to think how to ask the next question. "So you don't think any of us could have done it?"

"Oh, no!" Wilma compressed her mouth into a sad little bow. She got up, drifted over to the window, and stood with her back to me, one hand on the drape. Her shoulders slumped. Finally she said in a choked voice, "I mean, several people might have thought it, but they never meant it. I've said myself, 'I'm going to kill her!' when she volunteered for something and then put off what needed to be done until I had to help her with it. Willena could be lazy, you know, and dif-ficult when she wanted her own way. But I am going to miss her so much." She raised the pink handkerchief to her eyes, then turned with a bewildered frown. "You know what's silly? I'm almost as angry with her for dying as I am with whoever killed her. I keep thinking that if she hadn't spent so much time in that bathroom . . . She could have come out with MayBelle, or Meriwether. But it always did take her half an hour to fix her face." She sniffed and blinked back tears, then turned to stare out the window again.

"Anger is a natural part of grief," I assured her.

I was about to get up and leave when she turned around and asked in a funny little voice, "You don't really think one of us might have done it, do you?"

I tucked my clutch more firmly under my arm. "I was just wondering," I said.

She shook her head like she was trying to think that through. "I can't imagine any of us doing such a dreadful thing. Of course Nancy has been dreadfully jealous of Willena lately, because of Horace."

When I didn't say anything, she explained. "Horace wanted to marry Willena before he met Nancy, you know. Willena turned him down, of course — he had no charm whatsoever, and she had no need to marry him for his money. But Horace was set on marrying Willena. He married Nancy on the rebound."

If I stretched my mind back twenty years,

I could remember Horace and Willena dancing together at country club dances, but I'd never seen them as a couple. For one thing, he was three years younger. That's a lot at that age. For another, he was already a plump young man with unruly hair, beads of moisture on his forehead, and sweaty palms. Only an egoist like Horace would think he had a chance with Willena back when she was still fresh and lovely.

Had she begun to have second thoughts?

"I thought she and Grover —" I began.

Wilma's pink handkerchief sketched a graceful wave. "Oh, no. They are" — she gulped and soldiered on — "they *were* friends. Nothing more." She turned back to the window and her shoulders shook.

The transition from present to past tense is one of the most painful lessons in the school of grief. If Wilma had been almost any other woman, I'd have gone and put my arms around her, but I could not imagine touching Wilma Kenan. Nor that she would want me to.

I hated to seem ruthless, but I pressed her. "Had Willena and Horace become . . . er . . . friends again?"

Wilma sniffed and wiped her nose. "Oh, yes. You should have seen them dancing at the spring country club dance. Nancy got quite upset." She turned back to stare out the window at her lovely yard. In a moment she added, "I suppose that Rachel Ford might have killed her, too. There is something about that young woman I do not trust. Do you feel it? Willena did. She said Rachel was extremely pushy."

I myself had found Rachel surprisingly reserved for a New Yorker, but I wanted to encourage Wilma to talk. "New Yorkers are more aggressive than we are. I think they have to be that way simply to get through the crowds on their way to work. Did Rachel do something particularly pushy?"

Wilma turned, her eyes bright with tears and pink spots on each cheek. "Oh, my, yes. Not long after she got to town, Grover told Willena that Rachel had been a prominent attorney in New York before she moved here, and he thought she would appreciate it if we made her feel at home. Willena said we'd do what we could, of course, so she invited Rachel for coffee one Sunday afternoon. She invited me, too. Do you know, Mac, that young woman wandered all over the downstairs of Willena's house! Willena wondered if she was considering making an offer on the place, but it looked to me like she was casing the place to come back and rob it. I warned Willena to be careful about locking up after she left."

"How did she get into the investment club?" I hoped I wasn't stepping over some invisible boundary, being too pushy myself.

Apparently not. Wilma pursed her lips and answered readily. "It was not my doing, I can tell you that. She became friends with Meriwether, who nominated her, and then Gusta said having a lawyer in the group might come in handy. You know good and well that what Gusta wants, Gusta gets. I was the only dissenting vote. Even Willena voted for her. But if you could have seen the way Rachel sucked up to Willena after she got in! After every single meeting I was left to cool my heels while they talked. Rachel could not seem to leave Willena alone." Wilma sat suddenly in the nearest chair. "I cannot like her," she repeated.

"But she never threatened Willena or anything, did she?" It sounded to me like Rachel wanted to make a quick entry into Hopemore society without realizing that those things take time in Georgia. Or maybe she and Willena were becoming friends.

"No, she never threatened her. . . ." Wilma let her voice trail off. I got the impression that Rachel had done other things, but Wilma wasn't ready to reveal them to me. She continued, "And at least she's not common, like Sadie Lowe. Willena and I both spoke against *her* invitation, but again, Gusta insisted. She said Sadie Lowe isn't experienced in handling large sums of money and we have a responsibility to make sure it doesn't just flow through her fingers." I translated that to mean "flow out of Hopemore."

Wilma's mouth curved into a prim little smile. "But after we voted her in, Willena told Sadie Lowe in no uncertain terms that she'd have to dress appropriately for meetings." She gave a tinkling artificial laugh. "We didn't need her sitting there on the front row with her skirt hiked up and Grover able to see all her hidden assets."

I couldn't see that wearing too-short skirts made a woman a prime candidate for murderess. I couldn't even see that being interested in an old house with lots of charm qualified Rachel. Sounded to me like Nancy was the only good suspect so far.

I set down my tea and stood. "I'd better be going. Clarinda will be expecting me. She has strong feelings about people who are late for dinner."

Wilma hurried across the room and clutched my forearm. "Could I ask you a favor before you go? Say no if you want to, but Willena and I were supposed to go to

Augusta tomorrow for me to speak to a women's group about Granddaddy Will. I hate to disappoint them on such short notice, and it might do me good to get out of town, but I don't think I can bear to drive up by myself. Could you possibly ride with me? Chief Muggins has given me permission, and I know he'd let you go, too. Lincoln will drive." Which meant that "by myself" wasn't strictly accurate.

Still, I could understand how she might feel reluctant to go without Willena, thinking about her the whole way. It was pitiful, though, if I was the closest thing Wilma had to a friend. I scarcely knew the woman. I also wanted to hear her talk about her beloved ancestor about as much as I wanted to have an ingrown toenail cut out without anesthetic, but as I hesitated, she added, "You don't have to attend the meeting, if you have other errands you could be running."

That would be as good a time as any to look for recliners.

"I'll go if I can drive," I agreed. "I'll need my car up there." We settled on nine o'clock for me to pick her up, and I headed to the door.

Joe Riddley claims that folks usually save what they really want to say until you are walking out the door. Sure enough, I was actually standing on the porch and Wilma was in the doorway with her hand on the doorjamb when she said, "Of course, it certainly is convenient for MayBelle that Willena's dead, isn't it? Saves her the trouble of taking Willena to court."

I stared. "I beg your pardon?"

"Haven't you heard? Oh — you've been out of town. Well, last month I sold May-Belle fifteen acres of bottomland down by the river, on the express understanding that MayBelle would use them for a park. Then MayBelle turned right around and applied to the county for permission to build another one of her subdivisions down there." The way Wilma said *subdivisions,* I presumed she didn't appreciate MayBelle's developments. "When Willena found out, she was furious. She informed the county commission that those acres are wetlands and can't be built on. Then MayBelle pitched a hissy fit and threatened to take Willena to court. Willena was fixing to call the Environmental Protection Agency this week, to come down here and back her up." Wilma sniffed, reached into her pocket for a fresh blue handkerchief, and dabbed her nose. "I'm not accusing MayBelle, you understand, but it sure is convenient for her to have Willena out of the way."

I could see how it might be. Without Willena's passion for wetlands and her prestigious name, would the EPA care enough about a few acres in Hope County, Georgia, to spend its money and time on a lawsuit?

When I got to my car, I took out my list and added another item:

*8.*

MayBelle: Lawsuit over land?

I would see if I could talk to MayBelle that afternoon.

# 15

I headed straight home to dinner from Wilma's and arrived just before Joe Riddley. He came in tired from unloading sod and demanded, "Where in tarnation have you been? I called three times and Evelyn said you were 'out.' You promised to never go places without telling me where you'd be."

"I told you where I'd be. I went to Wilma's to deliver a casserole. And down to the detention center." While he tucked into shrimp, grits, and Clarinda's famous squash casserole, I hit the high spots of my visits with Wilma and Nancy. I didn't bother him with my standoff with feral dogs on Dexter's front stoop. I didn't want to bore him with every tiny detail of my day.

After dinner, I figured I'd better stop by the store long enough to let Evelyn know I hadn't run away with the payroll. "I'm going out again for a little while," I told her, "but I'll be back before closing time."

"Will you be down at the jail? In case Joe Riddley asks," she added. Color rose in her cheeks and one hand raked her hair. I knew he must have given her a hard time. On a few occasions lately when I'd gone out and not left word where I'd be, I had gotten myself in a little difficulty, and these days he worried. Joe Riddley used to be the most tolerant, kindly man you ever saw, but since he got shot his memory isn't good and his temper can be uncertain. We've all had to make some adjustments.

"I'll leave him a note," I promised. I did, too. *Running errands all over town. Back soon.*

Before tracking down MayBelle, I went to try to find Dexter again. I got back to his place around two. His car was still there, but again he didn't answer my knock. It occurred to me that somebody might have killed him as well as Willena. Maybe I ought to summon a deputy to check out his place to make sure he was all right.

Heading back toward my car, I saw the same two boys I had talked to earlier. They were hanging out near the Mustang again and had been joined by a third who looked younger. The two older ones eyed me warily, poised to flee.

I walked down to where they were. "You

all know where Dexter might be?" I asked.

"We seen him a while back," the fat one acknowledged. "Just before you come the last time."

"Why didn't you tell me that before?" I demanded.

Chubby shoulders rose in a shrug. "You didn't ask." He watched the toe of his worn sneaker scuff the dust.

"Do you know where he went?"

"I axed where he was going," the skinny one volunteered. "He said he was going to drown his sorrows."

The third one snickered. "Somebody oughta drown him." He looked like he might be eight, and had an air of hanging out with the big kids for the first time, wanting to show he was no baby.

The fat one jabbed him with one elbow. "Shut up! She's a judge!"

The little boy gave me a quick, scared look.

"I'm not on the bench right now," I reassured them. "Do you have any idea where Dexter might have gone to drown his sorrows?"

"Mad Mooney's," the skinny one said, as if anybody ought to know that. He pointed down the street.

I drove back to Mad Mooney's and pulled

into a dirt parking lot next to it. As I climbed out, I found myself peering around like I was doing something immoral or illegal. Actually, I was doing something extremely dangerous. If Joe Riddley found out about this, he would skin me alive and hang my hide on the barn.

The place was so small and dim, I had to pause in the doorway to let my eyes adjust. Also my nose. The air was thick with the smell of alcohol, boiled peanuts, and unwashed bodies. When I could finally see, I felt right at home. I recognized everybody there. They had all been up before me on one charge or another.

Two men slid off their stools and sidled toward the back and I heard a screen door slam. Two other men who had been talking loudly lowered their voices. I'd refused bail for one of them the previous Saturday night for starting a fight and cutting somebody with a bottle. I was surprised he was out already. He slewed a glance my way, then bent over the table and started talking loudly about the power of different car engines. I hoped it wasn't getaway cars he was discussing.

Dexter sat on the farthest of eight stools at the short bar, but he didn't look like his normal snooty self. At the community center he worked in a gray uniform. For most functions he wore a white cotton coat over black pants. Today he sported a faded maroon T-shirt, a pair of wrinkled gray pants, and black lace-up shoes without socks. From the way he slumped against the bar, he'd been drinking awhile.

As I approached, he dispensed with his usual deferential little bow and "Evenin', Judge. How you doing this fine day?" To some folks in the South, anything after noon is evening.

Instead, he waved both hands over the bar and shook his head. "I didn't do it, Judge. I swear to God. No matter what they goan think, I ain't killed Miss Willena." He swayed back and forth on his stool, trying to establish his equilibrium. "Ain't killed any of t'other ladies, neither, though it gets mighty temptin' at times. You cain't arrest me."

"Judges don't arrest people," I reminded him. "I just want to ask you a few questions about Monday night."

"Got nothin' to say. Nothin' a-tall." He'd had enough drink to slur his speech and remove whatever wall he kept between his behavior and his true feelings, but not enough to dull the edge of what was bothering him. He noticed that his glass was empty and waved it toward the bartender again.

"You've had enough for now," the bartender rumbled.

Surprised, I turned. "I know that voice! Hey, Clarence."

The bartender grinned, his teeth a quarter moon in the dimness. "Wondered if you'd remember me."

"How could I forget, with all those red suckers you used to come by the store for?"

Clarence Johnson was now a giant of a man, but he had been a chubby little boy who was a whiz at math. Joe Riddley and I had played math games with him all through his school years, and had tried, unsuccessfully, to persuade him to try for a college scholarship after high school. "I don't need college," he had bragged. "I'm gonna get rich." I was sorry to see he had wound up tending bar in a place like Mad Mooney's. He might have done so much better.

He leaned toward me and rumbled in a confidential voice as deep and sweet as honey, "It's good to see you, Judge, but I hope you don't mind my mentioning that your presence here is bad for business." Two other men sidled out the front door as he spoke.

"I won't stay long," I promised. I slid up onto the stool beside Dexter and sat with my feet dangling. "Can I have a Co-Cola, please?" I was glad Clarence set it before me in a can with a straw. The notion of drinking from a glass in that place gave me the willies. The counter before me looked clean enough, but I had been surprised that my shoes hadn't stuck to the floor when I hoisted myself onto the stool.

I turned my attention to Dexter. "Did anybody come in the center Monday night after the members of our group got there?"

"No'm, except'n Miz Harnett. She was late, as usual. After that I went on back to my room to wait until you all was finished, so I could lock up."

"But you didn't lock the front door after we were all inside?"

Dexter's head lolled to one side on his scrawny neck. "Now, who been tellin' you that? Course I locked it, like I always do. Miss Wilma would of had a fit if I hadn't. She's nervous about unlocked doors."

"So who could have unlocked it after-wards? During our break several people went out. It wasn't locked then."

"Anybody can get out," he said, his voice rising with disdain for my ignorance. "Fire department regulations. All dey gotta do is press down on the bar. Gettin' in is another matter."

"But they got back in, too." I took a couple of swallows of Coke to let that settle into his befuddled brain. "You can't get in unless it's unlocked with a key, right?"

"I locked that door." He pounded his fist on the counter. "Anybody says I didn't is lyin'. Somebody else coulda unlocked it, but I doan know who it was." He froze and looked like he was trying to remember something. "Mighta been Miz Harnett. She usually sneaks out for a smoke, and I smelt smoke in the hall when the po-liceman came. But no, that was in the back hall."

He picked up his glass and banged it down on the bar to get Clarence's attention. "I need something to kill my thirst here, Clarence." He swayed as if trying to get me in focus. "I tell you de truth, Judge, whoever killed Miss Willena, it wasn't me. I ain't got no reason to kill *her*." He emphasized the last word, then his voice dropped to a mutter, as if he was speaking his thoughts aloud. "Mighta killed Miss MayBelle a coupla times, always sayin' the place needs moppin' or a toilet needs fixin' right this minute, actin' like I got nothing else to do 'ceptin' what she says. That's a big place for one man to keep."

I didn't say a word, although Dexter and I both knew there was a whole crew who came in to clean after big functions.

"And Miz Harnett, strutting in late to every single meetin,' makin' me sit by that door waitin' on her royal pleasure. Somebody oughta take her down a peg or two. Miss Wilma, too." Dexter's voice rose to a falsetto that wasn't unlike Wilma's. " 'Dexter, would you please run out in all that rain and tote in those milk jugs of punch from Willena's trunk?' 'Dexter, do you mind if we close your door? Your television is so loud.' 'Dexter, would you carry in these boxes for me?' " His voice dropped even lower. "Never mind dat dem boxes weigh a ton. Had to bring that big silver punch bowl and all dem trays. The ones at the center ain't good enough for her? And how come she gives Lincoln the night off when she's got all that stuff to tote? You tell me that."

I wasn't interested in Wilma's domestic arrangements. "Who says you killed Willena?" I took a drag at my Coke so he wouldn't think the question too important.

He answered without looking up from the empty bottom of his glass. "Nobody yet, but I seen the way that po-liceman looked at me dat night. He's waitin' to pounce on Dexter. You wait and see. He's waitin' to send me up the river."

I'd had too many fears of Charlie Muggins in my own time to tell Dexter he was imagining things. All I could do was assure him, "Nobody's going to send you anywhere without a fair trial. And I haven't heard anybody mention that you are a suspect. Those were terrible doings that night, though, weren't they?" I took another drag at my Coke.

"Terrible," he echoed. "If you ax me, the wrong woman got killed. They's several others deserve it more. Clarence! I'm powerful thirsty, man. Get your ass down here!"

Clarence looked at me. I looked away. It wasn't my business how much Dexter drank unless he committed a crime. When Clarence refilled the glass, Dexter gulped down the gold liquid like it was water. It was a sign of how drunk he was that he wiped his mouth on his forearm.

His dignity returned as the buzz hit his system. He sat up straighter and rubbed one hand along the fringe of gray fuzz that circled his shiny scalp. "Miss Willena was one fine woman. She surely was. She singing with the angels this evenin', sure enough."

If Willena sang like she did at church, the heavenly choir was now a trifle flat, but I didn't say that. Given how drunk Dexter was, I decided to conclude my business before he got maudlin or passed out. "So as far as you know, nobody came into the center after we all arrived? Nobody who wasn't in our group, I mean?"

He shook his head. "No'm, Judge. Not a single person after Miz Harnett got there. I was on the door the whole time, 'ceptin' when Miss Wilma axed me to run out to Miss Willena's car and bring in the refreshments and all that silver. She did come with me to hold the umbrella," he admitted grudgingly, "and Miss Willena said she'd take care of the door while I was heppin' Miss Wilma. She stayed right there until I got back."

"And you're sure you locked the door after we were all in?"

"Just like I always do. Ladies don't like bein' in that buildin' at night 'lessen the doors are locked. 'Specially Miss Wilma."

"What did you do after you locked the doors?"

"Went back to my room and watched *Upstairs, Downstairs.* I got the whole series on videotapes. It relaxes me, like, to watch them."

Maybe that was where Dexter got his airs. Did he fantasize that he was Hopemore's perfect English butler?

"Does anybody else have a key besides

you?" I asked.

"Oh, sure. Presidents of all the clubs that meet there got keys nowadays. That's a change since you was president of the Garden Club. But since I'm not there generally at night, the city council say last year that it's okay for each club to have a key if they check it out from me. I was there that night because Miss Wilma axed me special, since she had to tote all that silver and dem jugs of punch and Lincoln wouldn't be there to hep her."

"Do any of the women who were there that night have keys?"

"Most folks. Miss Willena's got one — or, I should say, had one — bein' how's she was president of the investment club. It will go to Miss Wilma next, I reckon, when the po-lice git through with Miss Willena's keys. Miss MayBelle's got one 'cause she's president of the community center board this year. Miz Jensen has a key for the DAR . . ." He paused while an idea worked its way through the foggy reaches of his brain. "I 'speck Miss Gusta's still got hers, too, from the time when *she* was president of the DAR some years back. She wasn't supposed to have a key back then, but she bugged me until I give her one. I don't recall she ever turned it in."

No, Gusta would never have turned it in without a direct request.

Dexter continued listing the keys. "Miss Meriwether's got one, 'cause she's president of the library board. I cain't mind right off if there are any others. I got 'em all wrote down back in my office. . . ." He thought another second or two, then added, "Oh, yeah — Miss Cindy's got one. She's president of the Junior League." He nodded at me like a wise, drunk owl.

I toted that up and figured that the two New Yorkers and I were the only members of the investment club who didn't have keys. That made me feel downright unimportant.

I also noted that Dexter called Nancy Jensen — an outsider before she married Horace — by her married name, while he considered himself on a first-name basis with the local plutocrats. I wondered what he called me.

"It's hard to believe that one of us killed Willena," I told him. "I hadn't met with the group before, but they all seemed nice." I bent my head to my Coke and waited to see if he was drunk enough to take that bait.

"Seemin' ain't the same as doin'," he informed me with the solemnity of a preacher. "Take Miz Jensen, now. Always acts so nice and proper? But I saw her get real riled up with Mr. Horace 'cause of the way he was jokin' and carryin' on with Miss Willena at the country club dance down at the center last month. Miz Harnett's not the lady she likes to pretend, neither, prancin' around like a bitch in heat. She was snickerin' real good, watchin' Miz Jensen. Wives in this town better hang on to their menfolks when that one's around. And Miss MayBelle? I'm surprised somebody ain't shot her years ago. She's fixin' to tear down this whole neighborhood. Says she's gonna put up fancy town houses. Who she thinks is gonna live in all them town houses? And where she thinks these folks already living here gonna find houses? Tell me that. They's two hundred people or more livin' in Pleasantville. Where's she 'speck us to go? Cain't buy anything with what she's offerin' for the houses. Ain't that right, Clarence? What she offer you for this here bar?"

"I'm holdin' out for more," Clarence allowed without giving anything away.

"Yeah, but you got . . . what? Two blocks here? You got somethin' to negotiate with." Dexter lifted his glass to his lips and dribbled liquor on the bar.

Clarence wiped the spill with a cloth that looked clean enough, but probably harbored a whole colony of germs. "I keep tellin' you,

Dexter, all you folks who own on Good Hope Lane better stick together and hold out for good prices. Otherwise she's gonna pick you all off like buzzards on a fence. And she's gonna win — you need to make your mind up to that. Since they've voted to four-lane the state road up to I-20? Folks gonna be movin' out to Hope County like flies, drivin' up to Augusta to work. Ain't that right, Judge?"

"You're probably right, although I hate to see it coming." I refused to dwell on the day when our town became little more than a bedroom community for folks who worked elsewhere. Instead, I honed in on something else Dexter had said. "So you've got property around here, Clarence?"

He continued to wipe the bar without looking at me. "A bit. Been buyin' a piece here and space there over the years. With this area being so close to downtown, I figured it stood to reason it would be developed someday, so I might as well get me a piece of the action."

"Gonna be a millionaire before he's through," Dexter boasted. "Old Clarence is a deep one. Ain't much to look at, but he's plenty prosperous."

I looked at Clarence with new respect. "He always could add two and two."

Clarence's teeth shone in the dim light. "If you do that often enough, it mounts up." He moved down the bar to take care of a new customer.

I leaned closer to Dexter, but not too close. I didn't want to get drunk on fumes. "Can you think of anything — anything whatsoever — that somebody did Monday night that was a little odd?"

"Sure. Somebody done kilt Miss Willena."

"Besides that. Something out of the ordinary?" I lowered myself to quote that old saw from mystery novels. "Sometimes it's the least little thing that provides the most important clue to a murder."

Dexter shook his head. "I ain't seen nothin'," he insisted. He lowered his gaze meaningfully to his empty glass.

As a judge, I would not buy him a drink if I'd wanted to, which I didn't. Without incentive, he shrugged and slid off his stool. "All I know is, I ain't done it. You tell that to the chief, you hear me? I ain't done a dadgum thing." He left, weaving from side to side.

Clarence didn't want to let me to pay for my Coke, but I insisted. "Judges can't take presents from people. But I appreciate the offer. I'm glad to see you prospering, too." I looked around the seedy little bar and wondered if *prospering* was quite the right word.

His laugh rumbled across the counter. "This don't look like much, but it's what folks in this neighborhood are used to. I got two more places over in Dublin that are nicer, and while I wouldn't want it to get around, I'm working as partners with Miss Brandison to develop this neighborhood. She wanted to buy me out, but I said, 'Nothin' doin'. You want my land, we become partners and work together to turn Pleasantville into something nice.' " He laughed again. "You may want to move in here yourself one day, Judge."

"I have a new house," I informed him.

"Yeah, but we're gonna make part of this area into a place for seniors." He gave me a speculative look, like he was counting up my years. "In another twenty years or so? You might find it real attractive to have a little place all set up convenient for you. My granny lived with us the last ten years of her life, and I saw what all she needed. I'm plannin' on building some places equipped for people with disabilities and who are getting old enough to need a little help. Wider doors, bars in important places, no steps, wide sidewalks so wheelchairs and scooters can get to town and back — can't you picture yourself on a little red scooter, putting off down to the BI-LO?" He laughed again. "Keep it in mind, Judge."

As I went back to my car, I couldn't help thinking that if Clarence had gotten his degree in math, he'd probably occupy a minor position in somebody else's company. It is lowering sometimes to discover how much your advice is worth.

# 16

According to her office, MayBelle was "in the field" that afternoon. When I followed the directions they gave me, I discovered they meant it literally. MayBelle was in the middle of what used to be two cotton fields separated by a stand of oaks, maples, and hickories. The trees lined a small creek and an unpaved drive that used to lead down to a house and a barn at the far back of the property. Seeing a gap where that old home place had stood all my life gave me a hollow feeling. I wished I had taken a picture before it got bulldozed. So often it is the unremarkable parts of life that we most regret not having recorded before they disappeared.

Up at the road sat a big green-and-white sign with a huge tree painted to shade the letters. OAK HILLS PLANTATION it announced, even though there were no hills, soon would be no oaks, and never had been what most folks would call a plantation —

merely a couple of ten-acre cotton fields and a small white house.

Oblivious to the deception, pickup trucks, a bulldozer, and a couple of backhoes crawled over the muddy fields like huge beetles while men swarmed over the place like ants.

I saw MayBelle's silver Mercedes crouched partway down the drive, so I pulled in beside it. When I saw how muddy the ground was, I wished I'd worn older shoes. I don't think Dexter had even noticed my good ones in the dim light of Mad Mooney's.

I minced my way down the track to where MayBelle stood in the middle of a cleared space beside a bulldozer. The space used to be filled with a tall stand of Formosa azaleas that blazed with color each spring. Now it, like the clearing where the house had stood, was a freshly scraped palette, ready for a new generation to build on.

MayBelle wore bright orange coveralls, but their resemblance to Nancy's prison jumpsuit was almost nonexistent. With MayBelle's mahogany hair, they called to mind the forests of mountain autumns — which was odd, considering that her primary relationship with trees was to cut them down. She must order the coveralls custom-made, too, the way they fit her shape. As I got closer, I saw that even wearing coveralls and sturdy work boots, she had put on mascara, eyeliner, eye shadow, and blusher. I'd roomed with her once at a chamber of commerce convention, and MayBelle scarcely got out of bed in the morning before she fixed her face.

"What you want us to do about all these here trees?" the bulldozer man called down to her as I trudged up.

"Push them over, except that big one up near the road with the divided trunk. It has a nice shape, so we can use it as a focal point at the entrance." She turned to me with a wide, professional smile. "Hey, Judge."

"Leave the tree behind it, too," I advised as I got close enough for her to hear me. "The divided tree is a silver maple, and they are apt to split, but the oak is at least fifty years old and probably good for another fifty. Besides, it looks like the tree on your sign."

"It's in the way." She gave the bulldozer man a wave. "Take the divided tree out, too, Billy. The judge knows more about trees than I do."

I looked at that poor silver maple and silently begged its forgiveness. I hadn't meant to cause its death. I'd hoped to save the oak.

As the driver growled away on his huge machine, she called to me over the noise, "Are you looking for a building lot for a new house? You can pretty much have your pick right now. We're just starting this development."

I wouldn't have one of her houses if she gave it to me. I'm not into ostentation for the sake of ostentation. Besides, I prefer homes with some light and air around them, and MayBelle built her monster houses so close together that if she had put windows in the sides, folks would only have to subscribe to the paper in every other house and let their neighbors read over their shoulders.

Still, Mama didn't raise me to be rude. "I've got all the house I need, but thanks. I wanted to talk to you a minute about Monday night."

She looked disconcerted, but waved toward a muddy green Land Rover with BRANDISON BUILDERS painted on its side in white. "Come ride with me. We can talk while I make sure folks are doing what they're supposed to."

Climbing up into that Land Rover in a skirt was an interesting experience, but at least MayBelle used the vehicle for the purpose for which it was built: riding over rough ground and fording the little creek.

"About that night . . ." I held on tight as she downshifted and headed down the slippery bank.

"I'm fixing to dam the creek about here and create a little pond down at the back, next to the clubhouse." She slowed down in the creek and waved toward the flattened field.

"That's nice. Do you remember where people were sitting when we passed around Willena's present?"

"The clubhouse will be over there." She waved to the right as the Land Rover lurched up the far bank. "With a swimming pool behind it. I'm thinking of putting swans on the pond. Doesn't that sound classy?"

"Real classy. Did you see who had the corkscrew last?"

She waved toward a string of small markers to the right. "We've already begun laying out lots down that street." She reminded me of a child playing in an imaginary playhouse who knows exactly where the living room, bedroom, and kitchen are. For MayBelle, those empty fields were already full of houses.

I suspected they were also full of illegal immigrants. Most of the workers looked Mexican, and my guess was that not all of them had green cards and none were paid a fair Georgia wage. MayBelle suffered from what Joe Riddley calls "slave owner syndrome," which makes employers believe other folks ought to work for a pittance so they themselves can live in high cotton. If they can't find legal workers willing to live in poverty so they can make the profit their lifestyle demands, they employ desperate people from other countries. This syndrome is so rampant in America today, I'm surprised the CDC hasn't declared an epidemic.

However, as the Bible says, there is a time and season for everything, and that afternoon I hadn't come out to discuss MayBelle's business practices. I had come to pump her about her quarrel with Willena — if she ever stopped talking and gave me a chance.

"I'm getting twenty-seven houses from each of the fields and six where the old house used to sit. Can you believe how much space people used to waste?"

I took a deep breath and plunged in. "I believe you are trying to avoid talking about Monday night. Somebody killed Willena,

MayBelle, and chances are real good it was one of us."

A red flush stained her cheeks, and she jerked on the wheel with such force, I was thrown toward the window in spite of my seat belt. By the time I had righted myself, she looked amused. "You think it was me?"

"You and Willena disagreed over a land deal, right?"

"Come on, Mac. Everybody disagreed with Willena at one time or another. That's what she was like. Nancy fussed at her for dancing three times with Horace at the country club dance, belly to belly. Sadie Lowe was mad at Willena for telling her she had to tone down her clothes if she came to meetings, and for landing Grover when Sadie Lowe wanted him for herself. Wilma and she often went hammer and tongs over Willena volunteering for something, then dumping it all in Wilma's lap. And you heard Willena and Cindy at the meeting Monday night. Hell, Judge, if you'll pardon my French, the only person in the club Willena didn't fight with was Rachel, and that's because Rachel toadied up to her. What I don't understand, though, is why Willena let somebody get close enough with that corkscrew to kill her. She had her purse with her, and she always carried a gun."

That was a good point. "Folks said she was feeling lousy. Do you think she could have been poisoned, maybe was too weak to resist?"

She shrugged. "We all ate the refreshments. Besides, I don't think she got any. And while I like Wilma as a killer, why should she poison Willena there when she could do it at home?"

Since those points had occurred to me, too, I didn't pursue them. I could call Charlie later to remind him to have the forensics people look for evidence of poison. Right now I wanted to talk with MayBelle about her own qualifications as a suspect for Willena's murder.

"Speaking of Wilma, she said you bought some land from her for a park, but then you decided to put a subdivision on it, so Willena notified the county commission that it is wetlands to block you from building there."

MayBelle gave a little snort of laughter. "That's what Wilma wants to believe now. I told her all the time I wanted to build Brandison Park down there, and she knew as well as I did that Brandison Park would be a subdivision. Do I ever build parks?" She didn't wait for me to answer that, because we both knew she didn't. "But after she had my check in her pocket, she had second thoughts. Claimed she'd be able to see the roofs from her back windows, and she didn't want a subdivision that close to her house. She called and told me to give her money back, but I refused. So she called Willena, and that's when Willena called the commission to tell them I was planning a subdivision on wetlands."

"Are you?" I couldn't help asking.

She shrugged. "Possibly. But Willena was being obstreperous. She knew well and good that all I have to do is swap off some other land for that parcel."

"How do you move the raccoons, fish, and tadpoles?"

She exhaled a derisive little puff of air. "We hire a moving van. Come off it, Mac. It's standard procedure, and Willena knew that. A little time and money, and I'll get my variance and a permit to build. She wasn't any threat to me, so I had no motive to kill her."

As I looked at her proud profile, the nose high and hooked like some Middle Eastern princess, I reflected that developers these days are like judges and lawyers back during Prohibition, who spent the day convicting people of buying and selling liquor and then went home to secret rooms where they could drink in private. Some folks firmly believe that rules and regulations apply to everybody but them.

"Did you hear that Nancy Jensen has been arrested?" I asked, to see her reaction.

Her face lit with amusement tinged with admiration. "Now there's somebody who could think she had a motive to kill Willena, the way Horace was carrying on with her at that dance. She didn't have the sense to see that for what it was."

"She wasn't arrested for killing Willena. She was arrested for shooting a gun into a motel room. She claims she was trying to scare the people inside."

MayBelle gave a wicked chuckle deep in her throat. "By which I guess you mean Sadie Lowe and Horace? If Nancy's going to start shooting up all the motel rooms those two inhabit, we won't have a decent room left in the county."

I stared at her in surprise. "You knew about them?"

"Half the people in town know about them. They —" She broke off and swore. Then she jerked the wheel again, to drive across the field toward a clump of men who looked like they were surveying for utility lines. She screeched to a stop and muttered, "Give me a minute. I'll be right back." She swung down from the driver's seat and strode angrily to where the men had stopped work and were watching her apprehensively.

I was glad for a chance to let my bones resettle. Whatever she said, a couple of men cringed and picked up their equipment to move over a few feet. I watched her with the same mixture of respect and distaste I feel for an army tank.

MayBelle's daddy had been a carpenter for Big Jim Brandison, who owned a small construction company — Big Jim's — in town. When MayBelle graduated from high school, Big Jim's wife, Bonita, offered to let her work in the office until she found a better job. Talk about inviting a rattle-snake into your home! At that time Bonita handled all the office side of the business, but May-Belle was so efficient that by fall, Big Jim suggested that Bonita take it easy and let MayBelle run things. In those days Big Jim built houses from four basic plans, making the changes each owner requested. Folks used him because he had a reputation for being honest and fair in his prices. By Christmas MayBelle had persuaded Big Jim to offer his clients a wider selection of floor plans. They were such a success that he had to increase his crews.

After that, there was no stopping the

woman. She set out to learn anything there was to know about the building trade, until Jim started bragging that she knew as much as he did. He was so proud of her that at Jimmy and MayBelle's wedding, if you hadn't known the families, you'd have had a hard time figuring out whether Big Jim was the father of the groom or the bride.

Poor Jimmy, he was a tall, lanky drink of water six years MayBelle's senior, with his mama's sweet nature. Jimmy never wanted to be a builder, but he didn't want to fuss with his daddy and didn't have a clear idea of what he would rather do. I'm not sure he ever wanted to marry MayBelle, either. I'd always suspected he simply didn't know how to get out of it when his daddy depended on her so much.

When Big Jim dropped dead of a heart attack five years after Jimmy and MayBelle got married, Bonita and Jimmy talked about selling the business. She wanted to move to Florida, and he thought he would like to try to become a pro golfer. Jimmy loved golf and played real well.

MayBelle had a conniption. Next thing we knew, she and Jimmy had bought out Bonita's part of the business, renamed the company Brandison Builders, and branched out into real estate development. Their first two subdivisions were modest and sold quickly as starter homes, but modesty was foreign to MayBelle's nature. She next persuaded the bank to lend them an amount of money that made Jimmy hyperventilate whenever he thought about it. With that money she bought land adjoining the country club golf course and built several large houses that would have fit right into a wealthy Atlanta suburb. Nobody thought they'd sell in Hopemore, but MayBelle convinced some of our up-and-coming young couples that hers was the best place to live in town. She used her profits to build more big houses, and to convince young professional couples to buy more house than they needed or could afford. She also persuaded our chamber of commerce to market our great Middle Georgia weather to retirees from the North until pretty soon, lo and behold, MayBelle had several retirement subdivisions around two new eighteen-hole golf courses.

Before we knew it, Hope County was dotted with Brandison subdivisions, MayBelle had moved into commercial development, and she was expanding like a plague into neighboring counties. These days Brandison Builders was the biggest developer in the region and one of our major employers.

Over the past fifteen years, MayBelle had taken over most of the business. She negotiated for land, arranged loans, designed houses, bossed the crews, and packaged and advertised the developments. Jimmy mostly played golf and seemed embarrassed by his wife's success — or was it her steamroller tactics?

Nobody ever knew exactly why things came to a head. Was it Bonita getting frail and asking Jimmy for money to move into a nice retirement community near Orlando? Or Jimmy winning enough golf tournaments that year that he decided he was ready to try the pro circuit? He was always reticent about his personal business, and all anybody heard from MayBelle was that, "If I'd let him, Jimmy would spend money like water." For whatever reason, that past winter, Jimmy had filed for divorce.

MayBelle didn't mind losing Jimmy. Some folks doubted she remembered what he looked like. But she claimed she deserved ninety percent of the business, since she'd built it up. Jimmy pointed out to the judge that since Georgia is a common-property state, and it was his and his daddy's business before she ever joined it, MayBelle wasn't entitled to more than half. He also argued that since the Brandisons' good name was on the business, and the foundation of its success was his parents' hard work and reputation for honesty, his mother deserved compensation if MayBelle planned to continue using the name. When MayBelle vigorously objected, Jimmy described right there in front of God and everybody the inadequate settlement MayBelle and he had given Bonita when she moved to Florida. The whole community was shocked. Jimmy took half the blame for that, but nobody — including the judge — doubted that MayBelle had been the one to insist on not giving Bonita more.

Needless to say, Miss MayBelle wasn't about to lose any part of the business she could hold on to, so we had some pretty scrappy courtroom scenes around here for a few months. Finally Jimmy offered to give her sixty-five percent of the business and sell her the rest if she would pay his mama five hundred thousand dollars for the rights to the Brandison name. That ought to let Bonita live in comfort the rest of her life.

Since then, MayBelle had taken any opportunity to complain about how poor she was now that she was having to buy her own business, and how you couldn't make as much in Hope County as you could up in Atlanta. Jimmy went around smiling like a man who'd been reprieved from death row.

As I watched MayBelle stomp back to the Land Rover, I almost felt sorry for her. Folks respected her — after all, she knew better than most how to turn Georgia clay to gold — but I couldn't think of a single person who really liked her. More than one called her Miss Kudzu, meaning she might have once been an economic necessity, but now folks wished they knew how to get rid of her.

She climbed into her seat with her face flushed but without the frown line she used to have between her eyebrows. "One more crisis averted. Fools were about to put the water line right under a whole row of houses instead of beside the street. You have to watch them every minute, Mac, or they make a mess of things." On and on she went, complaining about folks who were working hard for her under the hot Georgia sun while she reaped most of the profits.

I really hadn't planned to fuss at her, though, until we splashed back across the creek and up the bank between two magnificent triple poplars she had slated for destruction. "Did you flunk biology?" I demanded.

She'd been in my son Ridd's class all the way through school, so I expected at least raised eyebrows. Instead she laughed. "No, that was chemistry. Ridd tried to help me, but I was hopeless. Why?"

"Maybe you missed the unit on 'The Trees Are Our Friends.' The one where they talk about what trees do for us."

"We'll be putting trees in later," she assured me, flicking one hand like she was a fairy godmother who could raise towering oaks with a wave of her wand. "Magnolias, dogwoods, maples, even a few oaks. The dogwoods look real pretty, and magnolias and live oaks are what Northerners think of when they move south."

"Magnolias and live oaks take up more yard room than you're allotting whole houses," I told her bluntly. "Most of them will have to be taken out within twenty years. Why don't you just keep the trees you already have and work around them? At these prices, the owners deserve a tree."

"Oh, twenty years." She sounded like I'd said a hundred. "Until then, they'll shade the porches real good." She sounded utterly disinterested. "I'm going to put wide front porches on these houses, so folks can sit out at night with their neighbors."

"Considering how close you're gonna build them, they can sit out and spit on their neighbors."

I thought that would rile her, but she laughed. "If that's what they want to do, it's fine with me." She turned the wheel, and from our new angle I got a glimpse of the bulldozer up near the road, finishing off the silver maple.

I tried another tack. "Like you said, I know more about trees than you do, and trees don't merely shade porches, they cool the whole atmosphere. They also produce oxygen from the carbon dioxide we breathe out. What do you reckon we'll breathe when you developers have cut them all down?"

"Whoever's around then will figure that out. People are amazingly adaptable."

I pointed to a hickory with a trunk at least sixteen inches in diameter. "That tree's roots hold and build the soil. Have you ever seen pictures of mud slides in Latin America, whole bunches of houses sliding down a mountain? We're gonna have scenes like that in Georgia, if you developers don't stop cutting down big trees and putting in little ones with shallow roots. Without trees, soil is like snow, sitting on top of whatever's under it. Slides real easy. You really ought to leave the big trees. Think how classy they would make the place."

She narrowed her eyes and looked at the hickory. "There won't be any hills in this subdivision. And those big roots get in the way of sewers and underground power lines."

"Couldn't you put the clubhouse where the old house used to stand, with the pool where the azaleas were? It would look real pretty from the road, all surrounded with tall trees."

"It makes more sense to clear-cut and replant when we are done." Her tone chilled me. She had no appreciation whatsoever for the fact that that tree had been on earth longer than I had. All she saw was an obstacle to her plans. It took all my will-power not to jump out, dash across the muddy field, and fling myself between the tree and the dozer.

"I take it you're naming this place Oak Hills in memory of the trees you're killing?" If I sounded snide, I didn't care.

Her eyes grew stormy, but she didn't pucker her forehead like I expected. Then I remembered that at the beauty parlor, somebody had mentioned that MayBelle had gone to Atlanta for minor surgery while I was out of town. Must have been plastic surgery. Maybe that's why her eyes looked bigger, her crow's-feet were gone, and her face wore that flat, blank look.

She pulled to a stop again and got out.

"I'll be back in a minute." She slammed the door real hard that time, and I could tell she was mad by the way she strode over to talk to another clump of workers. They could, too, from the way they edged closer to one another.

I figured I might as well swing down and take a last look at those trees. I couldn't ever recall having hugged a tree, but that afternoon I felt like hugging several. When I thought of the oxygen and coolness those trees would not contribute to the air, the birds and squirrels those limbs would never shelter, the soil those roots would not hold and those leaves would not enrich, I could have sat down and howled. All those years of growing, only to be pushed over in their prime for nothing but greed and one woman's convenience.

The bulldozer roared like a huge, hungry monster with an insatiable maw.

I walked toward an oak and stroked its rough bark. It trembled beneath my hand. Were the ancients right about trees having dryads inside them? Did this tree sense its end was near?

Then I realized that the trembling I felt was the earth around me. I looked up and saw, on the other side of the tree, the bulldozer bearing down on me. It had selected my oak as its next victim, and the driver couldn't see me behind the thick trunk.

I don't know if you've ever been approached by a bulldozer, but I can tell you that my thought processes went into hibernation. I stood there watching that thing come my way, and my feet wouldn't jump to either side. Somebody yelled. That energized me, but instead of going sideways, my legs backed up. Next thing I knew, I had tumbled down a bank and was sitting on sharp rocks in twelve inches of muddy creek water with the most expensive skirt I owned hiked up around me. Red-orange water flowed across my legs and shoes and made the thick bandage on my left hand look like a repellent ketchup-soaked hot-dog bun. My expensive leather clutch purse floated out of reach while I waited for the tree to crash down on my head.

# 17

The air grew still. MayBelle yelled something to the driver and pelted toward me. Hands on hips, she glared from the high bank of the creek. "I thought you were in the Land Rover." I couldn't see her face for the sun in my eyes, but although it lit up her hair like a halo, she was no saint. I could tell by the way she stood that she'd like to throttle me.

I moved my arms and legs to be sure they were still intact. "I got out to say good-bye to the trees." How could I have been so stupid?

MayBelle obviously wondered the same thing.

She turned and spoke curtly over her shoulder to some of the workmen. "Help her out." Two men with thick, straight black hair, swarthy skin, and dark brown eyes slid down the muddy bank and put out caramel brown hands. "You're not hurt, are you,

Judge?" MayBelle finally thought to ask.

"Judge?" they repeated. Their eyes flickered in fear, then both whirled and scrambled back up the bank. I heard the thud of their feet pounding across the field.

I turned over on all fours and clambered to my feet, holding on to a couple of saplings for support. Good thing I hadn't fallen in a few days later. MayBelle would have probably flattened the saplings by then, as well. As it was, she didn't so much as lift a finger to help me.

I limped, wet and muddy, toward a place where the bank wasn't so steep, and accepted the bulldozer man's grubby hand to pull me up. "I'm sorry, ma'am. I never seed you a-tall."

I exhaled a sigh of relief and frustration. "It's okay."

I lied. Nothing was okay. My shoes were ruined. My outfit was soaked and covered in wet leaves. My hair was full of who knew what. I had skinned my good palm and banged my sore hand, and both hips ached from landing on sharp rocks. That was definitely not one of my best public moments.

As I squished back toward the Land Rover through the muddy field, MayBelle spoke behind me. "I've got your purse. But are you finished with what you came to talk about? I'm fixing to head out to another site."

"We're finished for now." I climbed in and settled myself on the seat of the Land Rover, glad we weren't in her Mercedes. My skirt was clammy under me and streaked with mud. I accepted my poor, ruined clutch and gave MayBelle a sideways glance. "But seriously, can you think of anybody who might have a reason to want to kill Willena?"

MayBelle barked a short laugh. "Besides almost everybody?" She slammed my door, went around to her own side, and climbed in. As she started the engine, she asked more seriously, "You don't think it was somebody from outside who found the door unlocked?"

"It's hard to believe a stranger would happen to come to the community center in the pouring rain on the off chance they'd find a door open, then go to the ladies' room on the off chance they'd find somebody there to kill, and win on every count."

"Perverts do exist."

"What pervert would have had access to Willena's corkscrew?"

She steered over the field and headed toward our cars without saying a word.

I tried again. "You have to admit that getting permission from the commission to build on the wetlands will be a whole lot easier without Willena showing up at meetings to talk about squirrels and raccoons. And without Willena bugging them, it's not likely that the EPA is going to care what happens to fifteen piddly acres in Hope County."

"Darned tooting," MayBelle agreed cheerfully. She pulled to a stop next to my car and cut her engine. "I need to get on to another project, Judge, but if you're looking for a bigger house, you couldn't do better than Oak Hills. It's going to be gorgeous when it's done."

I was tempted to retort, *It's going to look exactly like thousands of other subdivisions all over America,* but I didn't. I was too wet and grubby to think of much else.

As I opened the door to my car, MayBelle called, "Keep an eye on Nancy. She's not the goody-goody she likes to appear."

I drove home muddy and miserable, wishing I'd gotten the leather seat covers Joe Riddley had recommended. Would I ever get that red mud out of gray plush?

Clarinda was gathering up her pocketbook, fixing to leave, when I arrived home. When she saw me she put down the pocketbook, propped both fists on her ample hips, and demanded, "You been swimmin' in a mud hole? Don't you recall you put in a perfectly good swimming pool down at the big house that Ridd and Martha said you and the judge could still come down and use anytime you want?" Joe Riddley would always be "the judge" to Clarinda.

She went on without taking a breath. "And look at that outfit! If the cleaners can get them stains out, it'll be a miracle. And you might as well drop them shoes in the garbage right now and be done with it. You ain't never gonna get no use out of them again. What you been up to?"

I sighed. "You don't want to know and I don't want to tell you. Would you call Phyllis and see if she can work me in for a shampoo this afternoon?"

"What happened to your cell phone? Did you drop it in the mud hole, too?"

"No, it's still in the car. But everything else I own is ruined." I opened my new little clutch purse over the sink and water streamed out. Clarinda took charge of the purse. "I'll turn the oven on real low and see can we dry out the money and your pictures and such. You get in a hot bath before you catch your death of cold."

I didn't figure I was likely to catch my

death of cold in May, but I was too bedraggled to argue. "Phone Phyllis!" I called back as I headed to the tub. "Tell her it's an emergency."

I cannot remember when a shower ever felt so good — or necessary. I went ahead and shampooed my hair. If Phyllis couldn't see me, I'd have to stay home the rest of the day.

I stayed under the hot water so long, Clarinda finally banged on the door. "You okay in there? Phyllis says she can work you in if you'll go right on down. I'm takin' this here outfit to the cleaners on my way home, and I'll take the shoes and purse to Guy, but I doubt he's gonna be able to do a thing with them." Guy ran the local shoe repair shop.

"Tell him to do his best. And thanks. I'll be a new woman."

"You gonna be something new, all right, if the judge ever finds out you're meddling in this here murder," she prophesied darkly.

By the time Phyllis had finished with me, I looked better but felt stiff and achy, I was limping from my sore hips, and the day was basically shot. It didn't help to get a call from Isaac James, our assistant police chief, later that afternoon.

While Chief Muggins is one of my least

favorite officers of the law, Isaac is one of my *most* favorite. Six feet tall and built to carry his height, Isaac has skin the color of polished mahogany and one of the finest minds I've ever known. I sometimes wonder if I would dislike Chief Muggins so much if I didn't feel so strongly that Isaac should have been given the position back when our city fathers decided to import Charlie from Tennessee.

"I understand you called in a report on some feral dogs over in Pleasantville this morning and were sighted at Mad Mooney's bar this afternoon. Are you starting a campaign to clean up that neighborhood?"

"It could use it. I was over on Good Hope Lane and saw a rat and all kinds of junk lying around in those yards, with little kids out playing in it. I asked Chief Muggins to send some deputies to check it out, but I don't know if he will."

"We can make a sweep." I heard him writing and knew he was jotting a note on his desk calendar. "But you know as well as I do that as soon as we pick up one truckload of trash and haul one set of owners into court, the rest of the folks out there will be dumping another truckload on the yards."

"We still have to try. Now, who told you anything about Mad Mooney's?"

"A little jailbird. I had to book Stack Rogers again this afternoon for theft by taking and he mentioned he saw you drinking down at Mad Mooney's right after lunch."

"I was drinking a Co-Cola. Did Sheriff Gibbons hear him?"

If Buster knew I'd been spotted at Mad Mooney's, there was no doubt whatsoever that he'd be teasing Joe Riddley about it before suppertime.

"No, he was out. But seriously, Judge, if you want to tipple after lunch, you can find a more congenial place than Mad Mooney's."

"A more sanitary one, too, I hope."

"Clarence runs a pretty clean joint, all things considered. We've never cited him for a code violation yet."

"Well, the rest of the neighborhood could use an inspection. And Ike? If you see Joe Riddley, don't mention Mad Mooney's, okay?"

"He won't hear it from me, but you know you can't keep a secret in this town. I don't guess you want to tell me what you were doing there, do you?"

Isaac and I have cooperated on other cases, so I might as well tell him. "I was talking to Dexter, the custodian over at the community center. I'm puzzled about how the front door got unlocked while we were meeting Monday night. Dexter swears he locked it before he went back to his room, but when Cindy went out at the beginning of our break, it was unlocked."

When Isaac didn't say anything for a very long minute, I added, "Do you know if the forensics team has been alerted that Willena may have been poisoned? She was pretty sick in the ladies' room just before she died."

Another long silence. Finally I heard, "The chief is handling that investigation, Judge. Personally."

Isaac and I both knew that wasn't a statement. It was a warning.

# 18

Rain started again in the middle of Thursday night. I heard the first tentative patters, then a sudden rush that meant it was streaming down. I turned over, trying to get comfortable, wishing I were back in the old blue house with its tin porch roof. Rain on the porch roof always sent me to sleep, and tonight I sorely needed sleep. For the second night in a row I had tossed and turned worrying about Walker and Cindy, wherever they were, and all my bones ached.

It was not the rain but exhaustion that finally put me to sleep just before the alarm went off. I eyed the streaming window sourly. Why had I promised to drive Wilma to Augusta?

I dressed stiffly, again putting on nicer clothes than I usually wear to work. Joe Riddley gave me a considering look over the breakfast table. "You aren't running around on me, are you, Little Bit? All this dressing up during the week?"

I went to fetch the coffeepot. "It would serve you right if I was, the way you sent me off to Scotland by myself. But not today. I just wish it wasn't raining."

His mug stopped halfway to his mouth. "Rain gets in the way of your running around?"

"No, but I've promised to drive Wilma Kenan to Augusta for a meeting. She's talking to some women's group about Granddaddy Will."

He chewed his toast and thought that over. "Never knew you and Wilma were such particular friends."

"We aren't, but Willena was supposed to drive with her, and she said she didn't like to drive up by herself. She even managed to get us both dispensation from Charlie to go."

"Oh. Has Lincoln retired or has he finally *gotten* tired of Wilma and quit?"

"Neither. She said he'd drive, but I thought I'd use the time while she's speaking to look for new recliners. Clarinda's been asking when she can have yours."

"Did you remind her of the addendum to the tenth commandment, 'Thou shalt not covet thy employer's recliner'?"

"Yeah, but she reminded me of the second

greatest commandment, 'Thou shalt love thy cook as thyself.' "

Our new house was so small, we could see the living room from our dining room table. He eyed his old brown recliner with a thoughtful look, and I could tell he was within a hair of telling me he liked it fine as it was. He surprised me, though. "You get comfortable ones, now. I don't want to have to go all the way over to Clarinda's when I want to watch TV."

"Come with me," I urged. "It would make the trip up a whole lot more fun."

He reached for his red cap. "For you, maybe. Can't say I would enjoy that much of Wilma's company."

I didn't either. While I steered through sheets of rain that made it hard to see the lines between lanes, she talked incessantly about anything under the sun except Willena's murder. The closest she came to mentioning it was when she said with a shudder, "They are cutting her up. Did you hear that? They are cutting her up to see what killed her. I can't stand it!"

"Don't think about it," I advised. "She is beyond caring."

Her voice was small. "I know." Then she started talking about how much better Grover was than her former stockbroker, and why I ought to move my account to him. In addition to trying to see the road and avoid a wreck, I also had to come up with replies that were polite without committing me to something I had no intention of doing.

I have wondered since if it was the coziness of being shut up surrounded by rain or the fact that I couldn't pay her much attention that kept Wilma talking — almost like a Catholic confessional where you can't see the priest. Anyway, while most Southern women would never talk about their finances to their casual friends, by the time we reached Augusta I had learned that Wilma, like a lot of people, had lost money during the crash of tech stocks around the turn of the century and blamed that on her old broker. That was why she was now using Grover. Of course, she thought his smile was real sexy, too, and didn't he have the smokiest blue eyes?

Reading between the lines, I figured the former broker probably thanked his lucky stars that Wilma had moved her account. From the way she kept repeating, "I told him . . ." I deduced that she had tried to micromanage her account and that her poor broker was probably now recuperating at the state mental hospital over in Milledgeville. I hoped Grover was prepared for what working with Wilma would entail.

It was a relief to drop her off and go looking for recliners. Even with the rain, shopping in the middle of a workday made me feel as carefree as those boys I'd seen the day before playing hooky from school. I found recliners I liked in the second store I visited, arranged to have them delivered the following Monday, and discovered I still had nearly an hour before I needed to pick up Wilma. I drove back to that part of town and, spying a coffee shop, decided to treat myself to a cup of cappuccino and a biscotti. Myrtle's in Hopemore has great coffee and chocolate pie, but her menu doesn't stretch to cappuccino or biscotti.

I settled at a table by the window and watched droplets run down the windowpane while I sipped the frothy drink from its thick paper cup. After a nibble at the biscotti, I peered around to make sure nobody was watching and I dunked it. There I was, pulling my dripping biscotti from my cappuccino, when I spotted Grover in a booth over at the side. Fortunately, he didn't spot me. He was leaning across the table listening intently to a companion I could not see. While I watched, a slender hand with bright red nails reached out to touch his. A dia-

mond on the hand looked as big as a blueberry.

Seemed like Wilma was right — Grover
and Willena had been nothing but friends.
Or was he the kind of man who flitted from
one rich woman to another, so long as he
could manage her account?

Reminding myself that it was no business
of mine whom Grover had coffee with on a
rainy business day, I turned back to contem-
plate the streaming scene beyond my window.

However, when I'd drained the last dreg
and brushed my crumbs neatly into a
napkin, I had to toss the cup and napkin,
and the only trash can was near their table.
As I approached, I heard a husky voice
murmuring, "So you think I'm safe?"

Grover spotted me before he replied. It
would have been rude of me not to speak.

"Fancy running into you here," I exclaimed.

From the other side of the table, Sadie
Lowe Harnett gave me a wide, lazy smile
through lips as scarlet as her nails. "Why,
hey, Judge. What brings you to Augusta?"

She wore a short black skirt and a red cotton sweater cut to call maximum attention
to her magnificent bosom.

"I drove Wilma up for a meeting and did

a little shopping," I told her. "And you?"

She put up one hand and touched the hair behind her left ear. As a girl I used to want hair like that, black and shiny. Today it was piled on top of her head with little curls cascading down her neck. "I came up to see Grover." Not by so much as a blush did she reveal that she'd been caught with Horace one day before. But then, the woman had acted in soaps. Maybe she thought that in real life women had to have an affair with any male who came on their horizons. I remembered, too, that she had left Hopemore in the first place because she had gotten herself taken into custody several times in tenth grade for having sex in the backseat of a car down near the water tank. Her parents were already lost in the alcoholic haze that would eventually lead one of them to burn down their mobile home with both of them in it, so our juvenile judge and Joe Riddley — who was a magistrate at the time and concerned about troubled teens — put their heads together and arranged for Sadie Lowe to go live with an aunt in Atlanta.

Now she gestured toward papers on the table between them. "He's such a sweetie about helping me figure out what to do with all my money." Her voice was more breath than sound, and she gave Grover a smile more appropriate for a bedroom than a business meeting.

He turned the color of a boiled lobster. If he wasn't careful, he could wind up in hot water, too. Still, his mama had raised him right. He slid out of the booth and took my hand with a smile like he'd been hoping to see me all morning. "MacLaren! Good to see you again. Everything going well in Hopemore?"

I have to admit, that threw me. "As well as can be expected the week of a murder," I agreed, "but I'm still trying to figure out how the dickens that door to the community center got unlocked Monday night. Do you have a key?"

Grover looked puzzled.

Like hot air, Sadie Lowe rushed in to fill the vacuum. "I still can't believe it about poor Willena, can you? I mean, who would do such a thing?"

"Do what?" Grover looked from her to me, then back at her in confusion. Sadie Lowe ran her tongue across her upper lip and waited for me to tell him. "I've been trying to call her all week, but she doesn't answer," he added.

I didn't know if Grover had been romantically involved with Willena, but she had certainly been his client. He didn't need to hear this news standing up.

"Could we sit down?" I moved toward the bench he had vacated. He stepped back to let me slide in ahead of him. When he was sitting beside me, I said, "I'm surprised Chief Muggins hasn't already called you. Somebody killed Willena during the break at our meeting Monday night."

His eyes widened and his mouth fell open, a perfect picture of shock. Either he truly hadn't heard or he was a great actor and had prepared for this.

"Oh, hon, you mean you really hadn't heard?" Sadie Lowe's voice oozed sympathy, and she put out a hand to cover his.

Just before she touched him, he lifted his coffee cup and raised it to his mouth. He didn't drink, only held the paper cup against his lower lip.

I didn't mind sounding skeptical. "How could you not know? It's been all over the national news."

He tried twice before he got words out. "I . . . I haven't seen a paper or TV since Monday. My son had a school thespian society competition this week up in Atlanta, and I went along as a chaperone. We left early Tuesday and came back last night." When we neither one said anything, he added, sounding defensive, "I was with the kids the whole time." He pressed his free hand to his mouth and swallowed hard, then set his cup down and rubbed his hands together, as if to warm them. "Willena knew I was going, but I tried to call her around suppertime both nights anyway. When she didn't answer, I figured she was out."

Again, neither of us said a word, but he went on explaining, as if we had doubted him. "The group went to plays both nights, then tooled around Atlanta. We got in so late, all I wanted to do was fall into bed. Last night when we got home, I was still so exhausted from living with twelve teenagers for two days that all I wanted to do was sleep, and I got up too late this morning to watch TV or read the paper."

Sadie Lowe leaned across the table, giving us a view that could have raised Grover's blood pressure considerably, had he been looking her way. He was studying the table-top like he found beige Formica fascinating. "Maybe it's a mercy you didn't know before you left," she said. "It would have spoiled your trip. Somebody went to the ladies' room and stuck Willena's new silver cork-screw right through her throat." She made a fist of one hand and struck the base of her own throat.

Grover groaned and grabbed the knot of his necktie.

I sat swamped by memories of that horrible night. I saw Willena lying on the floor, the flash of silver, the backs of her plump white knees. I covered my mouth and nose with one hand and took long, deep breaths.

"The judge, here, found her," Sadie Lowe added.

Grover slid his water my way. "Here."

I took an appreciative sip. "Thanks. Looks like you need some, too." I slid it back and he gulped down the rest.

Sadie Lowe leaned farther over and wiggled a little to settle her breasts more comfortably on the tabletop. "The police came and everything. It was like on TV. But you'd already gone. And Nancy." She dragged out the last two words suggestively.

Grover wasn't listening. He was bent over the table with his eyes closed. I didn't know if he was praying or trying not to cry. To give him time to recover, I turned to Sadie Lowe and said in a low voice, with what I'll admit was a little spite, "I understand you had some trouble with Nancy yesterday morning."

Her eyelashes rose to meet her wispy bangs. "*Some* trouble? She could have killed me! The woman is mad."

"Or real upset that you were with her husband."

Sadie Lowe's right shoulder rose in a shrug that caused the young man at the register to nearly fall over the counter. "Her marriage is over. She needs to accept that and move on." She reached out for Grover's hand again. "Are you okay, sweetie?"

Grover recovered the hand and clasped his coffee cup between both palms, moving the cup around the table in little circles. His voice was husky as he said, "I didn't even say good-bye. She was in the ladies' room and I wanted to get home. My son is only fifteen and I don't like to be away late. Besides, we had to pack for the trip." He turned to me, his eyes pink with unshed tears. "Do they know who did it?"

"Cindy," Sadie Lowe replied. Then, seeing my look, she added, "At least, that's what the police think."

"The police don't know a thing yet," I snapped. "Which brings us back to the front door. The custodian swears he locked it before he went back to his room, but it was unlocked during the break. Did you have any trouble getting back in, Grover, after you went out?"

"I didn't . . ."

I would have sworn he was about to claim

he hadn't gone out. Maybe he had forgotten for the moment, or maybe he was going to deny it but figured out that Rachel might have told the police he had. Or maybe he was remembering, as I was, Wilma exclaiming, "You're wet!" and his own reply that he'd forgotten his umbrella when he ran out to his car for something.

"I don't have a key." He frowned. "I hadn't given the door any thought until this minute."

That was probably true. When you go in or out a door, you aren't usually surprised to find that it opens unless you expected it to be locked.

I was so busy with those thoughts that I nearly missed Grover's most important sentence.

"Cindy was outside. Maybe she unlocked it when she went out."

"Did you see her?" I hoped I didn't sound as eager as I felt.

"Sure. When I went out with Rachel to give her something, Cindy was down the sidewalk under an umbrella, using her phone. Rachel and I went back in and had some refreshments, and when I left later, Cindy was still there. I don't know why she didn't step into one of the empty rooms."

"That building is a dead space. There's no

signal inside, and the reception isn't much better on the porch."

"Oh." He sounded like he didn't know where to go with the conversation from there.

I did. "Did you see Sadie Lowe outside smoking?"

He looked over at her. "No. Where were you?"

"Down at the end of the porch. It was real dark, and I had on black. Oh, Grover, I'm so sorry you had to hear about Willena like this. I didn't realize you didn't know."

She leaned over and grabbed both of his hands before he could draw them away.

That was my cue. I gathered my pocketbook and left them. Grover was staring at the table with no expression whatsoever on his face, and Sadie Lowe was clasping his hands and leaning across the table so far that he could have seen down to her navel if he'd been paying her a speck of attention. I kept waiting for some director to shout, "Cut!"

Only when I got to my car did I remember that Sadie Lowe had been wearing white on Monday night.

# 19

Wilma insisted on taking me to lunch to thank me for driving her. I was delighted until she directed me to a fast-food seafood place, where we had to eat mass-produced greasy food out of paper baskets. I sat looking at my lukewarm shrimp and silently named several moderately priced places in Augusta where I'd rather be eating.

Wilma fastidiously wiped ketchup from her fingertips. "I love their fried clams, but I almost never get by here."

She sounded like the place was out near Seattle and opened only once a decade. I refrained from pointing out that she could employ their chef by offering slightly more than minimum wage. *Heck,* I thought as I ate my soggy fries in silence, *she could buy the whole dadgum chain.*

When we got back to my car, she said, "I'd like to drop in and see Grover while we're here, if you don't mind. I have a few suggestions about my account."

Poor Grover.

"I saw him this morning, having coffee with Sadie Lowe," I mentioned as I headed in that direction. "Do all the women in the club have their accounts with him?"

"I have no idea." She flared her nostrils. "That woman is man-crazy, you know. We should never have let her in the club." She pulled out a compact, added a little powder to her nose, and inspected her face. "On second thought, I have an appointment for this afternoon. We ought to get on back. I can talk to Grover later."

The rain stopped on our way home, leaving the world soggy but brilliant, as if the whole shebang had been spray-washed. Normally that lifts my spirits, but today my thoughts were so full of Willena and her death, I scarcely noticed the sunshine except to be grateful that driving was easier.

Wilma kept up a steady stream of chatter about all the important people who had been at the meeting that morning, complimentary things they had said about her speech, how sorry they all had been to hear about Willena, how they couldn't believe she had actually been murdered, and how brave Wilma was to have given the speech in her hour of grief.

She took out a pale green hankie and dabbed at a drop on the end of her nose. "It was hard, but I told them that you can't give in to your emotions. That's what Daddy always said."

Her daddy had been a cold stick who looked like he'd never had an emotion in his life, but I didn't mention that.

As we got near Hopemore and I turned onto the road that led to her house, she said, "You can drop me off at Willena's." She sounded so casual that for one startled minute I thought Willena was still alive and I'd imagined the whole murder.

I must have looked as surprised as I felt, because she added, "Jed DuBose is coming over, and he'll drive me home afterwards. Willena changed to him when he came home. I'm still with Shep, of course."

I applauded Willena for giving Jed a chance — and recognizing superior quality.

Of course, Willena had been no fool. She gave the impression that she resided in a land of ease and relaxation, but she wasn't sloppy in handling her affairs. I'd heard her say more than once, "If you don't want to be bothered with something, find the best people you can to take care of it for you, then let them do it."

Willena's house was half a mile nearer

town than the Kenan home place, built on land old Will Kenan had deeded to his younger son, Frank. From what I'd heard, Frank Kenan was a boisterous man who had loved to entertain, so in 1915 he had built a square brick home with two stories of living space and servants' quarters in the attic. In 1939, when his children were in their late teens, he had built a four-car garage with servants' quarters over it and turned the attic into a large ballroom with dormer windows. Before we built the community center in town, Willena's family had often let groups use their ballroom. Mama said they had enormous ceiling fans to cool it before air-conditioning.

My senior class used the school gym for our senior prom, but Joe Riddley was in Willena's daddy's class, and they held their prom in John Kenan's ballroom. I got to go, of course, and it was magical to dance up among the treetops with the full moon making leafy patterns on the dance floor. We were given the run of the downstairs, as well, and I felt like a princess strolling through the high, comfortable rooms in my prom gown. We sat out several dances laughing and joking with our friends on the wide cement front porch lined with wicker chairs and rockers. He and I finally sneaked back to a little gazebo beside the fishpond, and it was there that he first said, "Oh, Little Bit, I do love you."

Since I didn't like to tell Wilma that, I said, instead, "My mother once came to a big dance at this house. In honor of your aunt, I believe."

Wilma pursed her lips and drew in her nostrils like something smelled bad. "Probably her wedding dance. Uncle Frank built the ballroom for the occasion, but she married a most unsuitable man and died not long after." The way Wilma bridled, I knew not to pursue that any further, especially when she added, "She was only eighteen. She should never have left Hopemore."

As we pulled into Willena's long driveway, Wilma looked out the window and commented, "Her yard hasn't gotten too bad yet."

You'd have thought the yard had been neglected for weeks instead of serviced the prior Monday. Furthermore, it looked great. Years ago, Willena had hired our lawn service and told us, "I don't care what you put in, so long as it looks nice." After that, she never made another suggestion or complained about a single bill. And while it wasn't full of perennials and theme gardens like Wilma's, the trees and shrubs were in proportion to the house, and scattered beds of annuals made bright splashes on the lawn.

I was surprised to see an elderly blue BMW parked under the porte cochere between the garage and the side of the house. Wilma didn't seem to notice it. She was gathering up her pocketbook and a little leather folder with her speech notes from behind my seat.

I pulled on around to the front steps.

"We're going to walk through and take a quick inventory," she informed me. "I told Jed that with all the antiques Willena had, we ought to know exactly what's here."

How like Wilma to tell somebody else's lawyer what to do. Still . . .

"I guess it will all be yours now," I hazarded as we rolled to a stop.

She glanced toward the house, and her mouth drew up in distaste. "Until I dispose of the place. I have always wished Uncle Frank had built something with charm."

I turned off the engine and waited for her to get out. "You ought to be able to sell it real easy," I told her. "Folks will appreciate how little maintenance it requires." I didn't mention that I found it as charming as her own.

She sniffed. "Maintenance is the price we

pay for being stewards of history."

Wilma had used that phrase the year Joe Riddley and I decided to put permanent siding on the old Yarbrough house while we'd still lived there. She had paid us a personal visit when she'd heard about the siding, to remind us that our house was a historical landmark in Hopemore (it had been built the same year as the Kenan house) and ought to be authentically preserved, even if that meant pouring gallons of paint over it every few years, because "Maintenance is the price we pay for being stewards of history." Joe Riddley had pointed out to her that we, like four generations of Yarbroughs before us (and Ridd and Martha, who lived there now), were more concerned with comfort than preserving history. Wilma had left with her panties in a wad and hadn't spoken to either of us for months.

I didn't see any point in renewing hostilities now, so I changed the subject to one I thought she'd find more congenial. "Willena had some lovely furniture."

Willena had been collecting antiques for years — or, rather, had been having somebody in New York and London collect antiques and ship them to her. Lately she'd been relying on Maynard Spence over at

Wainwright House Antiques. (Gusta had sold him her antebellum home on the condition that he put her name on the sign.)

Wilma shrugged. "I suppose, but not a single piece came from Granddaddy Will. All of that was left in my house."

You'd have thought her family had cut down trees from their own land, designed and crafted their own furniture, and never bought a piece from anybody else. She certainly implied that any chair that had not been blessed by her great-granddaddy's skinny rump or any table that had not held his meals was not worth owning.

"Well, if you need help disposing of any of it, call Maynard," I suggested. "He's been helping her buy things."

Wilma tightened her lips. "I'll have to see what's here first."

I should have worded that differently. Nobody told Wilma Kenan what to do. She'd probably pick an antique dealer out of the Yellow Pages to prove she knew better than me.

As she climbed out, though, she surprised me. "I appreciate your taking me this morning, MacLaren. I dreaded making that drive alone." She sounded sincerely grateful and a little forlorn. I told her it had been no trouble at all.

She looked toward the house and stiffened her back. "I hate going in there alone, too, but it's got to be done." She stopped as if it was now my move.

I knew good and well what she wanted, but I needed to get back to the office. On the other hand, I wondered if that old BMW belonged to Rachel Ford and what she was doing there, and figured Wilma might not be too gracious at finding her inside. I might need to referee.

"Do you want me to come in with you and wait until Jed gets here?" I offered.

"Would you?" Wilma sounded relieved.

"Just until Jed arrives." I grabbed my pocketbook and followed her up the brick steps to the wide front porch. Willena still had wicker chairs out there, I was delighted to see. "I suppose you have a key?" I asked.

Wilma reached for the bell, rang, then turned the knob. "Hetty and Baker are here. And Willena never bothered to keep her door locked. I kept telling her it's not safe in this day and age."

Instead of which . . . I wondered if Wilma was thinking the same thing I was.

She opened the front door and called, "Yoo-hoo? It's me, Hetty."

I'd forgotten about Baker and Hetty, who had worked for Willena for the last fifteen years or so and lived in, like Wilma's Linette and Lincoln. I was about to say something about how lucky we all were to have faithful people working for us when Wilma added — without lowering her voice, "That's one reason I want to go through the house. I don't want them taking anything before we get a list made."

I was too stunned to reply.

She looked at her watch. "Before I call Jed, shall I ask Hetty to bring you some coffee?"

"I'm fine," I told her. "I had coffee in Augusta." I would be too embarrassed to look Hetty in the eye at the moment.

"Then I'll call Jed and tell him to come on over."

As she trotted toward the living room, I reflected that it must be nice to take it for granted that a lawyer would come as soon as you called.

Willena's house might not be as old as Wilma's, but it was a lot more welcoming. Willena had a knack for combining antiquity with comfort. Her walls were a soft yellow instead of Wilma's chalk white. Her wide front hall was bright with paintings of flowers and landscapes rather than gloomy ancestors, and the golden oak floor was covered with one large and two smaller matching Oriental rugs that glowed in soft shades of red, green, and cream. A creamy brocade sofa along the left-hand wall suggested that if walking in from your car had tired you, you could pause and catch your breath. I particularly admired the staircase, which went up along the right side of the hall and made a graceful U-turn at the landing before climbing to the second floor.

That was as far as I had gotten with my admiring — which took all of five seconds — when Wilma demanded, "What are you doing here?"

I hurried to the living room arch. Rachel Ford sat on one end of the sofa clutching a photo album to her chest. Additional albums were piled beside her. She looked wan and tired, and the circles under her eyes were darker than they had been Monday night. But her chin was up in defiance at Wilma's tone. "Hetty let me in. Willena said last week that I could come look at some of her old pictures for an article I am writing on clothes of the 1930s." She gestured to the albums. "I was going through these to see what the people were wearing."

Were those tears on her cheeks? She wiped them away as if they were dust.

Wilma primmed her lips. "Hetty should never have let you in without my permission. At the least, she should have stayed with you."

Red stained Rachel's cheeks, and her blue-gray eyes glittered. "I'm not stealing anything, if that's what you're implying. I don't want the pictures, I just wanted to look at them."

"Nevertheless . . ." Wilma dragged the word out and gave Rachel a long, cold look.

I took the chance to peer around the living room, which was filled with an eclectic mix of old and new. The chairs and sofas looked comfortable, with thick, soft cushions. Some had footstools for those who liked them. Instead of Wilma's fixed, formal setting, Willena's furniture looked like it had been shifted around until she found the most pleasing arrangement. Antique china plates and marble busts on pedestals were interspersed with souvenirs from trips around the globe, so that a new handwoven basket held magazines beside an eighteenth-century wing chair and looked right at home there.

Rachel, however, appeared decidedly ill at ease as she closed the album she'd been examining and put it on top of the stack. She rose. "May I ask you not to throw these out until I've had a chance to look through them?"

"Those are family photographs. I have no intention of throwing them out." Wilma stepped slightly back and waited. The instructions were clear. Rachel obediently headed for the hall, but at the doorway she turned.

"May I have permission to look through them at a later date?"

Wilma's voice promised nothing. "We can discuss it after I've gotten through all this." She made a little gesture to encompass not only Willena's house, but her death.

Through a long front window I watched Rachel descend the front porch steps and head around the side of the house for her car. Had Wilma noticed that she carried neither pen nor notebook? Odd, for somebody researching an article.

# 20

"Can you imagine the nerve?" Wilma demanded. "After I've called Jed, I'll have a word with Hetty. We can't have every Tom, Dick, and Harry barging in here."

I turned. "You'll be busy, then. I really need to get on back to the store." I didn't think I could stand to spend another ten minutes in her company at that point.

Back at the office I managed to get through a good bit of work before the phone rang.

"MacLaren? MayBelle Brandison here. I wanted to see if you're all right after that wetting you got yesterday."

I allowed as how I was fine.

"No cold or anything?"

I couldn't tell if she hoped I had one or that I didn't. "Nary a sneeze," I assured her. "I spent the morning driving Wilma to Augusta so she could give a talk, and got back only a little while ago."

"I need to drive in sometime this week and talk to Grover about my account. I don't know if you've got a good broker, but he's wonderful."

"He must be. Wilma uses him, and this morning Sadie Lowe told me she uses him, too."

"Where did you see Sadie Lowe?"

The devil gave me a little nudge. "Oh, she and Grover were having a cozy little chat in a coffee shop when I dropped in for some cappuccino and a biscotti."

"I see."

I had no idea what MayBelle could see from that.

"Have you heard that Nancy is in jail?" she asked.

"I told you that yesterday," I reminded her. "I went to see her before I came to see you."

"Oh, that's right. How is Wilma holding up?"

"Sad, but managing. You know Wilma."

MayBelle's laugh wasn't the least bit humorous. "Oh, yes. Competent to the bone."

Before we hung up I had to assure her again that I had no interest whatsoever in buying a small plot of ground to build a big house on in Oak Hills Plantation. I hung up wondering what on earth that call had been about.

When the phone rang again almost immediately, I thought maybe she was calling back to tell me whatever she had forgotten to tell me before. Instead, it was Chief Muggins.

"Hey, Judge. I'm trying to get in touch with Mrs. Yarbrough."

"You've got her." I aimed for a light tone and willed my voice not to shake.

Impatience poured through the line. "The other one. Mrs. Walker Yarbrough. I keep calling, but nobody answers. I stopped by, too, but there's nobody there."

"Which is probably why nobody answers the phone." My voice didn't wobble, but I was glad he couldn't see me. My hands had started shaking so badly, I could hardly hold the phone, and my stomach was doing flip-flops.

"When did you see her last?" He sounded like he suspected me of hiding Cindy in our office safe.

I paused as if I needed time to think. "Monday night, I guess. I've been real busy catching up from my trip. You know how things pile up when you're gone."

He gave a grunt I suppose he meant for a laugh. "Is that why you were drinking at

Mad Mooney's yesterday? Whatever you were pouring down your throat must have been mighty strong to make you take a dip out at Mrs. Brandison's new subdivision before she dug the pool."

I forgot my manners enough to snap, "Seems like you'd have better things to do than listen to gossip. I nearly got run over by a bulldozer. Did your sources include that tidbit?"

"No, they neglected to mention it."

"Well, tell your deputies they'd do better to hop on over to Pleasantville and clean up the trash. You can fill the city coffers for the next month with fines."

You can push a vicious animal only so far. "When I need you to tell me how to do my job, I'll ask. Meanwhile, if you see your daughter-in-law, tell her to keep herself visible. And she'd better not leave town. You hear me?"

"I hear you. But every other member of the club except Rachel has left town since the murder, and I haven't heard you squawking about that."

"They didn't say they hadn't been in the bathroom when they had."

"She didn't —" Just before I said something I might regret, I remembered what Joe Riddley had said: "Do all in your power to keep the peace."

I clutched my manners in both fists and muttered between my teeth, "Sorry. I don't mean to tell you how to do your job. But before you get too set on Cindy, have you talked to Nancy Jensen?"

"Yeah. She's down at the detention center for firing at her husband."

"She didn't —" I bit my tongue. *Do all you can to maintain the peace,* I reminded myself silently, so I took a deep breath and said in as casual a tone as I could muster, "She might be connected to Willena's murder. Remember? She left our meeting early, upset about something."

He gave me an impatient huff. "She didn't leave her keys under the body, or claim she was out in the rain talking on a cell phone when nobody saw her."

"Grover saw Cindy." I was so delighted to hand him that piece of news, I felt like dancing a jig. "When I was up in Augusta this morning with Wilma, I ran into Grover Henderson, our stockbroker. He said he saw Cindy standing in the rain while he was at his car getting something for Rachel, and Cindy was still out there on the phone when he left just before the end of the break."

"Judge, butt out of this case. I don't need you traipsing all over Georgia interviewing my witnesses. I do need to tell you that your daughter-in-law is going to be in a passel of trouble if she doesn't give me a call in the next twenty-four hours to let me know she is in Hope County."

*Click.*

# 21

That call scared me to death. I couldn't sit there and work like nothing was wrong. Chief Muggins is nobody to mess with when he's mad. Walker would be in trouble, too, for taking his wife out of town. When I pictured my son's picture hanging in the post office with a number under his face, I sent up a frantic prayer. "Help! Show me what to do!"

Nothing happened.

My eye fell on my calendar, and I saw that my next monthly garden column for the *Hopemore Statesman was due Monday.* Maybe writing it would take my mind off Charlie.

If you are a subscriber, you may remember that particular column. I told readers to put a pound of ammonium sulfate around each blueberry plant instead of an ounce, and forgot to warn them to leave it six inches away from the trunk to prevent burning.

Thank goodness it rained a lot the week the column came out and I could print a correction the next week. Otherwise, we could have lost a lot of good blueberry bushes in Middle Georgia that summer.

When I was finished, I couldn't bear to sit in my office any longer, so I decided to run the column down to the newspaper office even though it wasn't due for three days. I hoped I could walk off some anger, fright, and tension on the way, but although the day had turned out lovely after the rain, with a cloudless sky and blossoms practically bursting into bloom as I passed, I kept thinking about Walker and Cindy and wondering how I could get in touch with them.

Nothing had occurred to me by the time I reached the paper office. I planned to leave the column at the front desk and go on back to work, but Slade heard my voice. "Mac," he called, "come on back. I want to ask you a question."

I trotted around to his office. He greeted me at the door, but as soon as I was seated he resumed what he called his "thinking position," lying back in his chair with his shiny loafers propped on his desk. The office had improved since Slade took over. The old green walls were now a soft cream, the battered metal desk and filing cabinet that had been there all my life had been replaced by a walnut desk and an attractive computer table, and wall-to-wall white Berber carpet covered the scarred gray linoleum. A dark green blind hid the view of the paper's parking lot, and several nice prints hung on the wall. Slade had good taste in everything except picking women.

I wriggled to get more comfortable in the green chair across from him and wished somebody in town would buy chairs for short people. "Ask away. But if it's about Willena's murder and you quote me in next week's paper after what you did to me this week, I'll hang you up by the finger-nails and let the pigs eat your toes."

"Ouch." I saw his loafers bulge as he curled his toes under. He studied his toes a minute, then blurted a question that, by his expression, wasn't what he had intended to ask. "What do you know about Rachel Ford? I can't figure her out. I mean, she shows up here after working in a New York law firm, where you know she had to have made more than she gets here, she takes a dead-end job in this —" He stopped, rubbing one temple with his forefinger like that would stimulate his brain to get him out of the hole he'd just dug.

"Dead-end town?" I supplied.

He had the grace to flush. "Well, you have to admit it's not New York. She drives a car almost as old as she is, doesn't seem to care a thing about clothes or how her hair looks —"

"I think her hair is attractive. I used to wish I had naturally curly black hair."

"You would. But I mean she doesn't go to the beauty parlor, or get manicures —"

"She has lovely hands, even without polish."

"That's beside the point. She doesn't seem to care about fixing herself up, doesn't seem to have many friends, so far as I know she never dates —"

"She's fixing up a house. That can pretty fully occupy your free time if you let it. But I know little about her. Maybe you ought to ask her some of these questions. Get to know her better." Seeing his expression, I added, "I know — she's neither rich nor classically beautiful —"

"She's almost plain except for those eyes," he said bluntly. "Besides, she's from New York. Give me a soft Southern girl anytime."

"Okay, I know she's not your type. But there can be other relationships between a man and a woman than romance. She might become a friend. She is, after all, an intelligent woman with a number of interests.

You've mentioned a time or two how few of them we seem to have around here."

He put his fingers together in a way that made me wonder if he, too, had played "Here is the church, here is the steeple" when he was a kid. "My mama used to tell me, 'Don't put it on your plate if you have no intention of eating it. That's a waste of good food.' "

"Well, my mama used to say, 'You'll never know if you like it until you try it.' Is that why you called me in here, to ask about Rachel?"

"Heavens, no. I wanted to ask if you've heard that Charlie got the initial autopsy report on Willena Kenan."

"Already?" Given the backload of cases, I was surprised they'd gotten to it so quickly. On the other hand, it wasn't every day that a Kenan heir got murdered in our part of Georgia.

Slade knew I was dying to hear what they'd found, so he looked up at the ceiling and whistled a few notes like he had nothing on his mind.

I sat there and waited, refusing to ask.

Finally he grinned at me. "The corkscrew didn't kill her, her heart just stopped."

I stared. "I never heard she had heart problems. Did they check for poison?"

"I don't know, but 'natural causes' is what the medical examiner is calling it. Chief Muggins will be announcing it on the six-o'clock news."

"He didn't say a thing about this when he called me not an hour ago."

Slade looked smug. "Ah, but the report just came in. I went by his office to see if there was anything new on the case, and he was hanging up from talking to you as I got there. The autopsy report came in while I was there, and he was on the phone with the television networks when I left."

"Telling them he's solved the case, probably. How does he plan to explain a corkscrew through her throat — or has he overlooked that little detail?"

"I asked about that. He said he doesn't plan to mention it. He figures that somebody found Willena dying and took perverse pleasure" — he caught my expression and held up both hands — "I swear, Mac, that's what he said — somebody took perverse pleasure in settling a score." Slade paused and touched his throat. "Macabre, isn't it? Do you have any opinion about who might have done it?"

He was watching me closely, so I picked up a pencil and played with it as if I were thinking. MayBelle Brandison was my first choice. Even if she hadn't killed Willena, she was irritated about the lawsuit and she had a coarse sense of humor. She might have felt the corkscrew delivered an appropriate message. But I knew Chief Muggins preferred Cindy. She and Willena had had a fight, and Cindy was strong. She worked out and played tennis several times a week.

I shook my head. "I've known some perverse people in my life, but nobody perverse enough to do that sort of thing. Where did the chief come up with that word?"

Slade grinned. "Where does he come up with any of them?"

"What about you? You got any suspects?"

"Not yet, but I'm working on it." He considered his finger-nails, buffed them against his slacks, and asked without looking up, "Do you have any idea where Cindy might be? I understand the chief is looking for her, and I thought I'd like to get her story from the other night."

I didn't like his juxtaposition of *I'm working on it* and Cindy's name.

"She could be anywhere," I said truthfully. "As busy as folks are these days, we don't try to keep up with our kids during the week. Weekends are mostly when we see them."

He nodded. "Well, if you hear from her, tell her I'd like to talk with her."

"I'll do that." I figured my chances of hearing from Cindy anytime soon were about the same as my chances of turning twenty-one my next birthday.

As soon as I got back to my office, I called Wilma. She ought to know if Willena had heart problems.

"Miss Kenan is not at home," Linette informed me formally.

"Is not at home, or is not talking to people?" I asked, adding, "It's Judge Yarbrough."

"She isn't with you? She hasn't come back yet since she left with you this morning."

"She asked me to drop her off at Willena's — something about taking an inventory with Jed DuBose. But that was right after two."

"She did mention something about goin' over there this afternoon to look around, and she hadn't come back yet."

I wondered whether Linette knew that Wilma didn't trust Willena's servants, and how Linette felt about that. It would make me mad enough to spit, if I were her. However, that wasn't why I'd called. It occurred to me that if I asked the right questions, I might not need Wilma after all. "Speaking of Willena, did you ever hear that she had a bad heart?"

"No'm, but it's funny, you asking that. Not two weeks ago Miss Wilma was after her to go get it checked. She was supposed to be leavin' next month for a cruise up the Amazon or some such, looking at rainy forests — seemed like a funny way to spend a vacation to me, but Miss Willena was always crazy about stuff like that, like her daddy."

"And Wilma was telling her to get her heart checked before she went? Her heart, specifically?"

"Yes'm. Miss Wilma was worried because her daddy — Miss Willena's, I mean, not Miss Wilma's, hers was strong as a horse — but Miss Willena's daddy dropped dead on one of them picture-taking trips he took to Africa. Miss Wilma didn't want the same thing happening to Miss Willena. Mr. Kenan wasn't but thirty-six at the time."

I had forgotten how Willena's daddy died. Now I remembered that he'd had a heart attack during a photo safari that coincided with one of the African coups. At first people thought he had been murdered. Even after they knew the real cause of death, the family had had a difficult time getting his body released and shipped back home. I suppressed the question of whether Wilma had been more worried about Willena's heart or the trouble of shipping her body.

Linette was still talking. ". . . laughed and said her daddy's heart problems came from rheumatic fever he had as a boy, and she ain't never had rheumatic fever, so her heart was fine. Miss Wilma got real upset with her and called to mind that Miss Willena's mama wasn't real strong, neither — she died before she made sixty, if you remember. But you know what Miss Willena was like — as soon as you told her to go right, she'd go left. She told Miss Wilma to mind her own business, she was in perfect health."

"I didn't know her real well . . ." I let my voice trail off.

As I'd hoped, Linette was bored with being home and out of the excitement, so she was eager to talk. "She could be real ornery when she wanted to. Miss Wilma likes things done right, you know?"

For *right* I substituted *her way* and kept listening.

"But no matter how much Miss Wilma told her the right way to do things, Miss Willena did the opposite. As a girl she'd come over here strewing her things every which away. Miss Wilma told her and told her to hang her sweater in the closet, but Miss Willena would laugh and drape it over the sofa. If Miss Wilma told her to put her schoolbooks on the table in the back room, she'd leave them on the floor for folks to trip over. No matter how many times Miss Wilma told her not to eat in the living room, I had to vacuum after every time she was here. Crumbs all over the place. And she was the same way after she grew up. If they had something to do for one of their clubs, Miss Willena would rush through her part so slapdash and sloppy that Miss Wilma had to do it over, to be sure it got done right. I don't like to speak ill of the dead, but Miss Willena was spoiled by her parents, so she could be real headstrong at times. It doesn't surprise me that somebody finally killed her."

In Linette's book, apparently, leaving books and crumbs on the floor were capital offenses.

I hung up and thought about what I'd learned. If Wilma had been concerned about Willena's heart, and bad hearts ran in her genes — but Willena hadn't simply had a heart attack and died. Whatever had killed her had given somebody time to twist a corkscrew through her throat before she actually died, because she'd been clutching it and the wound had bled. Chief Muggins wasn't going to be able to ignore that for long. Then, Cindy would be his favorite suspect again.

What could I do?

# 22

I slept better Friday night, which was a good thing. Saturday would turn out to be one of the longest days of my life.

I woke at seven, because we allow ourselves an extra hour's sleep on Saturdays and don't open until nine. My first thought was, *I still haven't interviewed Gusta or Meriwether.* They had gotten back from the beach the night before. I hadn't talked to Rachel or Sadie Lowe, either. Running into Sadie Lowe with Grover didn't count.

At breakfast I told Joe Riddley, "I'll be late getting to the store."

"So what's new?" He slathered so much butter on his toast that we'd be smart to buy a cow. "You haven't done enough work this week to justify your salary."

"Not to worry. Not to worry," Bo told him, mincing around his own place mat picking up bits of grain and fruit in his beak. Beneath the table Lulu lay curled at my feet, hoping somebody would drop something.

"I'm recovering from my vacation," I informed him, moving the butter dish to the other side of the table, out of his reach. "Jet lag and all that. Takes some getting used to at my age." I pushed down a guilty thought that he was right. We both work hard at the business, so we don't generally mind if one or the other slacks off a little, but if I didn't spend more hours in the office pretty soon, our employees would be welcoming me at the door like a stranger: "Can we help you, ma'am?"

He got up, walked around the table, picked up the butter, returned to his chair, and added another layer to his toast, simply to prove that he could. Then he munched a few bites while he considered me thoughtfully.

I expected great wisdom after all that, but what he said was, "You never mention your age unless you are about to do something you shouldn't. Got any plans to go drinking in Pleasantville again, or will you be sitting down in another creek?"

I was so startled, my jaw dropped. He waved away a question I hadn't gotten around to formulating. "You know good and well you can't have any secrets in this town. You might as well tell me what you're up to and get it over with. Otherwise, I might have to lock you down in the cellar and throw away the key."

"Sic 'em, sic 'em," Bo advised. I wasn't sure which one of us he was addressing.

"We don't have a cellar," I reminded Joe Riddley. "That was in the old house."

"I know a man who can dig me one mighty quick, if I need it. And it looks like I might. You've been investigating Willena's murder, haven't you? In spite of Isaac warning you, Buster warning you, and me warning you. Probably poor Charlie, too."

"Poor Charlie? Pooh! He's the problem. He's got me so worried about Cindy and Walker that yes, I have been asking a few questions. But that's all. Actually there wasn't a murder. Haven't you heard? Willena died of a heart attack. So that means that what I've been doing is mostly what you told me to — getting to know the movers and shakers in the investment club. If I'm going to hang out with the hoity-toity set, I need to get better acquainted."

He lifted his cup and drained his last inch of coffee, then got up and refilled both our mugs. "I understand you were down at the jail getting better acquainted with Nancy. Did you know she's already out?"

I was so astonished, I spilled my coffee.

"How?" I asked as I went to fetch a dish cloth to wipe up the coffee. Clarinda would have a fit at having to bleach that cloth again, but I keep telling her that coffee in our house has unreliable habits.

As I sat back down, I added, "She can't be. The charge was attempted murder."

Joe Riddley shook his head. "Not anymore. She hired Jed, he talked to Horace, and with Buster's support they talked to Judge Stedley and got the charge reduced to disturbing the peace. Buster gave you most of the credit. He told Judge Stedley you had reminded him that Nancy is one of the Three-Ds, so if she'd really wanted to shoot Horace or Sadie Lowe, she'd have made a better job of it."

"Darn tooting. But poor Nancy. Imagine that . . . that pig of a husband running around with Sadie Lowe. I hope Nancy didn't go home to him after she got out." I reached for the strawberry jam. "Tell me this: Why would anybody with Sadie Lowe's various assets bother with somebody who looks like Horace?" I spread jam on my toast and thought how much it looked like blood. I'd buy grape next time.

Joe Riddley placed one hand on his heart. "High school sweethearts, honey chile. Just like us." He leaned over to give me a kiss, but I backed away. He had jam on his chin.

"Back off," Bo warned. "Give me space."

Joe Riddley laughed and fed him some peach. Then he looked over Bo's flaming head at me. "Don't you remember why we sent Sadie Lowe away?"

"She kept fooling around with boys down by the water tank."

"Not boys, one boy. Horace Jensen."

I was so surprised, I dropped my toast. Lulu gulped it up. "No joke?"

"Nope. Apparently they'd been at it since they were thirteen. And you know who kept turning them in? Willena Kenan. She must have sat down there every night waiting for them."

"Do!" I added Sadie Lowe to my list of Members with a Motive to Murder. Then I frowned. "Back then she probably saw Horace as her ticket out of the mobile home park. But why on earth would she look twice at him now? She's got all the money she'll ever need."

"That kind never has enough money," said Mr. Know-it-all.

"How many of that kind have you ever known?"

He gave me a wide, smug smile. "Ask me no secrets, I'll tell you no lies."

■ ■ ■ ■

Joe Riddley headed to work, Bo on his shoulder. He often took the bird if he didn't have meetings during the day. As soon as I'd done the dishes, I called to see if I could visit Meriwether. I figured that with an infant, she might have the baby back down for his morning nap by nine.

Instead, Meriwether was already gone. Jed answered the phone and I could hear Little Zachary gurgling in the background. "She's over at Gusta's having a cup of coffee," Jed told me. "We men are having a bonding session."

"Have fun," I told him. "But listen, while I've got you, I have a question. If you can't tell me, don't, but I am presuming that Willena left everything to Wilma, right?"

He chuckled. "Why do I suspect you are looking for surprise bequests that might have led somebody to do her in?"

"Nobody did her in. Haven't you heard? She died of heart failure, the medical examiner says."

"What about the corkscrew?"

"It was a nasty touch while she lay dying, apparently. Which is still a punishable offense, especially since whoever it was didn't call for help. They might have saved her."

"Yuck!" I could almost see him shudder. "That's horrible. Is that why you are still asking questions?"

I had to think fast to come up with an answer. "Maybe. Or maybe I'm nosy. Or maybe I don't like loose ends. I wondered, that's all."

"Well, don't spread it around, but Willena didn't write a will. It's going to be one hell of a mess before I get things straightened out."

"What?" I tried to imagine how a woman could have even a little bit of money and not want to decide what happened to it after she died. And when a woman had as much as Willena Kenan . . .

"When I took over her business, I suggested that we go over her will to be sure it was up-to-date. She told me she hadn't gotten around to writing one, that it gave her the creeps to think about wills. And you know Willena — she was never one to bother herself with things she didn't want to do."

"No, she sure wasn't. I've always said that Willena was so laid-back, she practically lived lying down."

Jed chuckled, then grew serious again. "I kept pestering her, and she had finally agreed to come in to draft a will, but she never made it." He heaved a sigh. "I keep telling my clients that wills are like fire extinguishers — if you wait until you need one, it's too late. But do they listen?"

"Apparently not. But you're preaching to the choir, hon. Mine is up-to-date." I thought over the ramifications of what he'd said. "Still, I presume that Wilma will get what the state doesn't. I guess it's been proven that there are no other heirs?" I found the thought of all that money going to a woman who already had more than she knew what to do with too depressing to dwell on. Without even thinking hard I could name ten charities that would put it to better use.

"Like who? You thinking of trying to establish kinship?"

"No, but Robison, Willena's grandfather, had a sister. She got married to an unsuitable husband, then died young, according to Wilma, who told me she should have stayed in Hopemore. But it's conceivable she has a child or even children."

"Are you trying to complicate my life, Mac?"

"Always glad to oblige."

He turned away from the phone to say something to Zachary. Zachary laughed, and I listened with delight. Jed grew up without a dad and with two old reprobate uncles in the house, so I was astonished at what a good dad he was turning out to be.

When he got back to me, I asked, "Speaking of Wilma, how did your inventory go yesterday? She told me you and she were going through the house to make one."

"At Wilma's pace, it took all afternoon. She kept calling out instructions to Hetty to polish some of the silver or clean a mirror, and she made a list of each item. She literally had me count the teaspoons."

"Wilma doesn't want Willena's servants walking off with any of the silver."

"Hetty and Baker? They wouldn't!"

"You know that and I know that, but Wilma thinks they might." All of a sudden little Zachary let out the kind of wail that said he was ready for some full attention, so I hurried to wind up our conversation. "I guess I'd better go over and see if Gusta has any coffee left in her pot. Happy bonding." I hung up before he could suggest I come over and do something about the wail. I'd helped raise my two sons' children. I had no desire to be at the beck and call of another crying infant.

When I called to see if it was all right for me to come to Gusta's at once, Florine said in a superior tone, "Of course. Miss Gusta is always up and dressed by six. She's with Meriwether out on the porch, having coffee."

"Tell them to save me some." As I hung up, I wondered why some folks think it's virtuous to get up early. Personally, I've seen enough dawns to last me a lifetime. If I live to Gusta's age, I plan to sleep late every morning and enjoy my fill of the midnight sky.

I found Gusta with Meriwether on the front porch of Pooh's enormous yellow Victorian house, rocking, sipping coffee, and watching a few cars amble down Oglethorpe Street. Technically, the house was now Jed's, but since he and Meriwether preferred their one-story gingerbread house over on Liberty Street, I figured Gusta could live in Pooh's house as long as she liked.

I have failed to tell you that Meriwether is one of the few truly beautiful women I have ever known. She has a cloud of golden hair, lovely blue-green eyes in a heart-shaped face, and long, slender limbs. At one point she used to be far too thin, but since she had gotten married and had little Zach, she had filled out enough to be stunning. Today she looked a lot fresher and lovelier than the mother of an infant usually does, wearing a pink floral skirt with little white buttons all the way down the front and a pink cotton sweater.

Gusta was dressed, as usual, so that if she had to step in and chair an important meeting, she wouldn't have to change. Today she had on a soft blue cotton dress that accented her silver hair, with a matching cotton jacket. Need I remind you that those women owed their wealth to cotton mills? And that both had maids who did all their ironing?

I had scarcely taken a third rocker when Florine came out with a Limoges china cup and saucer for me. Gusta nodded to Meriwether, who poured steaming coffee from a silver coffeepot. Gusta had told me years ago, "I firmly believe that when a woman reaches sixty-five, she ought to throw away her second-best dishes and flatware and use her best china and silver every day." Augusta Wainwright was one woman who lived by what she believed.

As I sat stirring cream in my coffee with a sterling spoon and put the delicate cup to my lips, it occurred to me that Gusta might be right about a few things.

Of course, she could be tiresome, too. She consulted a small gold watch that hung from a gold bow on her chest and said, "It's nine thirty, MacLaren. What brings you to us when you ought to be working?"

"Good coffee," I replied.

"It is good," she agreed, indicating by a nod to Meriwether that she would like more.

"But I also wanted to see if either of you remembered anything about Monday night that might shine some light on what happened." These were such good friends that I dared to confide, "I hated it when Charlie was focusing on Cindy back when he thought it was murder . . ."

The expressions on their faces made me realize they hadn't heard the news, so I backtracked and filled them in on Willena's heart attack. I continued, "So if Charlie was looking at Cindy as his prime suspect for the murder, because MayBelle told him she and Willena had a fight at the meeting, now he's likely to think she used the corkscrew. I'm looking for anything that would prove she didn't."

"She wouldn't!" Meriwether exclaimed. "Cindy would never hurt anybody."

"She couldn't have used the corkscrew," Gusta declared. Her tone left open the question of whether Cindy would or would not hurt anybody, which made me want to smack her, but she pointed out, "Cindy left before Willena got her present. Remember? While we were holding the election of officers, Cindy got up and dashed out. She never came back to the room."

I had forgotten that elections were held right after Willena shamed Cindy about buying Walker's company stock. Now I remembered that during the elections Cindy had seethed, her eyes full of unshed tears. Finally she had muttered to me, "I want to check on the kids," and rushed from the room. She hadn't seen Wilma give Willena the silver bar set.

"I could kiss you, Gusta," I declared.

"Have more coffee instead," she suggested, nodding for Meriwether to refill my cup.

I felt so relieved that I held out my cup without hesitation, although it was my fourth of the morning. "I had also wanted to ask you a few questions about Rachel Ford," I told Meriwether. "But now I think I'll drink my coffee and go to work. I can ask about Rachel later."

Meriwether filled the cup and handed it back. "What did you want to know?"

"Anything, actually. All I know is she used to be a hotshot international lawyer in New York and came down here eighteen months ago to take the job of director at the Poverty

Law Center. I don't know a thing about her family, where she grew up, where she went to school — all the stuff that gives you something to talk about with a stranger. Joe Riddley has suggested I get to know the women in the club," I added, in case they wondered about my sudden interest.

I could tell by the glint in Gusta's eye that she didn't believe a word of it, but Meriwether has always had the better manners of the two.

"Well, let's see." She set her cup down on a little wicker table beside her and stretched her long legs out before her to soak up the sun. She was wearing pink flats to match her skirt and sweater.

"You look good enough to eat," I told her.

Gusta sniffed. "If she isn't careful, she's going to get as bad as Wilma, with shoes to match each outfit."

Meriwether grimaced. "Call me anything but Wilma, Nana. I'll even give up my pink shoes."

"Honey," I told her, "you are beautiful and you know it. And you have a gorgeous baby and a husband who loves you dearly. Keep the shoes. You will never end up like Wilma. Wilma is fifty percent pride and fifty percent bitterness, all wrapped up in postponed living and tied with the bow of discontent."

"Mac is a poet!" Meriwether told her grandmother admiringly. "Shall we nominate her for poet laureate of Hopemore?"

"Nominate me for a new job, if I don't finish talking to you pretty quick and get down to the store." I set my cup down on the table. "Quick, tell me what you know about Rachel."

"She grew up in New York City. Manhattan, I think. Her mother was Jewish and her daddy an Italian Catholic. Their name wasn't Ford to start with. She and her brother changed it when they grew up. I don't know why."

"She has a brother?" Rachel seemed more alone than any woman I knew.

"She did. He was in the army and got killed in Iraq. It's his car she drives. He wasn't married, so he left her what she calls 'his bits and pieces.' His death pretty much shattered her. Their mother had died the year before, and their dad had been gone for several years, so when her brother died, Rachel was utterly alone. She says she decided to start over somewhere without so many memories."

"But why Hopemore?"

"Why not?" Gusta demanded, bristling.

"We aren't exactly the center of the universe," I reminded her. "Finding the place would take some doing from New York."

Meriwether sipped her coffee with a thoughtful expression. "I don't think she ever said. I got the impression that she read an ad for the job, came down to interview, and liked it here."

I sat there thinking all that over. "Even after losing her brother and her mother, it's hard for me to believe she would give up a successful job in international law to head a poverty law center down here."

Meriwether's laugh was like a bell. "She didn't have a successful career in international law. She was one of a zillion lawyers in a New York firm, and she hadn't been there but three years, so she was way down on the totem pole."

"What was she doing before that?"

"Taking care of her mother. She was an invalid. I don't know what she had, but she got confined to a wheelchair while Rachel was in law school. Rachel's brother took care of her until Rachel finished, and then Rachel took over. She cared for her mother for years and years. I don't know what they lived on. But eventually her mother got so sick that she needed full-time care. Rachel took a job in a law firm so she and her brother together could afford enough to hire somebody to look after their mom."

"I'm presuming from all this that the family didn't have much money, and that Rachel bought her house here with her mother's and brother's estates. So how did she get in the investment club?"

"Meriwether nominated her," Gusta spoke with asperity. "I told her it wasn't suitable, but —"

"But Rachel is smart, and she needs to learn how to invest money. Besides, she knew Grover in New York. He and her brother went to Haverford together, and he used to come home with her brother for holidays or something."

"Then her brother must have been a lot older than she."

"I guess so." Meriwether obviously hadn't given that any thought.

I remembered something. "Wilma told me Thursday that Grover asked Willena to help make Rachel feel at home here. Maybe he was the one who told her about the job at the law center."

I could not imagine our Poverty Law Center board advertising in New York City, but they might have run an ad in the Augusta paper. Wilma had also said that Grover told Willena that Rachel had been a prominent attorney in New York. Was he doing a favor for his old buddy's little sister? Or was there something between them that nobody knew about? I remembered that the two of them had gone out into the parking lot together in the streaming rain. That merited more thought at a later time.

Right now, Meriwether was setting her cup on its saucer with a delicate click, and then she stood. "It's been great, Nana, but I'd better get back before Zach kills Jed or vice versa."

"I keep telling you that man knows nothing about raising children," Gusta snapped. "Growing up with those two awful Blaines, he'll probably be pouring whiskey down that infant's throat any day now. Next time, you bring the baby with you, you hear me?"

"Shall I give you a lift?" I offered.

When Meriwether had moved into her own home and out of her grandmother's, Gusta had carried on like she was moving to Iowa. She actually lived three long blocks away.

Meriwether hesitated. "I could walk, it's so gorgeous, but I am tired. Zach is teething and was up most of the night." She plucked her sweater away from her chest. "And if I don't get home soon to feed him, I'm going to be one sopping mess."

As Gusta let out a scandalized "Do!" Meriwether gave me a wink.

# 23

The young DuBoses lived on Liberty Street, a five-block stretch of comfortable one-story houses built between 1890 and 1920. The area had gone through a dismal period beginning in the 1950s, when the fashion was for small brick ranch houses farther out of town, but had been rediscovered in the eighties and nineties by young couples with an eye for charm and more energy than money. They had restored the old houses, and painted them in pleasant shades of blue, green, yellow, white, and cream, with contrasting shutters. Children now played on the sidewalks and in small front lawns, cats sunned on porches, and patches of flowers brightened almost every yard.

As I pulled to a stop in front of Meriwether's house, she pointed to one diagonally across the street. "Rachel's front door is standing open. Do you want to see her house?"

"Won't she mind?" I hated the idea of going up to an almost-stranger's house to invite myself in.

Meriwether laughed. "On this street? It's downright neighborly to go see what progress has been made on a house. I understand that several years ago, a favorite pastime if you got depressed was visiting your neighbors to see how much worse their places looked than your own. I really need to feed Zach, or I'd take you over. Knock and call through the door. She'll be glad to show you around. Don't expect miracles, though. She's doing most of the work herself. But she started inside, so she's accomplished more than shows from here."

I certainly hoped so. The place had been owned most of my lifetime by a grim old widow who had let the place deteriorate as her eyesight and resources failed. Yet whenever a young couple had approached about buying, she had declared, "I don't aim to sell this house till I die."

"And how," Joe Riddley had asked me in private, "does she plan to sell it then?"

She had finally died a year or so before, and her grandson in Atlanta had been delighted to sell it to Rachel. Why Rachel wanted it, I could not imagine. What I could see from the street wasn't enticing, except for one corner made up of curved windows. We'd had a corner like that in our big blue house. Otherwise, it had a plain front with double windows on either side of a narrow door, a pointed tin roof, peeling white clapboard siding, and a small front porch with banisters like a chorus line of fat women's legs. Whoever had built it lacked originality and flair.

As I crossed the street, I noticed that the chorus line was missing several legs, and the sidewalk was cracked and had lifted in several places. Rachel hadn't done a thing about the peeling white paint or the yard, which was little more than a small plot of patchy grass and scraggly bushes. I wondered if she would be offended if I offered to send my son Ridd over for a consultation. Ridd is legendary for his ability to transform barren yards into showplaces, and if he weren't already happy as a high school math teacher and part-time farmer, he could make a good living helping other folks landscape their yards.

This did not look to me like the house of a prosperous attorney, but in front sat a shiny black Lexus that looked suspiciously like Slade's. Had he come this early on a Saturday to try to wring blood from this particular turnip?

I stood at the front door and knocked. "Hello?"

"Come in," Rachel called from somewhere inside. "We can't come to the door right this minute."

I walked hesitantly into the front hall. The hall was dim and chilly out of the sun, and smelled of sawed wood, Sheetrock mud, and some kind of chemical that made me suspect she had opened the door to let fumes out. The floor was rough and littered with scraps of wood and drifts of sawdust. One doorjamb was fresh and unpainted, while white patches on the dingy blue walls indicated the plaster had needed numerous repairs.

"We're in here." Rachel sounded out of breath. I found her standing on a couple of boards laid across two sawhorses in the middle of the living room, screwing a large brass light fixture to the ceiling. It gleamed in the dim room. Brass polish was what I had smelled.

Slade stood on the boards beside her, holding it up while she screwed it in place. Her breathlessness, I deduced, came not from standing so near him but from the exertion of standing so long with her arms overhead. "Okay," she announced with satisfaction. "That ought to hold." She turned and looked down at me in surprise but no special delight. "Hello, Judge."

"Hey, there. I was dropping Meriwether off, and she suggested I come look at your house."

"Sure." She squatted and jumped down, then bounded to her feet with an agility that made me envious. Her face, however, was not as energetic as the rest of her. She still looked pale, and even sadder than she had the day before. I wondered if her run-in with Wilma the previous afternoon had anything to do with that.

For construction work she had pulled her hair carelessly back and secured it with a rubber band. Tendrils of curls were escaping, but they looked messy rather than charming. She wore paint-stained jeans and a T-shirt, and hadn't bothered to put on a speck of makeup, even lipstick.

Slade, of course, was immaculate in tan coveralls that set off his swarthy good looks. I suspected that underneath he had on pressed khaki slacks and a pretty polo shirt in yellow, green, or tan. He descended more cautiously from the boards across the sawhorses and brushed his hands together. "The place has a long way to go before it's finished," he warned. "Rachel's doing most of the work herself."

I tried to count up how many days it had been since they were going at it hammer and tongs in my parking lot. Certainly no more than four. And as recently as yesterday afternoon he had been maligning her name. Yet today he followed her into the kitchen like he half owned the place. I will never understand men if I live to be a hundred and raise a dozen of them.

However, I couldn't help remembering that he had followed Meriwether around her house the same way back before she and Jed got engaged, and how Slade had even taken it on himself to supervise Meriwether's workers while she was out of town.

"I haven't started the kitchen yet," Rachel apologized, standing in the middle of a dingy assortment of elderly appliances and cabinets. "I began with my bedroom and bath, so I'd have a haven to escape to, and then did my office, because I can't stand to work in chaos. But now I keep tracking stuff in on the carpet." She led the way to a pretty yet austere bedroom done in sage green and cream with a creamy Berber rug on the floor. The carpet looked a lot like the one Slade had in his office, except this one had trails of sawdust crisscrossing it.

The bathroom next door (for this house was too old to have a bath adjoining the master bedroom) sported a new tile floor and freshly painted woodwork, but the walls were bare. "I plan to paper in here," she explained.

Slade stepped back to let Rachel lead the way into a small bedroom converted into an office painted taupe and cream. She looked so weary and sad, I wondered if she was getting dispirited at having taken on so much alone.

"It's always a toss-up whether to do one room at a time or all the rooms at once," I comforted her. "We had the same problem when we redid our house several years ago."

Rachel sighed. "It's a mess, whichever you choose. But I've painted the ceilings in the living room, dining room, and hall now, and with Slade's help this morning I've gotten all the light fixtures in, so I can paint the walls and sand the floors. Or sand and paint. I don't know which to do first. I don't want to get sawdust on painted walls or paint on the newly finished floor."

"Paint first," I advised from experience. "The sanding machines vacuum up most of the dust."

I followed her around, excessively admiring the work she had done and plans she had for what she still had to do, trying to strike at least one spark of enthusiasm in her face, but she continued to look like somebody who had swum halfway across a lake and realized it was going to be a long way to shore no matter which way she turned.

Finally she stopped in the front hall and asked, in a tone that was more duty than desire, "Would you like some coffee? I've got a pot made."

Inwardly, I groaned. Much more coffee this morning and I'd get a quivering chin and shaky hands. But then I remembered I needed to talk to Rachel. I checked my watch. Ten thirty. I could stay another half hour. "That would be nice."

"Do you want some, too, Slade?" she asked.

"No, thanks. While you're on break, I'll work in the bathroom taking down the lights over the lavatory and the towel bars. Then we'll be ready to put up paper."

"Fine." She displayed no personal interest in him whatsoever. Maybe she knew Slade was looking for a rich and beautiful woman, or maybe she genuinely wasn't attracted to him. I got the feeling, though, that she had something else on her mind, something so immense that it left no room for anything else. Could it be a certain corkscrew?

Slade moseyed back toward the bathroom,

pulling a screwdriver from his overalls. I followed Rachel to the kitchen. While she poured coffee and found milk, I called the office to check that the store hadn't burned down before I got there. "I'll be in soon," I promised Evelyn.

As I hung up, the sun glinted off something on the window-sill. I laid my cell phone on the counter and leaned across the sink to look closer. An emerald ring glowed in the morning sun, a large solitaire with two small diamonds on each side. "That's gorgeous!" I exclaimed. "Weren't you wearing this at the meeting the other night, with matching studs?"

Rachel picked it up, slipped it on her right hand, and held it to the sunlight. Her hands were large and well-shaped, with oval, unpolished nails. "I wear them a lot. They were my grandmother's, all I have of hers."

"Were you close?"

"No. She died when my mother was seven."

"Was that the Jewish side of your family?"

She was setting out a plate of cookies, so she spoke without turning. "Not then. My grandfather was only nominally Jewish when he married my grandmother. She was Presbyterian, and they were both very young. After she died, though, he married a

315

Jewish woman, and the family became observant. My uncle and his son both had bar mitzvahs and proper Jewish weddings, and my mother was raised as a Jew."

"But she married an Italian Catholic? I guess that makes you . . . ?"

When she grinned, she was almost pretty. "An Episcopalian." She handed me a mug of steaming coffee and her smile disappeared. She held out the plate of cookies. "Will you carry these? I'll get the cream and spoons." Once more she was the hostess taking time from a busy day to entertain an uninvited guest. "The best place to sit is on the porch. Slade?" She raised her voice. "I'll be on the porch if you need me."

As she led me to a couple of green plastic lawn chairs with a plastic table between, I said, "I'm glad to see you all have made up your differences. How did that happen?"

She shrugged. "Last night we ran into each other at the BI-LO frozen food section. We were both buying TV dinners, and I felt bad about yelling at him. I actually was going a little too fast in your parking lot, so I apologized and invited him to come over here to heat up his dinner. He's not bad when he's not yelling at you, and he said he likes working on houses, so he came over today to help with parts of mine I can't do alone."

"Papering a bathroom?" If I sounded skeptical, it was because I've papered a few bathrooms in my time and never found it a two-person job.

"I'll need him for the border. It's almost impossible to do alone." She seemed uninterested in him except for his help.

I wondered what Slade's motive was. Since chances were good it wasn't romance, he must think there was a story somewhere in Rachel Ford. Unless she was really an heiress.

"Was your father a lawyer?" Maybe Slade had discovered she had inherited money from her parents and merely chose to live simply. Meriwether and Jed did, after all.

"No, he managed a drugstore." She reached up to drag the elastic from her hair so it fell around her face like a wavy curtain. A bid for privacy? Nevertheless, she continued her life's story without prompting. "He died when I was fifteen. I had a brother, too, but he was killed in Iraq. And Mama died a year or so before." She looked across her patchy lawn, but her blue-gray eyes were focused on the past. "Now I have nobody left. Nobody at all."

I scrabbled around in my brain for some happier topic of conversation. "Do you enjoy the investment club?" That was the only thing I could think of that we had in common.

She shrugged and gave me a wan smile. "I don't have much to invest, but Grover has been helpful in making suggestions."

Her voice warmed when she spoke his name, and the angular lines of her face softened. "Did Meriwether tell me you've known him a long time?"

"He went to college with my brother, Gary." She sounded casual enough, but once she started speaking about him, she couldn't seem to stop. "Since Grover was from down here, he couldn't get home for Thanksgiving, so he came to our place with Gary their first year. After that he'd visit for a few days once in a while. Grover and Gary stayed good friends all these years, and when Gary was on overseas assignments, Grover kept in touch with Mother and me. You know, he'd pop in from time to time." Maybe she aimed for casual, but she couldn't conceal how important those visits had been. "After Mother and Gary died, he was the one who heard about this job and recommended me for it," she added.

I sipped my coffee and wondered exactly what she felt for Grover. Maybe I could test that with her reaction to one piece of news.

"He seems to handle the portfolios of most of our members. MayBelle and Wilma both said he handles their accounts, and I saw him having coffee with Sadie Lowe yesterday morning. Of course, maybe they weren't discussing business." I let my voice broaden to imply more than I said.

She didn't reply, but I saw her hand tremble as she lifted the cup to her lips.

"You don't have any theories about who might have stuck the corkscrew into Willena's throat the other night, do you?" There was no way I could make that sound like a casual question.

Finally Rachel grew animated. Her eyes flashed and her straight dark brows drew together in a frown. "Not at all. It was a vile thing to do."

"Yes, it was."

After that, I couldn't think of anything else to say. I set down my mug and stood. "I know you're busy, so I won't keep you. I wanted to welcome you to town, a bit late."

"Better late than never." She held out her hand, gave mine a businesslike shake, and bent to retrieve the mugs and plate of cookies to take them inside. No drawn-out Southern departures for this young woman.

I reached my car before I remembered that I'd left my cell phone on her kitchen counter. I didn't bother to knock, just entered the open door and started down the hall. As I got to the kitchen, I heard her demand in a fierce, low tone, "What's this I hear about you having coffee with Sadie Lowe?"

I heard Slade working in the bathroom, so she must be on the kitchen phone. I backed out and went on to the office. I'd call later and ask Slade to drop off my own phone at the office when he left.

# 24

I picked up hamburgers for Joe Riddley and me to eat at the office. We don't usually go home at noon on Saturday, and it seemed like I hadn't seen much of him this past week. Maybe we could go out tonight, I mused as I paid and drove toward the office. When we lived in the big house, we used to have Ridd and Martha's family down on Saturday evenings. After we all moved, they started having us down there instead. This week, though, Ridd had called and said they had plans for Saturday night. He hadn't said what they were, but they must involve the children, because he had turned down my offer to babysit Cricket. Maybe I could persuade Joe Riddley to take me out for barbecue.

As soon as I got inside the store I heard shouting. As I approached our office, I realized it came from there. I hurried in.

Chief Muggins stood in the middle of the

office, his face red and his fists clenched. Joe Riddley sat in his big leather desk chair looking mulish, like he does when somebody is trying to make him do something he has no intention of doing. Bo was up on top of the curtain rod, squawking in distress.

When I came in the door, I spoke first to the bird. "You mess those curtains, boy, and you are dead meat."

"Back off!" he squawked. "Give me space." He gave a couple of wordless squawks, then said plain as anything, "Sic 'em, Little Bit. Sic 'em!"

Joe Riddley and I both laughed in astonishment. "Well, dadgum, bird!" Joe Riddley praised him, then added to the police chief, "That's the first time he's ever put 'sic 'em' and 'Little Bit' together."

"Sic 'em, Little Bit! Sic 'em!" Bo squawked again, a glutton for praise.

"The threat still stands," I warned him. "Don't you mess those curtains."

He flapped his wings and flew to the top of the filing cabinet. "See?" Joe Riddley told me proudly. "I told you he understands every word you say." He reached in his bottom drawer and handed Chief Muggins a cube of apple. "Would you pass that to Bo, please?"

Chief Muggins glared, but he held out the

square of fruit. Bo took it from him, muttering obscenities under his breath.

"You teach him those fancy words, Judge?" the chief needled me.

"Bo used to belong to Jed DuBose's uncle Hiram," I reminded him. But I had more important things to think about than a scarlet macaw and the old reprobate who used to own him. "What's going on?"

Chief Muggins narrowed his beady eyes. "Where are Walker and Cindy?"

"I have no idea." I hung my pocketbook on a hook by my desk.

"I know good and well you both know where they are," he raged. "I'll have you up for obstructing justice."

I glared at him. "The only obstructing going on right now is that you are obstructing the way to my chair." He moved over far enough for me to get by and sit down. I settled myself in comfortably, then added, "I already told you, I haven't seen or heard from Walker and Cindy since Monday night. We have enough to do without keeping up with our grown children."

He leaned down and pounded his fist on my desk. "They've left town!"

"Leave my wife alone," Joe Riddley snapped. "She doesn't know a thing and neither do I. I told you, I had one voice mail message from Walker on Wednesday, saying they wouldn't be available for a few days. That is all I know. And the judge doesn't know that much. I listened to the message and deleted it."

"Deleted it!" exclaimed the chief, gloating from one to the other of us like he'd caught us committing murder. "Deliberately erasing evidence in a criminal investigation."

"I'm clumsy," Joe Riddley corrected him mildly. "My finger must have slipped." Now that I was there he had lost his mulish look and was enjoying matching wits with Chief Muggins. Neither of us liked the man, but Joe Riddley seldom let the chief get under his skin like I did. Besides, have you ever noticed that whatever age married people were when they first met, they tend to relate to each other that way for the rest of their lives? Joe Riddley and I not only squabble sometimes like we're in elementary school, but he still enjoys showing off for me like he did back then. He can no longer walk on top of fences, but he can bait the chief.

"Your finger never slipped," the chief insisted. "You deleted that message on purpose and you know it. Judge, did you see him press that button?"

"I saw him press some button on the receiver, but I wasn't close enough to see which one it was." Which was true. "Why don't you sit down and fill us in on the case so far?"

He sank onto our visitor's chair with poor grace. "There's no murder case. Did you hear that?"

I nodded. "Slade told me yesterday that the medical examiner says it was a heart attack. But did they run any toxicology tests?"

He looked at me like I was a kindergartner in the justice system. "They don't do that when death turns out to be from natural causes."

"Unless they weren't so natural. What if somebody poisoned her with something that stopped her heart?"

"Leave it to the experts, Judge," he snapped. "Nobody but you has suggested she was poisoned, and the way the forensics folks are backed up, they don't have time to be looking for murder when somebody dies naturally." He stopped, then threw me a bone. "I do know they examined her intestines, and there wasn't a thing the matter with them. Poison leaves traces. Her heart stopped, that's all. But somebody put that corkscrew in her throat —"

"Before or after she died?"

"Before. That's why there was so much blood. She was in the process of bleeding to death when her heart stopped." We all sat a minute contemplating the horror of that.

"Fright from the corkscrew maybe caused her heart to stop," Joe Riddley suggested. From the way he clasped and unclasped his hands, I could see he was distressed. Who wouldn't be? Both the chief and I had automatically reached up to touch our throats. "In that case," Joe Riddley pointed out, "it would still be murder while in the process of committing another crime."

Chief Muggins rubbed his hands together. "Right. That's why I want to locate Cindy."

I felt a cold lump of fear slide down my windpipe and land in my stomach with a thud. But then I remembered that things weren't so desperate as they had been. "Cindy had nothing to do with it. Grover saw her in the parking lot, and Gusta remembers that she left the meeting before Wilma even gave Willena the bar set with the corkscrew in it. Cindy didn't know the corkscrew existed."

The chief thought that over for perhaps half a minute, then slapped both hands on his thighs and used them to help him stand. "Well, I've got a lot to do. But if you hear from Walker and Cindy, you tell them they'd better get their . . . ah . . . themselves back to town. I'm going to put out an APB if they haven't shown up by Monday morning."

Joe Riddley reached for his cap. "Now that you're here, Little Bit, I'm going to run down to the nursery for a little while."

"But I brought you a hamburger." I held it up, disappointed. I wanted to add, *I haven't seen you much this week,* but I didn't. He'd just reply, *And whose fault is that?*

He took it from me and bent to give me a peck on the cheek. "I'll eat it down there. Got a lot to do, now that you finally showed up." He left with Chief Muggins strutting beside him like he'd accomplished something.

I was almost finished with my hamburger when something Joe Riddley had said to Charlie finally sank in. He'd said, "*I* had one message from Walker." Had the chief noticed his emphasis on the pronoun *I?*

Somebody else could well have heard from Walker since Wednesday, and I knew who that was. I reached for my phone.

I wasn't surprised to get the answering machine down at Ridd's. Martha would still be at work. Bethany, their daughter, would be out shopping with her friends or doing all the other things high school senior girls do on Saturdays during their last month of school. Ridd and Cricket would be on the tractor, happily plowing or planting. I spoke sternly into the answering machine:

"Ridd. This is your mother speaking. Get on the phone to your brother and tell him to bring his family home pronto. Charlie Muggins is on the warpath, and threatens to put out an all-points bulletin on them if they aren't here Monday morning. But tell Walker, too, that Willena died of heart failure, and Gusta has reminded me that Cindy left the meeting room before Wilma gave Willena the corkscrew, so there's no way Cindy could have stuck it in Willena's throat —"

"Mama? It's me, Walker."

The voice was such a shock that it took me a few seconds to find my own voice again.

"You're at Ridd's?"

"Yeah. We have been since Wednesday. I didn't want Charlie bugging Cindy to death, so we decided to lie low down here for a few days."

Why hadn't I thought of that before and saved myself some sleepless nights? It was a perfect hideout, half a mile down a dead-end road outside the city limits. On one side of the road was a stand of pulpwood pines Joe Riddley had planted as part of our retirement plan. On the other side, the two other houses that shared the road were both vacant. The one up near the highway had been empty since its owner went to jail for murder. Nobody knew what would eventually happen to it. The other was a farmhouse, which was being converted into a shelter for battered or homeless women, but it had not started taking clients. The rest of that side of the road was pasture and a watermelon field. Beyond our house the road dwindled into a tractor track leading into acres of fields that Joe Riddley and I still owned, but which Ridd rented and planted each year. Nobody ever went down there except us. The house had a big yard plus a swimming pool surrounded by an eight-foot privacy fence, and Cindy's horse was stabled in Ridd's new barn. She and Tad had probably taken turns exercising him.

Relief made my voice sharp. "I was afraid you had taken her out of state somewhere."

"When she's a suspect in a murder case? Come on, Mama. You didn't really think I was that dumb, did you? After growing up with a judge?"

"I couldn't think where you might be." Time to change the subject. "Did you hear what I said on the machine?"

"Yeah. You said there's no way Charlie can

think Cindy did it."

"That's right, so be back in your house by Monday morning."

"We were going on back tonight, anyway. The kids both have tennis matches tomorrow, and all of us are ready to get home. Ridd and Martha were great, though, and it felt good to stay at the old place again for a few days."

He grew up in that house. I detected a wistfulness in his voice that I could identify with. "I know, son. It's a great house. I miss it too, sometimes."

"We'll both be singing another tune the next time Ridd has to paint. Then we'll be glad it's him and not us." We both knew he was lying, but we laughed together and hung up.

I sat still for a long while, taking deep breaths and exhaling like somebody was about to ration air. Walker and Cindy were safe. They hadn't left the county. And Walker was standing by Cindy all through this. When would I ever begin to trust that my sons were not only grown men but also responsible adults? And when would I ever begin to trust the thoughts that came after I'd been praying? If I had called Martha the first night I suspected Walker had left, she would have managed to reassure me without my having to ask a thing. Martha can be clever that way.

Now that I was no longer paralyzed by fear for my children, I could think more rationally about Willena's murder and what I had learned. I forced myself to remember the meeting of the investment club. Willena wearing her coat during the meeting. Willena lying facedown on the bathroom floor with the corkscrew in her neck. She had managed to get as far as the door to the hall before collapsing, but she had not bled to death. Had her heart seized up from terror when somebody stabbed her with the corkscrew? Or had something else stopped her heart?

I mentally went back through what each person had said when Charlie first interviewed us. Willena was throwing up in the bathroom because something at dinner had disagreed with her. Her hands were shaking so hard, she couldn't put on her mascara straight.

That still sounded like poison to me. I went to my bookshelf and took down a well-thumbed book on the plants of Georgia. I looked up something and read it twice.

I was certain Willena had been poisoned. I thought I even knew what had been used. I just didn't know who had given it to her, or why. And I needed the answer to two questions before I shared my suspicions with the chief of police. I reached for the phone, then changed my mind. What I wanted to know ought to be asked privately and in person.

I started to leave Joe Riddley a note, but checked my watch and decided not to bother. It was two thirty. He wouldn't come back until five. I could be there and back in half an hour and he'd never know I'd been gone.

It didn't occur to me that I'd said that very same thing before and almost didn't live to regret it.

# 25

As I pulled into Willena's drive, I had a sense of "been there, done that." Rachel's old BMW sat under the porte cochere.

I parked near the front door and tried to frame my questions as I climbed the shallow brick steps, crossed the concrete porch, and rang the bell.

Hetty answered, wearing a pink uniform and a white apron. "Why, hello, Judge. How you doin'?"

Hetty was some sort of cousin to Clarinda, and anybody could tell they shared genes. Both were short and plump, with wide, prominent cheekbones that hinted at an Indian ancestor somewhere back there. Both were excellent cooks and housekeepers. And each knew her own mind and was not afraid to speak it.

"I'm doing fine, but I wanted to talk to you a minute. Is this a good time?"

"Sure. Come on in." Hetty stepped aside

to let me enter, gave me a cynical grimace, and added, chin in air, "I guess I can still invite people in this door until Miss High and Mighty gets court authority to say otherwise."

"Is Rachel Ford here?" I asked, stepping into the hall.

Hetty hesitated, then jerked her head toward the back. "She's in the den looking at old albums again. I know Miss Wilma threw her out t'other day, but I can't see no harm in her lookin', can you?"

"Not a bit," I agreed.

"But I put her in the back room this time, so if Miss Wilma comes, she can sneak out through the kitchen without gettin' hassled again. Were you wantin' to talk to her?"

"No, actually I wanted to talk to you. I have a couple of questions."

"Would you mind comin' back to the kitchen, then? I was cleanin' out cabinets and drawers. I figure if we're gonna have to vacate, I want the place to be as tidy as I can make it."

I followed her down the hall and into the kitchen, which looked immaculate to me, although several drawers stood open, and pots, utensils, and the odds and ends that every kitchen accumulates were piled on the granite-topped island in the middle of the room.

It was a pleasant, happy room. The windows, of which there were three, were wide open to the breezes and birdsong. Sunlight glinted off the brass handles on high walnut cabinets and streamed through a garden window over the sink, where a Christmas cactus, a petticoat fern, and a couple of jade plants flourished. I moseyed over to inspect them. "Willena's plants look healthy."

"Yes'm, they's healthy, but they's actually mine. Miss Willena never cared a thing about plants. I ought to take them up to my own place now or Miss Wilma will be carrying them off like she's been carrying off everything else."

I wrinkled my forehead. "She shouldn't be removing things from the house until the will is read."

"You tell her, then. I plan on going on living a few years longer."

Hetty bustled over to pull out a chair at a table set by a double window overlooking the backyard. "Come on over here and sit. We can talk while I work. I'm putting new paper in the drawers and wiping down the cabinets, but I don't know what to do with all the stuff. I guess I'll put it back until somebody comes to box it up to sell it off. Seems a shame, don't it? Somebody picking over Miss Willena's stuff like that."

I suspected that was the closest she would come to grieving for Willena. Clarinda had said for years that Hetty and Baker privately called her Willena the Witch and often debated whether it was worth having to put up with her temper to get good wages. Baker felt they could stick it out a few more years. But, as Clarinda pointed out, he was mostly outside and didn't have to put up with her all the time.

"Can I get you some tea? I made a pitcher fresh this morning," Hetty offered.

I sat down and set my pocketbook beside my chair. "That would be wonderful."

I accepted the glass of chilled tea over a full glass of ice. I squeezed in a fat wedge of lemon and stirred with a sterling spoon while Hetty set a small plate of lemon wafers and a green paper napkin in front of me. Willena might be gone from the house, but gracious living had not. I got the feeling that Hetty was enjoying lording it over this kitchen without Willena in the background. I hated to break the mood with what I needed to know.

She may have sensed my unease, for Hetty moved over to the island and started sorting through the stuff. "You were wantin' to talk to me?"

"Yes, I was. Last Monday night, what did Willena eat for supper?"

"A big green salad. She was trying to slim down a little, so she could —" She broke off and turned to wipe out a drawer with a sponge. "Anyway, she said they'd be having refreshments at the meeting and Miss Wilma was taking her special crabmeat cheese puffs, so she wanted a salad for her supper. I put an egg and some cheese in it, to give her some pro-teen, but she wouldn't even take a hot biscuit after I made them up special for her. Baker and I had to eat the lot."

"What did she drink?"

"Tea, as usual. She hadn't gotten so desperate yet that she'd given up tea."

Hetty made her tea like Clarinda did, sweetening a gallon with two cups of sugar while it was still hot. Strong and sweet with the tang of lemon or lime, it's one of the last things a true Southerner forgoes in a diet.

"Why was Willena dieting?" I hoped I sounded casual.

Hetty hesitated. "I don't rightly know whether I ought to be telling you this or not, but Miss Willena and Mr. Grover were planning on getting married come August. She'd already got her dress, and she'd

337

bought it a size small, so she'd have to lose weight to get in it." Her eyes danced at the foolishness of that.

I mulled it over. "Who knew they were getting married?"

Hetty shook her head. "Nobody, that I heard of, 'cepting Miss Willena and Mr. Grover. And Baker and me, of course, because she wanted us to know there'd be a few changes around here, with the family increasing and a boy coming and all. I wouldn't have minded having the boy — Jamison, his name is, a real nice boy — but I don't think they'd even told him yet. Mr. Grover was worried about how Jamison would take it, moving out to Hopemore and away from the city. But Miss Willena was plannin' to send him away to boarding school next year. I heard her asking Miss Wilma for the name of the school her daddy, Mr. Billy, went to. I figured Miss Willena wanted to have a school in mind before she talked to Mr. Grover about it. He's mighty attached to that boy and not likely to take too kindly to sending him away."

*Two more motives for murder,* I thought, sipping my tea. A disgruntled teen and a prospective groom who might have begun to realize he was getting not just a wife, but a steam-roller.

"Did you and Baker have any of the salad?" I asked. "Or drink the tea?"

Hetty wasn't dumb. Her eyes narrowed. "You thinkin' Miss Willena was poisoned? You can think again. Baker and I finished off the salad — I made a big one, on purpose — and drank tea from that same pitcher. We weren't sick."

"I understand she may have had a heart attack."

"Pooh!" Hetty let out her breath in a puff of disdain. "Weren't nothin' the matter with her heart. Strong as a horse. I know Miss Wilma wanted her to get it checked before her trip to the rain forest, but that was just Miss Wilma's nonsense." Hetty picked up a stack of pots and set them into a lower cabinet with a crash like the final cymbal in an orchestral piece.

"If it *was* something she ate, it was Miss Wilma's crab puffs," Hetty added as an encore. "That woman's so cheap, she could have used old crab."

"Willena didn't have any refreshments," I pointed out. "She went to the bathroom to fix her makeup before Wilma set them out."

"Well, it wasn't anything I fixed." Hetty sounded miffed that I'd even think such a thing. Her voice changed to a welcoming lilt. "Oh, hey, Miss Rachel. Would you like some tea? I made a pitcher fresh this morning."

Rachel stood in the doorway. I didn't know how long she'd been there. She drifted in and leaned against the island. "Is it sweet or unsweet?"

"Sweet." Hetty spoke in the tone of one who knew the right answer.

Rachel disappointed her. "I'd like a glass of water, please. Hello, Judge." She took the glass Hetty handed her and ambled over to take a chair across from me. She looked around the room as she reached for a cookie. "Do you have any idea what will happen to this house?"

"My guess is, it will be sold. It will be up to Wilma, I suppose."

"It's a great old place, isn't it?" Rachel looked around the room like she was thinking of buying the place. She must have a false idea about how cheap things go in Middle Georgia. Chances weren't good that she could afford even the down payment. But she could dream.

Hetty added more lemon wafers to the plate. "Eat up, now," she urged. "You're too skinny. Need some meat on your bones."

She hadn't said anything like that when she'd handed me the first cookies.

"Did you find the photos you were looking for?" I asked. I hoped so — it would be nice if somebody was successful that afternoon. I hadn't learned a thing I could use. I was convinced Willena had been poisoned. She had all the symptoms: nausea, chills, tremors, eventual paralysis of the heart. But if she hadn't eaten anything for supper that Hetty and Baker hadn't eaten, and she hadn't had any refreshments — which the rest of us had eaten without harm — then how could it have happened? And why hadn't any signs of poison shown up in her body? Of course, the forensics folks may not have looked that far. As the chief pointed out, labs were swamped these days. Somebody probably worked overtime and moved Willena up to the head of a list to get her results as quickly as they had. Once they had a good diagnosis and no reason to look further, why should they? But her intestines should have shown something.

When Rachel said, "I found several that were real helpful," I had to think a second to remember what I'd asked.

"Why would a lawyer write an article about clothes?" I wondered aloud. Especially, I felt like adding, one who dressed with so little flair. This afternoon Rachel had on black slacks, a black shell, black sandals, and a lightweight taupe cotton jacket with lumpy pockets, like she crammed things into them without thinking. She looked stylish, but drab.

But then she smiled, and I was again surprised at how attractive she was when she bothered to lift her lips. "Writing is a hobby of mine, and vintage clothes are another. I decided to put them together, and a historical magazine agreed to take an article on spec. Did you get what you came for?"

I shook my head. "Not really. I was thinking that Willena had a lot of the symptoms of cardiac poisoning, but Hetty assures me she didn't eat anything here that could have poisoned her."

"If it had happened in South America, we could blame one of them poisoned darts," Hetty reflected. "But folks don't use them much around here."

Before I could speak, Wilma asked at the doorway, "Hetty? Who are you talking to?"

She had come in mighty quietly, for none of us had heard her in the hall. As she took in Rachel and me sitting cozily at the kitchen table, her thin nostrils flared in displeasure. She turned back to Hetty. "I told you this house is not open to the public. You were instructed not to let anybody in. Besides, you and Baker need to be packing. Go on, get your things together. Leave me your house keys now. And I want the two of you off the property before five o'clock."

Hetty untied her apron, folded it neatly, and laid it on the counter. She pulled a ring of keys from the pocket of her uniform and laid them on top of the apron. Then she gave Wilma one long look in which there was neither subservience nor respect, and walked out.

"What are you all doing here?" Wilma demanded. Her face looked more pinched than usual that afternoon, and her cheeks each had a bright red spot of color. Fury, I supposed.

"I came to look at the pictures again," Rachel admitted. "I was almost done, and I knew you weren't likely to let me see them once you got your hands on them." Her tone was almost insolent.

"I came to ask Hetty a few questions," I said quickly. "I had a theory that Willena might have been poisoned."

"Willena died of a heart attack," Wilma snapped. "I kept telling her to get it checked, but she never did a blessed thing I asked her to do. In the end, she paid for that." Her voice was full of self-righteous satisfaction.

"Somebody drove the corkscrew into her neck," I pointed out.

Wilma put a hand to her cheek. "Don't! I don't want to think about that. I won't think about it, do you hear me? It was terrible. Terrible!" Her face grew pinker and pinker and her voice rose.

I stood. "I think we ought to go, Rachel."

Rachel slid her chair back and stood as well. But before we could take a step away from the table, Wilma said, "You aren't going anywhere."

We were looking down the barrel of a small silver pistol.

## 26

She smiled so pleasantly, you'd have thought she was offering candy, but the way her hand trembled, she could shoot us without meaning to. I calculated the distance from the table to where she stood. She was unlikely to kill us from there, but she could hurt us pretty bad.

I was trying to figure out how to get out of the situation safely when Rachel asked, in a voice that was amazingly steady, "What's this about, Wilma?"

"It's about nosy, trespassing busybodies." Wilma spoke in exactly the tone she used when she was exasperated with somebody on a committee. "I told Hetty not to let anyone in."

"We were going," I reminded her. "You can put the gun away now. You don't want to shoot anybody by mistake."

"People are always telling me what I want to do and don't want to do. I know what I want to do, Mac. I'm a planner. You know that. Life is all a matter of planning. I kept telling Willena, 'You need to plan. Don't go off helter-skelter without thinking things through.' But she never listened, of course. From the time she was a tiny thing, she always thought she knew best. Now look where it got her." She brought a delicate blue hankie from her pocket with her free hand and dabbed her forehead. "It is warm in here. Hetty shouldn't have turned the air-conditioning off and opened the windows."

Grief takes different people in different ways. Looked to me like Wilma had either gone off her rails or was wobbling on them.

"Hetty's probably saving you a few pennies. I wish Clarinda cared about that." I aimed for a cheerful tone and to keep Wilma's attention on me. Rachel had begun to edge away from the table.

Unfortunately, Wilma noticed. "Stop!" She gestured with the gun toward a door in the back corner of the kitchen. "Walk toward the back stairs. Both of you."

"How long is this going to take?" I asked her. "Pretty soon Joe Riddley is going to begin to wonder why I'm staying so long and come looking for me."

Wilma laughed. "Don't try that old trick,

Mac. We're going upstairs."

"It's not a trick," I protested. "He is firm about my writing him a note whenever I leave the office, stating where I'm going and when I'll be back."

"You'll be back when I say so. To the stairs, please." She gestured again with the gun.

Rachel hesitated. The way her eyes narrowed, I suspected she was calculating whether a tackle would succeed. "Humor her," I advised, thinking. *Maybe on the stairs . . .*

I led the way to the door and opened it to reveal a narrow pine staircase varnished to resemble mahogany. It climbed straight up into darkness. The air inside was close and warm. I flipped a switch and one dim light showed a landing far ahead where the stairs turned back on themselves. The walls were varnished beaded board up to the narrow handrail, a dingy gray above it. They were so close on both sides that I felt like I needed to press my elbows to my waist.

"Go on. Get up there." Wilma stood behind us and gestured for us to climb.

I'm not the athletic type, but it's amazing how fast you can climb steep stairs with a gun at your back. We were soon half a flight ahead of Wilma. I turned and saw Rachel close at my back. "When we reach the second floor," I murmured, "dash toward the first open door."

Unfortunately, the door to the second floor was locked. We both tried the knob, but the door didn't budge. "What now?" Rachel asked, looking down at Wilma, inexorably climbing.

Once the top floor was converted from servants' quarters to the ballroom, Frank Kenan's servants must have used the back stairs for serving food up there. I shuddered to think of all the heavy trays that had gone up that steep staircase, but I'd have given a great deal for one of them at the moment. Anything to throw down and distract Wilma. Why had I left my pocketbook on the kitchen floor beside my chair?

"Keep climbing. When we get in the ballroom, go right. I'll go left," I said softly. "She can't shoot but one of us, and that gun is far likelier to maim than kill."

"Comforting thought," Rachel muttered. Still, she didn't seem the least bit panicked. Maybe people who lived in New York were used to this kind of thing.

She wasn't gasping, either. By the time we got to the third floor I was seeing stars and sucking air. Below us on the landing, Wilma was panting worse than me. The staircase ended in a closed door with a dull iron knob. An old-fashioned skeleton key was still stuck in the keyhole. I had the fleeting question whether Frank Kenan used to lock his servants in at night, but Wilma was already calling, "It's unlocked. Go in and close it behind you."

I hesitated, puzzled. Rachel passed me and bolted up the last few steps. As I followed her I tried to snatch the key, but it wouldn't come out easily, and I was in a hurry. As soon as I was through, we slammed the door and leaned our backs against it, although I didn't feel like much of an impediment if Wilma wanted in. I hadn't climbed so far at once in years. My legs quivered like the leaves outside the windows, responding to a light breeze.

Ahead of us the ballroom was stuffy, vast, silent, and very warm. Apparently the air-conditioning upstairs was turned on only for events. Dust motes danced in sunlight filtering through leafy branches. The hot space was empty except for a grand piano in one corner, a bar at the back, a table with two chairs near a front window, and one odd chair at the far wall.

"What now?" Rachel whispered.

I pressed my ear to the door and heard Wilma climbing up the stairs. Her steps were weary and her breath came out in little grunts. "Can you run over and bring that chair to put under the knob?" I couldn't run even to save both our lives.

Rachel sped to the solitary chair and was back before Wilma reached the top step. The back of the chair fit securely under the knob. Elated, we slid to the floor and exchanged a silent high five.

Our celebration was short. We heard a sharp click, then Wilma's steps going back down. "She's locked us in!" Rachel got to her knees and grasped the knob. The door wouldn't budge.

"Not to worry. The main entrance is over there." I wasn't sure my legs were ever going to bear my weight again, but I rose painfully to my feet and took a couple of experimental steps. I might make it to the other doors.

We staggered across the floor to big double doors that Frank Kenan had installed when he had extended the front staircase to the third floor and created the ballroom.

Those doors were locked as well.

Rachel and I stood looking at each other in disbelief. "What's this all about?" she asked.

"If I were to guess, she's holding us prisoner while she calls the police."

I could see Charlie Muggins's satisfied smirk when Wilma triumphantly flung open the door and he saw me. Like I said, he's been trying to catch me in some criminal activity ever since I became a judge. I doubted that Wilma could make a trespassing charge stick, since Hetty had invited me in, but hauling me before another judge's bench would give Charlie enormous satisfaction.

"Do you think we could . . . you know, push the key out on the other side and pull it under the door?"

"Like they do in detective stories?" I asked dryly. "No, hon. There's a step immediately beneath it, and no crack under the door. If there had been, we'd have seen light through the crack while we were climbing."

We circled the room, peering down from all twelve windows, four each on three sides. At the front, the porch roof prevented us from seeing the drive, but I presumed my car and Wilma's were both still there.

Speaking of seeing, I wondered what had happened to all the chairs that had lined the room for Joe Riddley's prom, small gold chairs with red velvet cushions. There must have been fifty that night. Were only three left? I considered the two sitting at the small table placed near a front window. Had Wil-

351

lena and Grover come up here for romantic meals and dancing?

As I moved over to the side windows, I heard a crunching sound from outside. "Oh, no!" Rachel exclaimed, and started banging on a front window. I hurried to join her and watched Wilma drive away in her silver Cadillac. Lincoln seldom drove her unless she was going a distance or had things to carry.

"Where's she going?" Rachel whispered, as if her voice had left with Wilma.

I tried to speak briskly. "Home, I imagine. She'll call the police and let them come and find us. I hope. It's possible she won't bother to call them, but plans to leave us here awhile to stew."

"Hetty knows we're here." Was Rachel trying to comfort me or herself?

"Hetty doesn't know doodley-squat," I said bluntly. "She's over in her apartment packing and can't see the front of the house from her windows. I'm sure Wilma will have locked up the house, and Hetty no longer has keys, remember? Besides, for all she knows, Wilma took us both somewhere with her and will bring us back later for our cars. We're in a pickle, hon."

The air felt warmer and closer every minute. I could tell myself there was plenty of oxygen, but I was having trouble believing it.

"Maybe we can get out a window." Rachel stripped off her jacket and dropped it onto the little table, then headed to look for a route of escape.

In opposite directions we circled the ballroom again like wallflowers in search of partners, but the windows were small and had been painted shut sometime since the advent of air-conditioning. No windows at all overlooked the garage and Hetty's apartment. That wall held the double doors at the front, a small one in the center, and the door to the kitchen at the back. When we opened the door in the middle, it led to a storeroom piled high with small tables and all the chairs I remembered.

Rachel peered through the gloom. "Are there windows behind all the chairs?"

I craned my neck, but saw not a glimmer of light. "Nope. This side was probably an attic storeroom when the servants' bedrooms were up here. Maybe if we break a front window and yell together, Hetty or Baker will hear us."

Rachel dashed across the room, hoisted a chair, and smashed a front window before I'd finished the sentence. Glass spattered the porch roof far below, and a blessedly cool breeze flitted in. We both leaned toward the window to savor moving fresh air.

But though we called until we were hoarse, Hetty and Baker did not respond.

"Let's wait until we hear them loading up their truck," I croaked. "Then we can yell again. I sure wish we'd brought our tea up with us. I need to wet my whistle."

Rachel gave me a rueful grin. "Anticipated death distracts the mind. The way Wilma was shaking, I was fully occupied with praying her gun wouldn't go off."

I grinned back. If you had to be imprisoned, Rachel wasn't a bad person to be imprisoned with. I scouted the room with my eyes. "I wonder if the bar at the back still has running water."

Rachel beat me there. She was rummaging beneath the counter when I arrived and gave a crow of delight. "Tonic water, unopened lime juice, and gin. Can you drink a gin and tonic without ice?"

"Hon, I could drink a gin and tonic without tonic right now. Mix 'em up."

She took a couple of glasses from inside a cupboard and wiped them on her shirt. "Don't be overly fastidious," I begged. "Just pour." I could feel my clothes sticking to my body and my face beginning to perspire.

We dragged the chairs over to the open

window and sat there, alternating sips of lukewarm liquid with gulps of cool, fresh air.

When we finished that drink we had another. What else was there to do?

I went exploring and found a bathroom in the far corner of the room, but there was no escape route in there.

I kept checking my watch. For over two hours we sat and waited to hear Hetty and Baker come out to their truck.

We chatted about this and that. I finally asked, "Did you and Slade finish your projects?"

"We started on the bathroom paper, but I underestimated how much I'd need. I'll have to buy another double roll."

"Those little rooms take a lot more paper than you ever think they will," I agreed. "The two of you seemed to be working in rare harmony."

She shrugged. "He's fun when he gets off his high horse. We discovered that we like a lot of the same books, movies, and music."

"Slade can be a nice man," I opined.

"For somebody," she agreed. "Not for me."

"Grover?" I hazarded.

She turned and gave me a puzzled look. "Grover?" She laughed. "Heavens, no. He's like a brother." Her voice softened. "I loved his wife, and Jamison is the nephew I never had."

"So you didn't mind that he was dating Willena?" I wondered how much she knew about their plans.

"They were actually planning to get married." She drained her glass and sighed. "And I'll admit I wasn't too happy about it. Grover seemed happy, but Willena —" She stopped.

"Not somebody I'd want my brother to marry," I agreed.

"She'd have run Grover's life for him," Rachel said bluntly, "and she would never have put him first in anything."

"My feelings exactly. But if Grover isn't the complication, do you mind telling me what your problem is with Slade?"

Rachel held her glass to her cheek. "It's awful hot, even with the window open. I'm tempted to break another to get some cross ventilation."

I was disappointed not to hear why she didn't like Slade, but all I said was, "Go for it."

She picked up her chair and went to the one catty-cornered from where we were. "Timber!" she shouted, and smashed the legs of the chair into the window.

"Timber?"

"What else could I yell, 'Glass'?" She brushed shards off the seat of her chair and brought it back to where I sat. She sat with her legs stretched out and wiggled her toes in her sandals. "Hot damn, that was fun. Now I understand why kids vandalize buildings. Makes you think you are a lot more powerful than you really are."

I lifted damp hair from the back of my neck. "I feel more breeze, too."

She picked up her drink and stared at the dregs in the bottom like they could tell her future. "And now, it seems, we have arrived back at your question. The short answer is, I didn't get a law degree to stay poor. I grew up that way, and it's no fun. So I don't want to work in poverty law all my life. I wish I were that noble, but I'm not. Therefore, I doubt I'll stay in Hopemore long. I like the town and the people, but I need to earn more than I do now, and there are already enough lawyers in this county, so I can't go into private practice and make much of a living. Marriage to a small-town newspaper editor wouldn't add much to my bank account, either. Do I sound mercenary?"

"You sound like Slade. He came up poor, too, and he has told me his three criteria for the woman he will marry. She needs to be rich, beautiful, and smart." I slid down in my chair and tried to stretch out my legs, too, but the chair was too high. Afraid I'd slide all the way off the seat, I sat back up straight. Then I squirmed, trying to get comfortable, but it wasn't any use. Those hard seats were made for sitting on between dances, not permanent roosts.

"In that order?" Rachel inquired, her eyes amused.

I had to think a second to remember what she was talking about. "Simultaneously."

She gave a short, not-funny laugh. "Well, I strike out on two of three. See? We are obviously not suited."

"Nonsense. You have a lot in common — you are both wrapped up in the wrong things. That ought to count for something." We were silent for a time, then I mused, "Wilma and Willena have always had lots of money. Do you think it's made them happy?"

"I have no idea, but I'd rather be unhappy and rich than unhappy and poor. At least you can be comfortable in your misery."

She had a good point. No matter how miserable a well-to-do person is, their misery isn't accompanied by the terror of not having a next meal, shelter, or transportation. Still, I felt compelled to point out that money isn't a panacea for all ills. "Sadie Lowe married for money and it didn't last."

"Bad defense, Mac. She got to keep the money."

"Well, look at Nancy Jensen. She married for money. Look where it got her."

Until then we had been talking in light, bantering tones. Now Rachel sobered instantly. "Slade said she almost shot Sadie Lowe Thursday."

"No, she only shot *at* her. If she had meant to kill anybody, she would have. And in her shoes, I'd shoot Horace, not —"

We both leaped to our feet as a motor roared to life below us. We pounded on what was left of the window and yelled for all we were worth. Rachel even leaned out and waved frantically, but Baker's black pickup growled down the drive without a sign that anybody knew we were there.

I checked my watch. It was five minutes until five. My hamburger was a distant memory. "I sure wish I'd eaten more of those lemon cookies."

"Me, too. Why do you think Wilma did this? Pure spite?" Rachel shoved her hair out of her face with one slender hand. Damp heat had created a mass of corkscrews curling all over her head.

I repressed the image of corkscrews.

"Maybe. I think this past week has made Wilma a tad crazy. She and Willena were very close."

"She's crazy, all right." Rachel began walking about the room with restless energy. I wished she didn't remind me of stories I'd read of prisoners of war who developed exercise rituals to keep their sanity. "She's making me crazy, too. She thinks I did it, you know — killed Willena." She had her back to me, so I couldn't see her face.

"Why should she think that?"

"Because I was trying so hard to get to know Willena. Wilma would never believe it was so I could look at those albums."

"I can see how she might consider that a weak excuse to cotton up to someone," I mused. I looked at Rachel through half-closed eyes and saw a strong young woman who certainly had the strength for the murder. She had gone outside with Grover but not returned with him. Had she stopped off at the ladies' room to kill Willena on her way in? "You would have needed a motive," I pointed out.

She laughed. "I've got a motive. What I'm missing is an alibi. Listen, how long before your husband will come looking for you?"

I sighed. "I didn't leave a note," I admitted.

"But you said —"

"I said Joe Riddley insists that I leave him a note saying where I'm going. I didn't exactly say I had. This was only supposed to take a few minutes. I thought I'd be back before he was."

She looked at me in dismay. "It is possible," she pointed out, "that we could die up here."

## 27

That spurred us to action.

"Maybe one of those chairs could break the door lock," I suggested. Anything to salvage self-respect after monumental stupidity.

Rachel seized the extra chair and crashed it against the double doors again and again until the lovely wood was scarred and one of the legs broke off. The lock held. By now she was dripping with sweat and I read desperation in her eyes. Or were they mirroring my own?

She eyed the red drapes that hung from each window. "Maybe we could make a rope and climb down to the porch roof."

I steadied a chair, and she climbed up on it to drag down a couple of lengths of heavy fabric. When we tried to tie them together, the knots were thick and unwieldy. "We could never trust those knots with our weight," I concluded, "but if we could cut the drape into strips and braid them . . ."

Rachel loped to the bar and began pawing through drawers. "Voilà!" She held up a short paring knife. She brought it back and plunged it into the fabric, then ripped the drape from top to bottom. She stabbed a second spot and soon had torn a long strip. I yanked it between my hands to see if it was rotten. It held.

"Are you good with knots?" I asked.

"Only in shoelaces," she said ruefully.

"Then you cut. I'll braid and knot them." I hoped I could remember distant Scout lessons on knots. I made several long, braided strips, then braided three of them together, knotted at intervals. Proudly I held up my crimson rope. "That ought to hold our weight."

"Not ours," Rachel corrected me. "Mine. If I can get down to the porch roof, I can break a window and get into the second floor. Then I'll come up and let you out."

"Do you know anything about rappelling?"

"Not a thing, but I'm willing to learn. I don't want to spend a night in this place. Besides, I'm getting hungry."

My own stomach gave a growl of agreement. We had only joked about hunger before. Now I felt like I had a ravening wolf inside.

We checked all the windows and chose one in the center. "More margin for error on each side," Rachel joked. Now that we had a plan, we were getting giddy with relief.

She took what was left of the drape and tore off a short strip to tie her hair at the nape of her neck, then gestured at the window. "Okay, Mac, smash it. Your turn to be demolition crew."

I enjoyed breaking that window so much that Rachel warned, "Don't get addicted. We don't want you smashing up Oglethorpe Street once we get out of here."

The thought of actually strolling down Oglethorpe energized us both.

Rachel was all for crawling immediately through the hole I had made, but I insisted on removing shards and splinters of glass from the frame. "I don't want you bleeding to death before you rescue me. You can bleed all you want to afterwards."

We started laughing, and laughed until we had to hold our sides. That was how glad we were to be getting out.

Until we realized we still had a problem. She looked at the windowsill in bafflement. "What can we tie the rope to on this end?"

We looked around the bare room in dismay.

"A piano leg!" I crowed, and headed in its direction. "Help me roll it over here."

By the time we had rolled the grand piano across that huge room, we were panting and gasping again. "Will you be able to do this?" I asked, anxious now that the moment had come.

"Just watch me. At worst, I'll fall to the roof and break a leg. But you tie the knot to the piano leg. I'm not good with knots."

"Thank God for Girl Scouts," I said fervently. I made the rope as fast as I knew how and handed it to her. "It's all yours. Good luck, hon."

Without another word we exchanged a fierce hug. As she climbed onto the windowsill and looked down, I saw a shiver pass through her body. Admiration welled up in me. I doubted that I'd be able to lower myself out that window into space. Could she?

She threw the rope over the ledge, then knelt and took it in her hands. "Here I go, Mac. Wish me luck."

"Mind if I pray instead? I usually find it more effective."

She didn't answer, just grabbed the rope tightly and lowered herself over the sill.

I prayed her all the way down. She more slid than rappeled, and from a yelp as she was halfway there, I suspected she had burned her palms, but one of the sweetest sounds I ever heard was the thud of her feet on the porch roof.

That sound was followed by silence.

"What's the matter?" I called down.

"I don't have any way to break the window. I'm going to take off my shirt and cover my hand —"

"No, wait a minute." I trotted over to where the chair leg had broken off and snatched it up, then dashed back and called, "Stand clear. Bombs away."

The leg clattered onto the roof. In another second I watched her swing the chair leg through the window, clear away the shards, and climb inside.

After that, nothing.

She left the ballroom at ten till six. By six thirty, I had run out of excuses — she stopped to go to the bathroom, she couldn't find the key to the door — and run a complete gamut of fears. She had fallen inside and could not reach a phone. She had cut an artery getting in the window and quickly bled to death. She had decided to go for help and had a wreck on the highway. She had forgotten all about me.

I never imagined the disaster that had really happened.

In between worrying, I sat looking at treetops and reviewing events of the past week. I mentally repeated all the interviews I had had: Wilma in her shabby but historical living room and powdering her nose in my car. Hetty downstairs. Linette at the old Kenan home place. Dexter down at Mad Mooney's. Clarence, with his unsuspected wealth. MayBelle in her Land Rover. Nancy, down at the detention center, wailing, "And all this time I thought it was Willena. I thought Grover was camouflage."

I remembered Grover trembling in the coffee shop booth, and Sadie Lowe leaning across the table to console him.

I remembered what Gusta had said, and Meriwether. I thought of Rachel, white faced at being caught looking at albums at Willena's and holding her emerald up to the morning sun.

I put the puzzle together in several ways. Eventually I knew who had killed Willena. I knew why, with what, and how. All I needed to do was tell Isaac James. He could do the rest.

"What I need around now," I told the Boss upstairs, "is a miracle. Somebody coming down that drive or Wilma changing her mind and coming back." But though I stared at the bit of the drive I could see until my eyes watered, I didn't see a soul.

My stomach figured my throat had been cut. It growled and growled, protesting that it should be feasting on barbecue by now. I decided maybe I'd better try for my own escape.

The sun wasn't going down yet, but it was heading that way, and this house faced east. Already the porch roof was dim and shady, blocked from the sun by the house itself. I picked up the rope and balanced it in my hand. Went to the windowsill and put one knee up. Tried to convince myself I could hang on and slide down it if Rachel could.

I couldn't. My sore hand wouldn't let me. But even if I had had two good hands, I knew I couldn't face that instant of leaving the safety of the windowsill and swinging into space.

Standing there racked by indecision, I shivered. The breeze was cooler now that the sun was behind the trees. I picked up Rachel's jacket from the table and draped it over my shoulders. Something thumped against my hip bone.

I debated with my conscience for half a second, then slid one hand in the pocket. It came out holding a miracle. My cell phone.

The question was, whom should I call? Charlie Muggins, to say I'd solved his case for him? The sheriff, since we were outside the city limits? Joe Riddley, so he could come kill me?

The thought of facing Joe Riddley or climbing down a ladder in front of law enforcement personnel was more than I felt up to. I could phone Ridd, but he was my law-abiding son, the one who would insist on calling the police or a rescue vehicle. What I wanted was somebody who wouldn't mind breaking another window. I punched autodial.

Walker answered on the second ring. "Hey, Mama. What's up?"

"I am. I'm up on the third floor of Willena Kenan's house, locked in. Don't ask how or why, but could you come over here and let me out? You'll need to break a window to get in, but there's nobody else around, and I've already broken several. Another one isn't going to make much difference. Then come up the back stairs from the kitchen. There's a key in that lock, I hope."

I heard the kind of silence on the other end that meant Walker was trying not to swear. "You want to tell me what you've been up to?"

"Nothing at all. I was having a glass of tea out here with Hetty, Willena's maid, when Wilma came by and took exception to my being in the house. She made me come up here —"

"Made you?"

I huffed. "Don't ask so many questions. She made me come up here and locked me in. You know how petty she can be. But I think she left the key in the lock. If not, it looked like a skeleton key. The kind in all of Ridd's doors. Borrow one of them on your way."

"Can I tell Ridd what I'm borrowing it for? He's likely to ask."

I hesitated. "Okay, you can tell Ridd, but not your daddy. Understand? Not a word to your daddy."

"Okay, but he's already looking for you. He's called here twice."

"I'll call and tell him I've been delayed but am on my way home. You get here as fast as you can. Oh, and son? Be real careful. Rachel Ford was up here with me until half an hour or so ago. She escaped by climbing down to the porch roof on a rope we made from the curtains" — I heard a noise that could have been a snort or a laugh, but I plowed on — "and she was supposed to go inside the house and come get me. But she hasn't shown up, which worries me. Wilma has a gun and doesn't know how to use it."

Now he did swear. Where he learned those words I have never known. Certainly not in our house. "Mama, how did you get mixed up in this? A person with a gun who doesn't know how to use it is the most dangerous kind of person in the world."

"I know, but I think Wilma is probably back at her house right now eating dinner, reflecting that she has certainly shown me a thing or two. Just don't come barreling down the drive without scouting things out first."

Cindy spoke on the other extension. I wondered how long she'd been listening. "Does this have anything to do with Wilena's murder?"

"Not really. I think I've figured that out, but we got locked in because Wilma got mad that we came in the house without her permission."

"And you don't think she's around now?"

"I haven't heard her. Look, could Walker come get me out? Please?"

I didn't mean for my voice to tremble, but I did sound pitiful. Walker's voice was gruff when he replied, "Hang in there, Mama. I'll be there as soon as I can."

"I'll love you forever if you'll bring me a Hershey bar and a Coke. I'm starved."

I spent a few minutes steeling myself, then dialed our house. To my great relief, Joe Riddley wasn't there. I left him a voice mail. "I'm sorry I'm late, hon. I got delayed, but I'll be home within the hour. Love you."

That wouldn't keep him from fussing, but at least he couldn't claim I didn't call.

I paced the floor and waited. Found a light switch and turned on the lights at the back end of the ballroom. Drank some more water. Used the bathroom. Started to wash the two glasses Rachel and I had used, then decided Rachel might want them as evidence. She was threatening to sue Wilma for all this. I tucked the glasses up behind some others, where they'd be obscure, and I stored the gin, tonic, and lime in a back corner beneath the bar.

By now it was too dusky outside for me to see anything on the driveway, but I strained my ears for the sound of Walker's car.

I still couldn't sit, so I began to pace again. Finally I heard the second-sweetest sound I'd heard all day. Somebody was turning the key to the ballroom's back door.

I headed in that direction. "Boy, I'm glad you finally got here!" I called.

The door swung open.

MayBelle stood in the open doorway with another little silver gun pointed straight at me.

# 28

"I thought you were . . ." My voice and my courage deserted me at the same instant.

She laughed, lowered the gun, and dropped it into her big pocketbook as casually as if it were a wallet. Heavens to Betsy, did every woman in the investment club go around armed?

"I thought *you* were a squirrel. A very big squirrel." We eyed each other warily. She seemed as discombobulated as I was. If she hadn't stood between me and the door, I'd have made a dash for it. But I didn't know if she was in league with Wilma or a possible deliverer.

She peered up at the high ceiling with its eight crystal chandeliers. "Isn't this marvelous? Wilma said we couldn't look at the top floor tonight because squirrels got in and made a big mess, but it looks . . ." Finally she spied the piano in front of the window with the rope still tied to one leg, the shattered chair near the double doors, three broken windows, and the pile of savaged drapery. She frowned. "That wasn't squirrels. Has she had vandals?"

I finally found a faint voice. "No, that was me. I was locked in, so I broke the windows and made a rope. But then I couldn't climb with my injured hand." I decided to leave Rachel out of the story. Where *was* Rachel?

MayBelle looked at me like I had escaped from some asylum. "How on earth could you get locked in? The key was right in the door."

I took a chance on the truth. "On the outside of the door. Wilma got annoyed with me for visiting Hetty."

MayBelle's eyes widened until her new face almost wrinkled. "Lordy, that woman has come plumb unhinged by grief."

"You can say that again." I edged closer to the door, desperate to leave. MayBelle started pacing off the width of the ballroom.

"How did you get here?" I peered down the staircase to be sure it was empty but was reluctant to go without her. Wilma could be at the bottom, ready to do to me whatever she'd done to Rachel. I found the thought of MayBelle's gun immensely reassuring.

She spoke absently from across the room.

"Wilma ran over to check on whether Hetty cleaned up their place before she left, so I decided to sneak up. I'd heard you moving around, and figured you were either the world's biggest squirrel or a prowler."

"But how did you get to the house? I didn't hear your car on the drive." I moved away from the door until she was ready to leave, not wanting to make a target of myself should Wilma appear on the landing.

"I used the shortcut from Wilma's. I had told her I wanted first refusal on the house, and she called today to say I could see it this evening while she checked to be sure Hetty and Baker had gotten all their stuff out. I stopped by her house to get her, but she'd already come ahead, so I used the back way."

I had forgotten there was an old tractor track that the Kenans had paved to connect the two houses so they could get from one to the other without going up to the highway. When Willena got concerned about the environment, she had replaced her driveway with pea gravel, but had left the asphalt on the shortcut. It would have been a stealthier way to come.

MayBelle completed her measurements and turned briskly. "Come on. It's too stuffy to stay up here long."

I could have smacked her.

We were too late. Wilma called up the stairwell. "MayBelle? Are you up there? I told you, the top floor is off-limits until we get rid of vermin. It's a real mess."

"It sure is," MayBelle called back. She chuckled. "But by vermin, are you referring to Mac, here?"

Wilma stood in the doorway, huffing and puffing like the little bad wolf. Between huffs, she explained, "I caught them trespassing, so I locked them up here for a little while to teach them they can't go into other people's houses whenever they want to."

She turned to me. "If you've learned your lesson, you can —"

She stopped and her jaw dropped. She had seen the front of the ballroom. She stood like a frozen child in a game of statues and said in a strangled voice, "You broke my windows? And Uncle Frank's chair?"

*We also drank up your booze,* flitted through my head, but I didn't say it. I didn't want anybody thinking we'd enjoyed ourselves. When Saint Peter comes to take me home, I still plan to inform him that Wilma Kenan stole four hours of my life that I want credit for.

She hurried across the room and picked up the red-and-gilt corpse of the chair.

"Why on earth did you break this? And where is the leg?"

"The chair broke when we were trying to open the double doors. . . ."

Wilma dashed to the doors and ran her fingers over the bruised and dented panels like they were a beloved face. "How could you? How could you?"

I finished, "And Rachel used the leg to smash a downstairs window to get back in the house."

Wilma ran to a broken window and peered down at the rope that still dangled there, and then she whirled, her face red with fury. "You had no call to destroy this house. You knew I wouldn't leave you up here forever. I will kill you for this! I will sue you for everything you've got. This is . . . is . . . unconscionable!"

MayBelle asked in an amused voice, "Did you expect Mac to just sit and wait until you showed up?"

Before Wilma could answer, the double doors opened a crack and a familiar deep drawl spoke through them. "Miss Wilma? I need to ask you a few questions."

Wilma uttered a little shriek and opened her purse.

I didn't know I could fly, but I seemed to cover the space between us in one leap and shoved her to the floor as Sheriff Gibbons came through the doors.

"She's got a gun in that purse," I gasped, sprawled awkwardly on top of Wilma.

In one motion he bent, retrieved the purse, and opened it. "Do you have a permit for this, ma'am?"

"It's Willena's. I was . . . bringing it . . . back to . . . the house." Her words came in gasps. She writhed beneath me like a bucking bronco, stronger than I would have suspected. "Get off me. Get off!" With one big shake she flung me off.

I grabbed the doorknob to keep from falling. The door swung wildly, and I thought for a second I'd take off again into outer space. When it finally came to a stop, I stumbled to my feet and found myself trembling in Walker's arms. He held me tight. "It's okay, Mama. You're gonna be okay."

Sheriff Gibbons held the purse out of Wilma's reach and extended his other hand to help her to her feet. "A few questions," he repeated.

Wilma staggered back to one of the chairs at the table by the window. "You nearly scared me to death!" She began to cry.

MayBelle hurried over and sat beside her. "Calm down," she advised. "The sheriff wants to ask you some questions."

I looked up at Walker and whispered, "I told you not to call him. He'll be sure to tell your daddy."

"I didn't call him," he whispered back. "He was here when I got here, already inside. He says he found the back door open."

"I found her!" somebody shouted downstairs. The voice dropped a notch. "Can you walk? What happened? Wait . . ." It got louder again and seemed to be coming our way. "Stay still. I've got you." It was Slade. He raised his voice to call, "We're coming up."

"I don't want to go back up there," Rachel protested. "Put me down! Let me go!"

We heard a scuffle, then silence. A moment later, we heard somebody heavily climbing the stairs. Finally Slade came through the double doors carrying Rachel in his arms. She had one hand pressed to the back of her head. Her face was pale and wore a strange expression. Her hair straggled out of the strip of crimson drape. "I don't know what happened," she said groggily. "I must have fallen. Everything went dark."

"Somebody hit her and put her in a closet under a pile of sheets," Slade told us angrily.

"I don't remember." Rachel looked around the room like she was having trouble focusing her eyes. She looked at me standing close to Walker, at the sheriff over by a broken window, at Wilma and MayBelle seated at the table. "Why is everybody here?"

"Wilma was showing me the house," May-Belle explained.

Wilma recovered her aplomb. She drew herself erect in her chair, nostrils flared. She reached up to straighten her hair, which had gotten a little mussed, then glared at Rachel. "Did you call the sheriff?"

Rachel wrinkled her forehead. "I don't think so."

"Well, I'm glad he's here." She turned to him. "I want you to arrest these two women for trespassing. They illegally entered my cousin's house."

Rachel shook her head, then groaned. It must ache.

I pointed to Wilma. "First, arrest her for abduction and imprisonment at gunpoint."

I could see the word *What?* on the tip of MayBelle's tongue.

"You had no right to force us up here and lock us in," I informed Wilma. "Much less to go off and leave us."

"Are we missing the party?" called a deep,

sultry voice downstairs. A stampede of feet
came up the stairs.

# 29

Sadie Lowe was at the head of the group that came in, lovely as always in a flowing red skirt with a white button-front shirt that covered up her assets but let you know they were there. Cindy was right behind her in jeans and a pink T-shirt. The anxious look in her eyes when they met mine told me she had called all these people and wasn't apologizing, but she hoped I wouldn't be mad. Nancy was behind Cindy, wearing a navy shirtdress that was too tight and the wrong shade of blue for her coloring. She kept her distance from Sadie Lowe, I noticed.

"Meriwether and Gusta will be up in a minute," Cindy announced. "Mac said she has figured out who killed Willena, so I thought we ought to all come find out who it was."

"There are chairs in that closet," I told Walker, jerking my head toward the door.

"Would you get some for Gusta and Rachel?"

He set one over by the side window where there was a little breeze, and Slade lowered Rachel onto it, then stood over her massaging one shoulder with his fingers. I remembered Joe Riddley doing that to me, but it seemed like a couple of lifetimes ago. Rachel put one hand up and covered his, then looked up at him with an uncertain smile.

If he hadn't kissed her right before he brought her upstairs, my days as a sibyl were over.

Most of the women had never been upstairs. Some didn't even know the ballroom was there. They milled around exclaiming at the chandelier and polished floor and gaping at the havoc Rachel and I had wreaked. Watching them, I got nervous. I moseyed over and whispered to the sheriff, "I know MayBelle has a gun, but I don't know who else might. Could you collect and hold weapons while we're all up here?" Only one of those people was a killer but after the afternoon I'd just had, any concealed weapons made me nervous.

He cleared his throat. "I understand that some of you carry weapons. While I am sure you have permits for them, I would appreciate it if you'd give them to Walker while we're all together up here. Walker, would you take them up and put them on the bar at the back?"

MayBelle promptly pulled hers out. "I wouldn't really shoot you, Mac," she joked.

"I might." Sadie Lowe took a deadly-looking little black number from her shoulder bag. "But not tonight."

Nancy glowered at me and reached with reluctance into her purse. "I know," she told the sheriff, "I'm not supposed to be carrying this after . . . you know. But I don't like to come out alone at night without it."

The sheriff looked around the circle. "Anybody else?" He stopped at Rachel.

She shook her head. "I have one, but my purse is still down in the den."

When Walker reached into his pants pocket, I looked at him in astonishment. All their lives our boys had heard their daddy preach, "Don't carry a loaded gun, and keep any guns you have locked up. It is families who don't think their kids will use guns who lose them to guns. Nobody, and I do mean nobody, knows what a child may do when pushed to a certain limit." And now the father of two of my precious grandchildren was carrying a gun?

He brought out a Hershey bar and handed it to me with a grin that said he knew exactly what I'd been thinking and he had set me up again. "Here. Your Coke is in my car."

I followed him to the bar, turned my back to the rest of the room, and tore open that candy like I'd been on a desert island for a week. You can say what you want about elegant chocolate. Right that minute, Hershey's was the elixir of the gods. Then I looked over my shoulder at Rachel and made the most generous offer of my life. "I'll save half for her."

Walker pulled out a second candy bar. "I brought her one."

"You are a prince among men." I popped another rectangle into my mouth.

When we returned to the front of the room, everybody was standing around looking at me expectantly. "Well, Mac?" Cindy asked brightly in the same voice she used to open the Junior League meetings. "Who did it?"

Sadie Lowe's sultry laugh seemed appropriate in that warm, thick air. "It wasn't me. I can tell you that much."

"No, but you played a part." I looked over at Nancy. "I don't want to embarrass you or Sadie Lowe, but I suspect that everybody here knows what happened Thursday. Nancy, you told me you thought Horace was having an affair with Willena. Why was that?"

Nancy was miserable, but she was no wimp. She lifted her chin. "Because she drove a white Jaguar convertible and I'd seen Horace's car parked near one like it at restaurants and motels. Then at the country club dance — I believe you were away for that — but she and Horace danced together and carried on like teenagers."

Sadie Lowe laughed again, a derisive sound this time. "That was camouflage. Horace was playing up to Willena to throw you off the track. He has never loved anybody but me." She switched her hips a little, and her skirt swished around her calves.

Wilma sat up straighter, and her nose went up in the air. "I'll have you know that Horace wanted to marry Willena in college. She turned him down, of course, That's why he married Nancy." Wilma crossed her legs in a genteel manner.

The expletive Sadie Lowe used was in no way genteel. "He married Nancy because he had to marry somebody to breed another Jensen. That's the same reason he looked twice at Willena in college. But Horace hasn't been able to keep his hands off me since we were in seventh grade, and he never will." She gave Nancy a pitying smile.

"You might have wed him, honey, but you'll never bed him like I do. Horace has me under his skin and I'm a permanent disease."

My guess was, those last two lines were from some soap opera she'd played in, but they were certainly effective. Nancy dashed across the room with her hands lifted like an angry cat's paws, and before the sheriff could stop her, she had raked her nails down Sadie Lowe's face. Sadie Lowe backed up, clasping her palms to her cheeks, then she seized Nancy's wrist with one hand, grabbed her shoulder with the other, and shook her so hard I expected to hear a bone crack.

"Keep away from me, bitch! You hear me? Keep away from me and Horace, or I'll give you something to remember." Was that Sadie Lowe or Nancy? I have never been certain.

The sheriff and Walker pulled them apart. They stood panting and furious, glaring at each other. "She's a tramp," Nancy gasped. "Make her leave my husband alone."

Sadie Lowe checked her nails and buffed them on her skirt in a show of unconcern. "He's not going to be your husband long. Get used to it. He'll be filing for divorce within a week. After what you did Thursday,

I told him I'm not playing games anymore. Either he marries me, or I'm leaving to find somebody who will."

"Horace needs me," Nancy said stoutly, her face flushed and her eyes glittering.

"She killed Willena!" Wilma whimpered. "She killed her, and it made her so sick she had to leave the meeting early!"

Nancy whirled in her direction. "I did not. I got a migraine." She looked around at the rest of us. "I wouldn't have killed Willena, even if she and Horace —"

"Where were you during our little break?" Gusta stood in the double doors, leaning on her silver-headed cane. I didn't know how long she had been there. She can climb stairs with the aid of a good arm and her cane, but it takes her a while. Meriwether held her elbow. Little Zach was a plump pill bug in a Snugli on his mother's chest. He was fast asleep.

Gusta stomped over to the vacant chair and sat down. Immediately it became a small gilt throne. Walker set one beside her for Meriwether, who sat cradling Zach's little head with one hand. The group fell silent.

Through the unglazed windows came the sound of cicadas tuning up for their nightly symphony. Even though the air was still warm and thick, there was nothing menacing about that ballroom when it was full of people. Rachel's eyes met mine, and I was certain we were the only two who could imagine how terrifying the place could be.

"Well," Gusta said, thumping her cane once on the floor, "get on with it, Nancy. My great-grandson needs to be in bed. Where did you go, and why did you leave early?"

"I thought Willena had gone to meet Horace," Nancy confessed sullenly.

Sadie Lowe laughed. "No, that would be me." She looked around the room and shrugged. "Okay, so I didn't go out on the front porch to smoke. I went out the back door to smooch. With Horace. In his car. I still wasn't killing Willena."

"Nobody said you did," I reminded her. "But what did you do all that time, Nancy?"

She raised both palms and shrugged. "Looked for Willena. She was gone so long —"

"It always took her a long time to fix her face," Wilma explained.

"I didn't know that," Nancy snapped. "I thought she and Horace were somewhere in the building. So I looked and looked, but I couldn't find them. I even went outside —"

Cindy, standing on the other side of

Walker now and leaning against him, spoke up to confirm, "I saw you. You came out, then went right back in. And you came out a little later and drove off."

"Did you look in the ladies' room?" Meriwether stroked her son's head with one gentle finger, but she looked with pity at Nancy.

Nancy shook her head. "That was the one place I didn't look. I knew he wouldn't be in there. But worrying about him gave me a migraine, so I left. I must have driven all the way to our beach condo, because the next thing I knew, it was morning and I had been sleeping in the parking lot."

"That eliminates Nancy," Gusta announced. "What about the rest of us?"

I gave her a wry smile. "Us? The police chief already assured us that you are innocent. How little he knows."

She huffed in arrogance. "He knows I didn't kill Willena. So who did? I'm putting my money on you, MayBelle."

"Me?" MayBelle's laugh was unsteady. "Why me?"

"General principles," Gusta replied.

"Without Willena, the zoning board will let you do anything you want with my land," Wilma pointed out with a sniff.

"Or maybe you killed her because you

want to buy her house," Sadie Lowe added.

MayBelle gave a little snort. "I wouldn't kill somebody for a house. I could just build one exactly like it."

Wilma was shocked. "But you wouldn't have the history of the house."

"Or broken windows and scarred doors," I added. "But you were, after all, the last known person known to see Willena alive. Do you know what convinced me you didn't kill her?"

"That I have absolutely no motive."

"No, that you flunked chemistry. I think Willena died from a cardiac toxin."

Everybody turned to look at Nancy. "I didn't kill her," she protested. "I was a chemistry teacher, but I never poisoned anybody."

"Of course not." Wilma gave me a frosty look. "Willena died of a heart attack. Why can't you accept that, MacLaren, and let her rest in peace?"

I gave her what my boys call Mama's Killer Look. "Because she didn't die in peace. She died with chills, nausea, sweats, and tremors — symptoms of a plant poison that stops the heart. I was puzzled because the autopsy showed no intestinal symptoms, but this afternoon Hetty said that if Willena had died in the Amazon, we'd suspect a poison dart."

"Ooh! Exciting!" Sadie Lowe squealed.

"It's ridiculous," Gusta said haughtily.

"Of course," I agreed. "But a hypodermic isn't. Administered by injection, a cardiac toxin is more deadly and leaves no intestinal traces."

"Where would somebody get a poison like that?" the sheriff inquired.

"Ask Little Miss New York," Wilma said spitefully. "Her dad was a pharmacist."

"He managed a drugstore," Rachel protested. She was less groggy now, but her eyes were still large and dilated, and her hand still rested in Slade's. "Daddy didn't know the first thing about chemistry. Neither do I."

"So, Judge?" the sheriff prompted.

"Mistletoe," I told him. "Some folks use it medicinally, but brewed correctly it is deadly." I looked across at Wilma. "Lincoln was cutting mistletoe last week for you."

"Of course. The trees are full of it. But I didn't use it to kill Willena. Why should I? I saw her every day. Why kill her with all of you around?"

"More suspects," I said bluntly.

Wilma appealed to higher powers. "Miss Gusta, Sheriff Gibbons, you all know good and well I wouldn't kill Willena. I loved her like a sister." She turned to the other women in the club. "Besides, how could I when I had my hands full fixing refreshments? I can't be two places at once. You all saw me the whole time."

MayBelle gave her a considered look. "Except when you were mixing punch. Could she do it in less than five minutes, Mac?"

"The poison would take a while to work, so she probably jabbed her with a needle while they were in the kitchen before the meeting. Willena kept complaining about feeling cold. But it wouldn't take but a second or two to drive the corkscrew into Willena's throat." I turned to Wilma. "It sure took you longer to mix the second batch of punch than the first. I had time to eat brownies, chat with Gusta, and talk with Grover before you came back."

Red spots had appeared on Wilma's sallow cheeks, a sure sign she was angry. "I had to combine a lot of ingredients."

"No, you didn't. They were already mixed. When I was at your place Thursday, Linette told the other maid to pour it down the sink because it had been mixed and wouldn't keep."

"Linette doesn't know a dadgum thing about that recipe." Wilma dabbed her eyes with a tissue MayBelle had given her, since the sheriff still had her purse. "Poor Willena died of a heart attack, just like her daddy. I told her and told her to get it checked, but she wouldn't."

"You knew she wouldn't, if you insisted. In fact, you ensured that she wouldn't get it checked so there would be no medical records of the recent condition of her heart. One more thing. Where did you get Willena's gun?"

Before she could answer, I turned to May-Belle. "When you left the bathroom, Willena was still fixing her face, right?" May-Belle nodded. "Using cosmetics from her purse?"

"Sure."

"So when did you get Willena's gun, Wilma? She kept it in her purse, which was in the bathroom while she fixed her face. The police took the purse away after she was killed. So when did you get the gun, if not right after you stuck the corkscrew in her throat?"

"Before the meeting. She didn't like for me to be alone back in that kitchen."

For the first time I found myself felling sorry for Wilma. She had laid such careful plans and come up with answers to everything. I almost hated to demolish her construction. "No," I said softly, "she had the gun right before the meeting. I saw it when she opened her pocketbook to give me a petition. I even asked if she had a permit to carry it, and she said she did."

Wilma leaped to her feet and fixed me with a furious glare. "You are an interfering busybody! I do not have to stand for this in my own house. Willena always said we should not let you Yarbroughs into the club. She was right."

Next thing we knew she had dashed out the double doors and down the stairs.

## 30

Several of us started after her, but the sheriff called, "Let her go. I have deputies at all the exits. She won't get far."

We milled around for a few seconds, then Sadie Lowe sidled up to me and purred, loud enough for the whole group to hear, "That was so exciting. Just like something on TV. When did you first know it was her?"

I shook my head. "Not until this evening, when I had a lot of time to think. That's one of the few advantages of incarceration." They laughed a little, as I'd hoped they would. We needed to lighten things up and get home.

"But how did you know?" MayBelle demanded. "What clues did the rest of us miss?"

"Could we all sit down?" Cindy asked. "Mac looks like she's about to collapse."

If truth be told, I felt like a balloon whose air had just gone out in one big whoosh. I hated what Wilma had done, but I also hated what society would now do to Wilma. I wished I hadn't been the one to turn her over to the law.

Several folks carried out chairs, and we sat in a circle with Queen Gusta at the head. One by one I enumerated the indicators that pointed to Wilma and mistletoe poisoning.

"Like I said, Willena was cold, nauseated, and sweating during the meeting. Those are all signs of ingested or injected plant toxins. Wilma also brought a big carryall that night to hold a small pair of galoshes, and it was still bulky when she left. I noticed that at the time, but it didn't register. I think it held the boots she wears to work in the yard — the boots she wore to kill Willena so she wouldn't get blood on her yellow shoes. Thursday morning I found her working in red mud in those same boots, and she washed them in my presence. Some of the drippings looked like blood, and I think they were. I believe, Sheriff, that if you have somebody examine those boots, you will still find traces of Willena's blood. And I suspect that an examination of MayBelle's blood-stained raincoat will show that Wilma wore it."

"Damn," MayBelle exclaimed. "Do you

know how long it took me to find one that color?"

"But why would she do it?" Nancy wondered aloud. "They were like sisters."

"Like sisters, but not sisters," I reminded her. "Two families, two fortunes. Gusta, when I first was considering whether to join the club, you mentioned that not all of you are as rich as you used to be. Were you referring to Wilma?"

"Primarily," Gusta acknowledged. "She was a greedy child and a greedy adult, so she invested almost everything she owned in tech stocks not long before the crash. We all tried to warn her, but nobody ever could tell Wilma anything."

MayBelle drummed her fingers on the table. "I tried to get her to give Grover her portfolio years ago, soon after Willena turned hers over to him and persuaded me to move mine, too. Grover's good. He's increased our net worth considerably. So there was Willena, getting richer and richer while lying on her couch, mean as a snake and never doing a lick of work. And poor Wilma was watching the markets every day, calling her broker several times a week with advice, and still losing a bundle."

"She also put a lot of money into bonds right after the crash because they looked real good," Nancy added, "but they went down to practically nothing afterwards."

Sadie Lowe spoke with uncharacteristic sympathy. "Poor old Wilma, anything she touched turned to dust."

"To dirt," Meriwether said softly. "I remember something Willena once said to me that makes sense now. She said, 'Wilma isn't smart. Plants die. Antiques appreciate.' I'll bet she told Wilma that, too. Poor Wilma."

"And her house would be in constant need of repairs," I added. "Right now it needs paint, wallpaper, upholstery — there's no end to keeping up a place like that."

"I know she asked Willena to help her with it." Rachel was finally ready to join the conversation. "Willena told me so. I mentioned to her that I was thinking of buying a house, and she said to buy a brick house like she had, because they required little maintenance. Then she said Wilma was hounding her for money to help keep up the old Kenan home."

Cindy spoke in a thoughtful tone. "I wonder if Willena's dating Grover had anything to do with the murder. When we were at the club for the seafood buffet last Friday night, Willena was telling us she was finally fixing to make a will. She winked at

Grover when she said it. Wouldn't it be dreadful, after all this, if she has made a will leaving all her money and the house to Grover?"

"Wilma can't profit from a crime," I reminded her. I wasn't at liberty to inform them that Willena never made a will.

"But how did she do it?" Walker asked, shifting his bulk on the little chair and resting one calf on the other thigh in an attempt to get comfortable. "I mean, you were all there; she was in full view most of the time —"

"Planning," I told him. "Wilma has always been a good planner. She knew the best time would be the election of officers meeting, when all the members would be there, because the more people, the more motives. She listed for me this week why any of several of you might have killed Willena." I ignored their gasps. "But she also unlocked the front door to allow for the possibility that somebody had come in from outside. Before she left home she mixed the punch so she wouldn't need to do that, and I would guess she filled one of her daddy's old diabetes needles with poison she had distilled from mistletoe leaves. Sometime during the evening she probably told Dexter his television was too loud and shut his door, so he wouldn't notice her in the hall, because he mentioned to me that she had complained about the noise. But you said something important, Nancy, on Thursday. You told me that when you were searching for Horace that you looked in each room *and the kitchen, and saw nobody.* Wilma was supposed to be in the kitchen at that point, mixing punch."

"She wasn't there," Nancy agreed with a surprised expression. "I never thought of that."

"What about my keys?" Cindy locked her fingers, turned her palms outward, and extended her arms to stretch. "How did they get under Willena?"

I shrugged. "Accident or deliberate attempt to incriminate you — one of those senseless things we'll probably never understand."

"Nothing is ever senseless," Gusta rebuked me in the tone I remembered from my kindergarten Sunday school days. "God used the keys to get you involved, Mac-Laren."

There was that. Sometimes the interconnectedness of the tiniest details gives me the shivers. Or was that a sudden breeze flitting through the ballroom's broken windows?

Meriwether leaned forward, holding Zach's little back. "What I don't understand is why Wilma would bother to give Willena that expensive bar set right before she killed her."

Sadie Lowe knew that. "To make her cry. You want to get a woman into a bathroom by herself, make her cry and run her mascara. That'll do the trick every time."

"Wilma told me herself that it always took Willena half an hour to fix her face," I added. "Since Wilma was in charge of refreshments, she could decide how long the break would be."

"And she knew we all always go to the bathroom as soon as the break starts, so we'd be back by the time she went to stick the corkscrew in Willena." Sadie Lowe was on a roll. I looked at her in admiration. I would never have suspected her of a having a wide practical streak.

"But why would she use the corkscrew if she'd already killed her with poison?" Slade was jotting notes on a pad he always carried in his inside coat pocket.

Sadie Lowe gave a bawdy laugh. "Maybe it was Wilma's ladylike way of saying, 'Screw you!' " Every single person in that room put a hand to the hollow of their throat and shuddered.

"And her motive?" Slade persisted. "In one word?"

"Covetousness," Gusta snapped. "Pure, unadulterated greed."

I leaned over and looked right into his eyes. "Let that be a lesson to you."

He gave me a saucy grin. "I'm a reformed man, Judge. You won't believe the new me." He draped one arm over the back of Rachel's chair like it had a right to be there. I noticed she didn't squirm or move away.

Sheriff Gibbons rose. "I think we have hashed this thing over long enough. The judge and Miss Rachel have been through an ordeal and need to get home. And I need to get over to the police station." Before he left, he looked across at me. "You'll come give a statement, too? And you, Miss Ford?"

"Tomorrow," I promised. "I'm exhausted tonight."

His eyes twinkled. "Plus you still have some issues at home to resolve."

I tottered down the stairs holding Walker's arm, feeling a hundred and two.

Nancy touched my elbow and murmured, "I'm glad you're okay, Mac."

"Will you be all right?" I asked in concern.

She gave me a sad smile. "God only knows. Literally. But I'll do the best I can."

She walked heavily out to her Cadillac SUV, climbed into the seat, and roared down the drive.

"Poor thing." Sadie Lowe spoke at my shoulder. "Horace has done her dirt, hasn't he?"

"You might take note of that," I suggested. "A man who does one woman dirt is likely to do the same again. And you can't live a lifetime on chemistry, you know."

Her lipstick was a curved slash of red under the porch light, and I could tell she didn't think I knew a thing about the kind of chemistry she and Horace had. I saw no need to enlighten her. But as she walked to her car, I felt pity for a child who had never known real love.

Cindy retrieved my pocketbook from the kitchen while Walker offered, "I'll get your Coke, Mama, but it will be warm by now."

"I couldn't care less," I assured him. "Wet and tingly will be fine."

Slade and Rachel stood at the bottom of the porch steps with me. "Give me your keys and I'll bring your car," Slade offered. "I came with the sheriff, so I need a ride home anyway."

When Rachel's gaze followed him, I asked softly, "You like him better now?"

She gave a little sigh. "Yeah. He's sweet."

405

"I can't understand how he got here, though."

"I called him. I wanted him to take pictures to support our case. I was telling him what had happened when suddenly everything went black. I guess Wilma hit me." She touched her bump gingerly. "She must have hung up, too, because he called back and got no answer, so he called the sheriff and asked for a deputy to come with him. When the sheriff heard you were here, too, he decided to come himself and bring several deputies. When they got here, they saw two cars parked out back and found the kitchen door unlocked, so Slade started looking for me while the sheriff went up the front steps for you."

I gave her a sideways look. "That silence just before you came upstairs sounded a lot like a long kiss. Did you and Slade decide that money isn't everything?"

"Yeah." One syllable, a volume of feeling.

"Well, I hope you all will be very happy. You won't starve. Will you mind staying in Hopemore?"

She gave me a funny look. "Can you keep a secret, Mac?"

"Sure, if I need to."

She held up her hand so her emerald winked in the porch light. "Remember I told you this was my grandmother's? Actually, her grandmother gave her a pin when she got married. My mother had the stones made into the earrings and the ring. Grandmother's maiden name was Willena Kenan, and she grew up in this house. I found lots of pictures of her in the albums. So I have roots in Hopemore."

I stared. "When did you find that out?"

"Three years ago. Mother used to talk about coming down south with her mother one summer when she was real little, to visit her grandparents. She could remember a big brick house, a cousin John, who was ten, and eating watermelon each afternoon out in the yard. They'd have contests to see who could spit seeds the farthest. That's all she remembered, except she thought somebody who was her 'other granddaddy' lived in a big white house with two porches."

"But she didn't know who they were?"

"No, she had no idea where or who those people were. Her mother died when Mother was seven, remember, and her daddy soon married again. When she asked about her mother, he said they'd talk about it when she was older. Unfortunately, he died before he felt she was old enough."

"And her mother's family never got in touch with them after her mother died?"

"Apparently not. Mother thought maybe they cast her mother off for marrying a Jew."

I remembered Wilma saying, "She married a most unsuitable man and died not long after. She was only eighteen."

"More likely for marrying a Yankee," I said wryly. "We had Jews in Georgia, but we didn't have many Yankees back then. But Wilma said she died right after she was married."

"No, she lived another eight years. When Mother was dying, she wanted to know who her mother's people were. Mother's half brother lives out in Seattle, and he has only one son, so Mother hoped maybe her cousin John might still be alive, with children my brother and I could get to know."

"So how did you find out about the Kenans and Hopemore?"

"I started digging around and turned up the marriage license for Granddaddy and Grandmother, issued in Hope County. Then I checked the phone book and found two W. Kenans living here now. I called and got Wilma, but when I told her I was Willena Kenan's granddaughter, she accused me of playing a filthy joke and hung up." Rachel smiled. "I didn't know about the other Willena, or that she wasn't married. Mother died soon after that, so I sort of forgot about it. But after Gary got killed, when there was nobody left" — her voice was small in the night, with a catch in her throat — "I decided to come down and check things out. I stayed with Grover and scouted out Hopemore. That's when I saw the ad for the job, so I decided to interview for it."

"Did Grover know then about your connection with the Kenans?"

"He still doesn't. He knows I was looking for ancestors here, but I didn't tell him the name. They could have turned out to be horse thieves or something, so I didn't want to tell him until I knew. And then I found him all involved with Willena . . ." She gave an unfunny laugh. "They were almost as bad as horse thieves, weren't they, Mac?"

"Not all Kenans," I assured her. "John was a dear, and his daddy and granddaddy. I never cared much for Wilma's side of the family. They suffered from what I call olderson complex, thinking they are better than others simply because they got born first. But if John had lived, Willena might have turned out differently. Her mother spoiled her once her daddy died."

"I wanted to get to know her, but I didn't like to tell her who I was. I didn't want her to think I was after her money or anything." Rachel turned back to look at the house, and her face was wistful. "But sometimes I wanted to say, 'My grandmother grew up in this house.' "

I stared at her in astonishment. "That's what you meant when you said you had a motive?"

She nodded. "I've been worried to death somebody would find out and think I'd killed her for her money. It was such a relief to find out she'd left it to Wilma."

"But she didn't." The enormity of the whole thing almost buckled my unsteady knees. "You are going to inherit the whole shebang." I didn't give her a chance to protest. "Willena never wrote a will, so as her first cousin, you are her closest living relative." I chuckled at her dazed expression. "I told Jed he ought to be looking for you. I even told Slade to go looking for you." I had a sudden thought. "You're sure he doesn't know?"

That changed the expression on her face to another kind of dazed. She gurgled. "Positive. He said, 'Dammit, I never wanted to fall in love with a poor woman. It's all your fault.' "

We looked at each other, started laughing, and could not stop. "I almost wish you didn't have to tell him," I said, gasping for breath.

"I won't," she cried. "I won't say a word until after . . . you know, if we decide . . . and then — wham!" She hit a palm with her fist. "Will you keep the secret?"

"Durn tooting," I agreed, "but tell Jed right away. And don't put off too long deciding. I just hope you'll let me be there when you tell Slade. I want to see his face."

The BMW came around the corner. Slade was peering anxiously through the windshield, but he relaxed when he saw she was laughing. As she climbed in beside him, I saw him take her hand and heard him ask in a tone I'd never heard him use before, "Are you feeling better?"

"Absolutely wonderful," she agreed.

I will not tell you what happened between Joe Riddley and me when I got home. Early in our marriage we decided we would never fight in front of the children.

I will tell you that since that night, I have felt a special sympathy for prisoners I see cuffed and in leg shackles. Joe Riddley says I'm lucky he doesn't take a leaf from Wilma's book and keep me locked in our attic.

Fortunately, we don't have an attic.

# THANKS

Although this book is a work of fiction, I owe a debt of thanks to an unknown toxicologist at a long-ago Sleuthfest for notes I took on mistletoe poisoning by injection, and to Jim and Joyce Lavene, who write delightful herbal mysteries, for pointing me in the right direction to check my facts. I also thank Ros and Mark Breitenbach, the proud owners of an electron blue Corvette, for initiating me into the world of Corvette cruises. And I assure the members of my own Jonquil City Investment Club that it in no way resembles the one in Hopemore, and I did not transplant any of our members to Middle Georgia. Please keep that in mind as I end my own term as senior partner. No corkscrews, please!

# ABOUT THE AUTHOR

**Patricia Sprinkle** grew up in North Carolina and northern Florida, graduated from Vassar College, and spent a winter writing in the Scottish Highlands before settling in Atlanta. Although as an adult she has also lived in Chicago, St. Petersburg, Mobile, and Miami, her mysteries and novels reflect her love for and the strength of her Southern roots. Sprinkle is a member of Sisters in Crime and Mystery Writers of America. Contact her at thoroughlysouthern@earth link.net or check out her Web site, www .patriciasprinkle.com.

We hope you have enjoyed this Large Print book. Other Thorndike, Wheeler, and Chivers Press Large Print books are available at your library or directly from the publishers.

For information about current and upcoming titles, please call or write, without obligation, to:

Publisher
Thorndike Press
295 Kennedy Memorial Drive
Waterville, ME 04901
Tel. (800) 223-1244

or visit our Web site at:

www.gale.com/thorndike
www.gale.com/wheeler

OR

Chivers Large Print
published by BBC Audiobooks Ltd
St James House, The Square
Lower Bristol Road
Bath BA2 3SB
England
Tel. +44(0) 800 136919
email: bbcaudiobooks@bbc.co.uk
www.bbcaudiobooks.co.uk

All our Large Print titles are designed for easy reading, and all our books are made to last.